STOLEN KISSES

He closed the book with a soft smack. She raised her eyes then. Looking into their glittering silver depths, he felt himself drawn in, wanting her. He set the book down and rose to his feet, stretching slightly. "Did you enjoy that?"

She nodded, silent.

"I shall take you to the theater. You've never seen a play, have you?" He smiled faintly as she shook her head. "But first the shops. As Lady Harcourt, you'll need fine dresses of velvet or silk. Perhaps in green to show off your hair."

She touched the coil at her neck. "I despise it!"

"Why? It's beautiful." She stood up and backed away as he approached her. He chuckled. "'Tis a small room, you've nowhere to go." Proving his point, he cornered her by the door. She averted her head, eyes closed, her breath coming in soft puffs. "I told you I wouldn't hurt you." With those soft words, his fingers gave in to the itch to unpin her burnished copper locks.

The thick braid unfurled down her back. She did not move as he combed his fingers through it, except to lick her lips. He bent to nuzzle her soft cheek, exulting in the shudder he elicited from her. His lips moved over the silken skin, easing toward her mouth, but not taking it.

She rewarded him by turning her head to him, opening herself to him with a soft moan. He embraced her gently as his tongue swept into her accepting mouth, twining with hers.

As their kiss deepened and roughened, his arms tightened, holding her to him. Her body nearly matched his for height, fitting perfectly against him. He left her mouth, searching for the sensitive point on her throat as she gasped and threw her head back . . .

To Be
Seduced

ANN STEPHENS

ZEBRA BOOKS
KENSINGTON PUBLISHING CORP.
http://www.kensingtonbooks.com

ZEBRA BOOKS are published by

Kensington Publishing Corp.
119 West 40th Street
New York, NY 10018

All Kensington titles, imprints, and distributed lines are available
at special quantity discounts for bulk purchases for sales promo-
tion, premiums, fund-raising, educational, or institutional use.

Special book excerpts or customized printings can also be
created to fit specific needs. For details, write or phone the
office of the Kensington Special Sales Manager: Attn. Special
Sales Department. Kensington Publishing Corp., 119 West 40th
Street, New York, NY 10018. Phone: 1-800-221-2647.

Zebra and the Z logo Reg. U.S. Pat. & TM Off.

ISBN-13: 978-1-4201-0867-5
ISBN-10: 1-4201-0867-0

First Printing: February 2010

10 9 8 7 6 5 4 3 2 1

Printed in the United States of America

To my three green-eyed blonds:
Paul, Irene, and Lauren

ACKNOWLEDGMENTS

I would like to express my immense gratitude to Sally Walker, Johnnye, and the rest of the NWW. All of you make me a better writer. And to Hilary and Peter, without whom this book would not be.

Chapter 1

January 1661

He had picked a prodigious cold day to abduct someone. Shivering in his full-length cloak, Richard, Baron Harcourt, hunched into the worn seat of the hired coach and cursed. No one heard him; he was quite alone, waiting for his accomplice to return with their prey. Much as he disliked depending on others, his face could be recognized in Stanworth, and that would ruin his plan to flee before any villagers raised a hue and cry. His long fingers lifted the leather window covering an inch to the side and he peered out. Only a few pockets of snow were visible on the rutted road. Winter-browned fields lay abandoned just beyond it. A bitter wind robbed the day of any pretense of pleasantness even though the sun shone. One chill gust buffeted his face as he let down the window and called up to the coachman, "Walk the horses, Jem. They've stood long enough."

"Aye, sir." He heard the slap of the reins and braced himself as the ungainly vehicle lurched into motion. Raising the glass pane into place in a vain attempt to keep draughts out, Harcourt swore again. The only thing worse than sitting in the middle of nowhere in the middle of winter in this miserable equipage was sitting in it as it jolted over a frozen road. He availed himself of a lap robe while he plotted his next move. The ancient coach and sturdy horses had taken nearly every farthing. This was his last throw. If he lost, it would cost him everything.

Despite his grumbling, Lord Harcourt was not in the middle of nowhere. Clearly visible from the coach, an iron gate opened onto the small estate of Abberley. From the entrance, a gravel drive curved around a copse of trees toward a red brick manor house built in the reign of Queen Elizabeth. Only mullioned windows and a pillastered doorway embellished the plain facade.

The oak door opened into the great hall, a room of dark wood panels and velvet hangings. Although richly appointed, it possessed a stern quality that discouraged lingering. A door to the right permitted escape to the dining room and kitchen and one opposite led into the library.

This afternoon, the library door stood ajar just enough to allow the conversation within to be overheard in the hall if one listened carefully.

Flattened against the wall, Bethany Dallison

knew that if caught eavesdropping, she would doubtless spend the next several days locked in her room. Custom forbade young ladies to know the terms of their marriage settlements. Hardly breathing, she braced her stockinged feet to run at the first sign of being overheard.

"I believe these terms will prove satisfactory to you, madam, while meeting my expectations of the portion due an affectionate husband." Her suitor, Mr. Daniel Ilkston, had ostensibly earned her mother's approval because of his sense of responsibility and excellent morals. Bethany knew the true source of her approbation was his own fortune and large property.

She herself found neither his person nor his manner pleasing. He persisted in wearing his thinning dark hair in the chin-length Roundhead style, and even on festive occasions, he clothed his plump form in somber black. His appearance combined with his habit of looking at her as if she were a particularly tasty morsel for him to snap up reminded her of a greedy hen. Mother insisted Bethany would grow to appreciate him, but she doubted that.

He treated her with cool condescension. They shared no interests, for she loved to read and socialize, while he made clear that his wife should occupy herself with supervising his household. And raising children. She shuddered. The thought of conjugal relations with Mr. Ilkston disheartened her greatly.

Her mother's voice, sharp with disapproval,

floated out the door. "This clause has not been changed, sir. I believe I mentioned that providing a suitable upbringing for dear Bethany caused a great expenditure from my own income. I do feel that as her only parent for these many years, it is only proper that I should be reimbursed those costs, particularly since I shall lose my only child upon your marriage." Bethany could imagine the scowl on her narrow face. Despite her generous jointure, Mistress Dallison intended to wring as much gold as she could from her future son-in-law.

"Dear lady, I agree in principle that you should not suffer because of the loss of your daughter, but I must protest! This amount seems excessive for the care and feeding of one girl, no matter how excellently trained." In his turn, Mr. Ilkston sounded downright petulant. Bethany heard the slap of papers on the massive wooden table that dominated the library as the argument continued.

She clenched her fists in her woolen skirt. They sounded like two old dames in the market haggling over the price of a prime piglet. Except the piglet was her. Or to be exact, her money. Her father's will settled a fine fortune on her, and with no other males in the family, she would also inherit the estate upon her mother's death. She looked down, fighting tears. The banns were not up yet, but if they signed the settlement today, the knot was as good as tied. The contract bound her to Mr. Ilkston as surely as if the wedding had already taken place.

Her mouth twisted bitterly. She had no living

relatives. If she cast herself onto any of the families in the neighborhood, they would scold her as an undutiful child and pack her right back home. She could not even use her own money to flee. Her father's London banker kept it in trust, except for a paltry amount designated for her personal use each quarter. The trust would be dissolved only upon her marriage, giving her husband control of her inheritance.

At length, her mother and Mr. Ilkston agreed to have the documents redrawn, and to sign them next week. Bethany had gained a reprieve.

She suddenly realized that she would have to join them before their guest departed and that her shoes were across the hall. She skittered along the floor, nearly losing her footing on the polished planks. Hastily slipping her shoes on, she plopped down on a high-backed chair next to a square table, folded her hands in her lap, and gazed serenely out the window, heart pounding. Thankfully, Mother noticed nothing amiss when she appeared and ordered Bethany into the library.

She entered the room. Three pewter goblets stood on the great rectangular table, along with a matching plate holding some small cakes. A pitcher of mulled cider warmed on the hearth before the crackling fire.

Mr. Ilkston attempted a weak gallantry. "Mistress Bethany, you look bright as a silver penny this afternoon. I trust you are well?"

She murmured a polite answer. Her plain bodice and skirt of agate gray wool denoted no special occasion. Nor did the white cotton whisk modestly hiding her shoulders or the muslin cap covering her hair.

Her mother forced a cheery smile onto a mouth tight with irritation. "We agree 'twould be most suitable for the wedding to be privately done here, dearest. Mr. Hay shall come from Highbury to perform the ceremony." She gestured for Bethany to offer their guest the plate of cakes. "Do have some Shrewsbury cakes, sir—made with my daughter's very hands."

Carefully selecting one of the sugar-dusted confections, Mr. Ilkston bit into it. Bethany watched his reaction with anticipation. She did enjoy cookery and was thought to have a fine hand with baked goods. He pursed his lips, taking on the appearance of an officious flounder. "Naturally, I do not partake of sweets often," he said. "One should avoid frivolity in diet as in other aspects of one's life."

Only her betrothed would consider his immortal soul endangered by a few cakes, although she noticed he helped himself to one more. She decided to change the subject.

"Must we send for Mr. Hay? The Reverend Mr. James could marry us at Saint Matthew's." Choosing a cake for herself, she nibbled it, enjoying the horrified expressions of the other two.

"Bethany! You cannot mean that, you wicked girl! Mr. James was assigned to Stanworth because he has embraced the popery imported from France." Mistress Dallison looked ready to collapse with an apoplexy. "Whatever will Mr. Ilkston think?"

With any luck, Bethany thought, Mr. Ilkston would withdraw his suit from so depraved a creature as herself.

"Mistress Bethany does not grasp the implications of her words," he stated. "It is not unusual for persons with red hair to lack a sense of proper behavior." His chill gaze swept over her. "However, I trust that I am capable of enforcing godly conduct within my own home."

Gray eyes narrowed and lips thinned, she bit back a retort. Setting his back up further would serve no purpose. To compose herself, she turned her gaze through one of the diamond-paned windows overlooking the front drive. Movement flashed beyond the copse and a moment later Mistress Gloriana Harcourt appeared from behind it. Bethany often found their neighbors' niece a silly chit, but just now she provided an excuse to abandon Mother and Mr. Ilkston, at least for a short time.

"Of course you are correct, sir." She forced a note of contrition into her voice. "I shall amend my actions in the future, and I beg you to forgive my flippancy. Perhaps you would accept fresh cakes as a peace offering?" Without waiting for a reply, she picked up the plate and left the library, pulling the door shut behind her.

In the hall, she hurried over to a window. Gloriana had just set foot on the doorstep and looked over at once when she heard tapping on the glass. Bethany pointed to the side of the house, relieved when the other girl immediately turned toward the rear door of the house.

She scurried to the kitchen to meet her. Mistress Magwort, the sour old soul who cooked for them, stood spitting a roast for supper. Bethany set the cake plate down on the scrubbed worktable. "Mistress Harcourt has come from the Rothleys. I am sure only grave necessity would send her out on such a cold day, so I shall go see what help I may provide." The old woman grunted without looking up.

As Bethany bundled up in the worn brown wool cloak and matching hood kept on a peg by the rear door, she assured herself that she had not lied to the cook, only speculated. It wouldn't get her out of trouble with her mother, but her own conscience might let it go.

Slipping out to the walled garden, she nearly ran into Gloriana, walking head down and clutching the hood of her black cloak to keep the wind out of her face. She reached out to steady the smaller girl. "Thank goodness you've come! I have no idea why you're here, but 'tis marvelous indeed." Bethany had to raise her voice to be heard above a strong blast of cold air.

In turn, Gloriana greeted her eagerly. "Aunt Rothley has been making me daft today! I told her I would take a jar of broth to old Mr. Lawton just to get out of the house." She brushed aside a strand of fair hair as she looked up. As usual, Bethany felt like a giant next to her petite blondeness.

"She must have been most demanding if you abandoned a warm fire on a day like this." Bethany eyed the girl curiously, for she knew well Glory's indolent nature.

The younger girl's cheeks reddened with more than the cold, but she nodded vigorously. "Indeed she has! That's why I came to visit you before going back."

"Do you think your aunt might be in a better humor by now? I hoped to return with you—Mr. Ilkston is here, and he and Mother are waiting for me to return to them."

She tried not to let her desperation show, but Gloriana's blue eyes gleamed with laughter. "What? The proper Mistress Bethany deserting her betrothed? I vow 'twill be the subject of gossip for the next month."

"He's not my betrothed yet. No announcement has been made," she snapped. Really, the girl possessed an impudent tongue for a mere sixteen-year-old. She relented an instant later. "Oh, Glory, do help me. I'll have to spend more than enough time with Ilkston after we're married."

The other girl grinned and peeped up at her speculatively. "How are we going to get to the road without being seen?"

"The road? You're right next to us! We'll take the bridle path to your uncle's land."

"No, we should take the road," Gloriana insisted. "Perhaps you'd like to go to the village and—and buy some hair ribbons." Taking her hand, she tugged Bethany toward the drive.

"On a day like this? Be sensible, you goose!" Still nervous at the thought of her mother discovering them, she chewed her lip. "If we stay close to the garden wall, I think we can run before they catch sight of us. Once we're past the copse, we might be safe."

The two girls hugged the brick wall of the kitchen garden, then sprinted along the drive, skirts lifted and feet flying across the brown grass. They stopped to gasp for breath once they were out of sight of the house, leaning on one another.

"We can't stop here. Mother has surely missed me by now. How I wish I'd thought to grab my gloves." Bethany looked back over her shoulder. She believed they were invisible from the library windows, but feared they might yet be observed.

"You could share my muff," puffed Gloriana. She paused as if reluctant to go on. "Don't you need to catch your breath?"

"No, I shall already be punished for leaving. I may as well take what pleasure I can before Mother catches me." Bethany straightened and walked toward the gate. Turning, she saw Gloriana standing in place, irresolute. "Do hurry!"

The younger girl caught up with her, grumbling under her breath about winter weather and doing favors for others. "Don't be so uncharitable," Bethany chided gently. "I'm sure Mr. Lawson was most thankful for some broth on such a day. Here, scandalize me with the latest gossip you've ferreted out. You always enjoy that."

Instead, silence fell between them as they trudged along. A few of last autumn's leaves whispered across their path, and the afternoon sun cast their shadows ahead of them. Bethany wondered if Gloriana

regretted their rash behavior just as the other
girl spoke.

"My brother is visiting for a short while." Her voice
squeaked with excitement. Glory hero-worshiped
the dissolute young man twelve years her senior.

Having made his acquaintance the summer previous, Bethany understood her companion's feelings. Even she had found it difficult to resist his
charming smile and manners, despite observing
his shameless flirtations. To her mortification, she
recalled wishing that he might indulge in the
same disreputable behavior with her.

"What a pleasant diversion for you. Lady Rothley had not said that he planned to visit," she said
in a tone of polite indifference.

"Oh, she wouldn't have," Gloriana replied airily.
"We did not know exactly when he'd be here, as
he is kept immensely busy in London."

"I can imagine," Bethany said dryly. According to
her mother's acquaintances, since the ascension of
the second King Charles, the city had plunged itself
into a plethora of lascivious behavior, drunkenness,
and public disorder. A man of Lord Harcourt's lax
ways would find much to occupy himself, most of it
immoral.

The road appeared before them through the
manor's open gate. She hurried between the massive brick and iron posts and turned to wait for the
smaller girl to catch up.

At her side, Gloriana smiled brightly and pointed
past Bethany's shoulder. "Look! I believe that is my
brother's coach down the road."

Bethany shook her head at the chit's transparent attempt at surprise. "For pity's sake, Glory, why did you not simply tell me your brother awaited you? 'Tis quite unmannerly of you, although I am surprised he did not escort you to the door."

Her companion looked sheepish. "I wasn't sure your mother would admit him after the escapade with your maidservant last summer. I am very fond of Richard and did not wish to subject him to embarrassment. Faith, he swore nothing more happened than a few kisses, and that the girl was willing."

Bethany snorted. "Knowing Joan, she proposed the meetings! But it's true, Mother would scarcely welcome him had he come with you." She smiled mischievously. "Although it might have been amusing to watch him puncture Mr. Ilkston's self-importance." While she could not approve of loose behavior, she appreciated Lord Harcourt's piercing wit.

She watched the shabby coach make its way along the rutted road for a moment before adding, "I think we had better go meet him. That contraption looks like it won't last all the way to the gate."

Gloriana nodded and they strolled to meet it. Bethany glanced at her. The younger girl's mouth was set in a determined line and her usually inquisitive eyes remained fixed on the ground.

However, when they reached the slow-moving coach and four, the irrepressible sixteen-year-old called out cheerily, "Rickon! I'm back, and look who came with me. Mistress Bethany thought to visit Aunt Rothley."

The door swung open, and Lord Harcourt himself stepped down to assist them. Bethany caught her breath. He remained unchanged from last summer. Instead of a periwig, he wore his own hair in long, dark gold waves. The same lazy smile highlighted his strong features as his gaze swept over her with unsettling thoroughness. His assessment reminded her uncomfortably of just how worn her brown cloak and hood were, and how drab she must look beside Gloriana's fashionable amber dress and black cloak.

"It is my pleasure to meet you again, Mistress Dallison." Even his voice unsettled her with its combination of honey over gravel. "Please allow me to convey you to our destination." He stepped forward in a fluid movement and took her bare hand in his gloved one. Gracefully he bowed over it, brushing her fingers with the barest kiss. They fluttered nervously at the unexpected contact and Bethany swallowed as Lord Harcourt tightened his grip. Feeling the strength and heat through his black leather gauntlets only served to make her blush. From the warmth in her face, it must be bright pink. He smiled and assisted her into the coach.

"Your hands are cold. We'll have to find a way to warm them." He pressed a kiss into her palm, his green eyes glinting at her wickedly. She gasped softly and snatched her hand away. He shrugged and helped Gloriana inside, then settled himself on the seat opposite them.

She pointedly placed herself as far from him as the cramped space allowed and stared out the window disinterestedly. His clear green eyes shot her an amused glance before he turned his attention to his sister.

The two of them chatted idly during the brief ride to Rothley Hall. Left to herself, Bethany observed the coach's interior. Stuffing burst from the cracked leather seats and dark blue paint peeled off the wooden sides. Warped window frames permitted a steady draft of cold air inside, forcing her to keep her hands inside her cape. She thought this must be the worst-sprung vehicle she had ever ridden in. She could not imagine enduring its teeth-rattling bounces for a lengthy journey. Lord Harcourt's purse must be lean indeed to have resorted to such a miserable conveyance.

Her ears pricked up when Gloriana teased her brother to fetch her back to London. To her surprise, Lord Harcourt's brows drew together in unexpected disapproval.

"That would be quite improper, as you should know. 'Pon rep, I've explained it to you often enough." His sister protested, but he ended the argument with a flat "No."

Lifting the window covering, Bethany recognized the stretch of road leading to Rothley Hall. She anticipated sitting by one of Lady Rothley's warm fires for an afternoon of amusing conversation before having to face her mother.

Lord Harcourt noticed they had reached their destination as well. He knocked on the top of the coach and it halted.

"Glory, we're here." His serious tone made Bethany turn to look at him. He held his sister's hands and gazed into her face, now white and frightened, as if he silently asked her a question. It was one she apparently understood, for she gave him a jerky nod of her head in return. "Good girl," he said softly. "You'll be well?" She nodded again. To Bethany's surprise, he opened the door without another word and got out to help them down. Surely he did not mean to have them walk to the Hall from the gate!

Glory looked over her shoulder with an apologetic expression before stepping out of the coach. Puzzled, Bethany prepared to follow, only to find her way blocked as Lord Harcourt placed an arm across the doorway. "I beg your pardon, my lord, but if we are to walk to the Hall, I should get out of the coach." Her cold voice clearly displayed her displeasure, but he did not reply.

Instead Gloriana looked up at her from the road. "Bethany, I am so truly sorry," she choked out. "Richard said he needed my help and I am obligated to—he's my brother and he took such care of me after our parents died. Please try to forgive both of us."

"Enough, Glory. You must go." At his flat statement, the girl pulled her hood up and trudged up the drive to her aunt and uncle's, her cloak wrapped around her. Lord Harcourt turned and leapt up into the coach so quickly that Bethany was forced to sit back down. "I regret to inform you, Mistress Dallison, that you will be coming with me." He knocked on the roof again.

"I—beg—your pardon?" Dumbstruck, Bethany scarcely noticed as the vehicle lurched into motion.

"You will accompany me to my estate in Yorkshire, where we will be married." His matter-of-fact tone did not stop the air rushing out of her lungs in shock. He looked at her sympathetically. "I'm very sorry, my dear. But I need a great deal of money very quickly, and you are the most accessible heiress of my acquaintance."

He continued to observe her minutely during the long pause that ensued. When she lunged to wrest the door open, his hand shot out to capture her wrist easily.

"No." The softly spoken word belied his iron grip. Trying to pull away from him only resulted in an agonizing stab up her arm, and Bethany yelped in pain and anger.

He released her at once, only to move across to her side and examine her slender wrist in the light of the window. "I apologize, madam." He looked at her ruefully. "I did not realize you have such delicate bone structure." He looked bemused as his gloved thumb and middle finger easily encircled her wrist.

She froze as his hand slowly moved to her face. His leather-clad fingertips grazed her cheekbone as his eyes looked soberly into hers. Bethany caught her breath at the intimate touch, but a blaze of outrage cleared her mind.

The arrogant blackguard was trying to seduce her! She glared at him. "Get away from me and stop the coach at once! I am most certainly not going to marry you."

Instead, he released her and leaned back against the seat at her side. "I believe you will have no other choice. Rest assured, I have no desire to harm you, but after two days and a night in my company, the world will assume the worst. You will either become Lady Harcourt or you will be ruined." Glancing her way at last, he raised his eyebrows suggestively. "A title and an estate, my dear. Many other females would snap me up without hesitation."

Fear seeped into her fury as Bethany realized his utter seriousness. She shook her head to dispel her sense of unreality. Giving in to fright would not help her. Or would it? Perhaps a bout of hysterics would convince him to turn the coach around and dump her back on her mother's doorstep.

As if reading her mind, her adversary smirked and pulled a small object out of his pocket. "A vinaigrette. French ladies carry them to use in moments of great distress." He offered it to her. "In case of faintness. We will both find the journey far more pleasant if you do not indulge in a fit of some kind."

She itched to slap that irritating smile off his face. "I am never faint." She lifted her chin and glared at him. Lord Harcourt simply shrugged and tucked the filigree oval into the depths of his greatcoat.

"My felicitations, dear Mistress Dallison. I am sure you are the first female of my acquaintance to say so." His voice quivered with amusement.

Bethany nearly ground her teeth but held on to her temper. She needed a cool head to convince him to return her to Abberley. She cringed to think what her mother would say, not to mention Mr. Ilkston. Her fortune would doubtless overcome his shock, but she feared he would make her suffer for it once they married.

The thought unexpectedly surfaced that life with Lord Harcourt would make the most intimate aspects of marriage very pleasant, but the idea flashed out of her mind just as quickly. Like Ilkston, he just wanted her money; he merely followed a more direct course of action to obtain it.

She wished again that she controlled her own money. Disgusting as the idea might be, she would have considered bribing him to return her with her reputation intact. But the law allowed only widows any control over property and income. Most women depended on funds settled on them by their fathers and husbands.

At this thought, Bethany straightened on the seat and blinked. Unmoving, she stared at the opposite side of the coach for several seconds. Suddenly facing Lord Harcourt, she took a deep breath. If he guessed at the idea that had entered her mind, she faced disaster.

* * *

Tucking the vinaigrette away, Richard congrat-
ulated himself on the success of the first part of
his plan. Despite the fierce scowl on her face, the
girl offered little resistance so far. Granted, she
had demanded he stop the coach, and then tried
to open the door while it still moved, but he
had expected no less. He had recognized the will-
ful streak behind her pretty face the previous
summer, but he had every confidence of mastering her. Once he wed her and bedded her, everything she had became his.

Expanding on this pleasing subject, he regarded
the young woman beside him. She refused to look
at him, pinning her gaze straight in front of
her. He satisfied himself with the view of her rigid
profile, even opening the window covering farther
to permit more sunlight into the coach. He had
thought her pretty enough last summer; he was
pleased that his recollections proved accurate.

Her fair skin glowed against the darker wood
and leather. A few pale freckles spotted the bridge
of her nose. He tamped down an urge to trace
them with his fingers. She had shied away from his
touch earlier and a frightened bride would not
suit his purposes at all.

He realized he had never seen her hair uncov-
ered and wondered what color it was. He guessed
brown from the brow and lashes turned so fixedly
away from him. The color of her eyes, he knew,
ranged from cool gray to silver lightning.

When she turned unexpectedly to face him, they flashed bright sparks of anger before hardening. The charming sight so disarmed him that he was not prepared for her question.

"How much money do you need?"

She might just as casually have asked how much he needed for a new shoe buckle. He stared at her.

The baggage dared to roll her eyes at him. "How much money do you need," she repeated, her tone of voice suggesting that she spoke to a person of limited mental capacity.

Richard stalled for time to assess this new ploy. "Why do you want to know?" He leaned against the back of the seat and cocked an eyebrow at her. Stretching one booted leg before him gave the appearance of ease, while his other foot remained firmly on the floor, enabling him to move quickly should she try to bolt again.

She did not try to bolt. Instead, she settled herself more firmly on the seat and looked him full in the face. "I might not have enough to meet your debts." A triumphant smile curved her lips.

Clever puss, to search for his most vulnerable point. "I'm quite sure your assets will more than meet my needs," he purred. "My uncle determined your worth to be a good fifteen thousand pounds, and I have immediate need of but five thousand."

"Ah." Bethany tilted her head against the back of the seat as if thinking. When she looked at him again, he guessed her next words.

"Very well, Lord Harcourt. I will marry you."

He'd won the throw.

Trying to hide his overwhelming relief at her capitulation, he pressed her hand between both of his. "Thank you for doing me the honor of agreeing to be my wife, madam."

"Indeed. Naturally, there are conditions." At her suddenly brisk tone of voice, his brows lowered. "In the first place, I wish to be married in London, so you'll need to turn the coach around. In the second place, I trust you will not pester me with unwanted attentions after the ceremony. I collect you planned to marry me and leave me in Yorkshire?"

He could not seem to find his voice. She continued, unperturbed. "I think under the circumstances that will do very well, although I might like to travel at least to York or Scarborough occasionally."

Lord Harcourt gathered his wits. "And just how do you think to enforce your—er, conditions, girl? Tell me that."

"Easily." How a slip of girl managed to look down her nose at him while sitting down, he did not know. "I shall say 'No' in front of the minister."

"And destroy your reputation? You're bluffing."

A delightful blush covered her face, but she did not back down. "I might be ruined, but you'll still be poor," she retorted. "And that would defeat your purpose, wouldn't it?"

She betrayed no sign of her anxiety as she waited for his response. Lord Harcourt underestimated her fortune. Perhaps he would underestimate her intelligence as well.

"I should think a God-fearing woman would wish to avoid the immoral atmosphere of London," he mocked. "Are you so eager to embrace the city's delights?"

"Certainly not," she replied stiffly. "Our former vicar now lives there, and I wish him to marry us."

"I suppose I must respect your sentiment in wishing to have your childhood pastor marry you." To Bethany's surprise, his lordship spoke in earnest She sniffed disdainfully.

"Sentiment has nothing to do with it," she said tartly. "'Tis simple enough to pay someone to act as a man of the cloth. You shall not wed me in a mock ceremony only to take my money and abandon me."

The insufferable man had the gall to take offense. "Good God, madam, I'm not a thief."

"I vow 'tis a burden off my mind to know that I've been kidnapped by an honest man," she spat.

For a few seconds Lord Harcourt's green eyes blazed with rage. Then his lips twitched into a reluctant grin.

"*Touché,* my dear," he chuckled. Opening the window, he shouted to the coachman to make for London. Now if he could just get his bride-to-be to the altar without throttling her.

Chapter 2

Some time later, Lane wheeled the coach onto the London road. His route, as far as Bethany could discern, had ranged over a series of ill-kept tracks in an attempt to remain hidden from everyone in the Stanworth area. The jostling she experienced in the rickety vehicle surpassed her earlier imaginings, and she prayed the smoother surface of the highway would bring some relief to her aching head. It did not, but the sight of Lord Harcourt bracing himself against the squabs next to her proved obscurely comforting. She stiffened her spine, determined not to complain.

As the coach traveled farther and farther south, her resolve dwindled. The ache in her head spread down and formed an alarmingly familiar heaviness in her stomach. For some time, deep breaths of the chilled air seeping around the window frame kept her nausea at bay. When the fresh air no longer helped, she turned to her new fiancé, trying not to show her distress.

"Excuse me, my lord. I believe I should like to avail myself of the vinaigrette you offered earlier." His only reply was an arched brow, but he produced it willingly enough. Bethany took it from his outstretched hand and held it under her nose, inhaling the acrid odor thankfully. The leaden ache in her stomach receded slightly, but she feared her relief would only be temporary. Attempting to distract herself, she spoke again.

"Will it take long to reach London?"

"We should arrive near midday tomorrow," he replied. Bethany felt another lurch in her midriff, this time caused by the reminder that she would be spending the night in an inn with a stranger, fiancé or not. At her choice, she reminded herself firmly.

Her companion looked out the window. "I believe we have another two hours of daylight. We should start looking for a decent place to stay before dusk."

Bethany nodded, hoping her stomach would remain calm that long. She cast about for another subject to speak of. "Where exactly are your lodgings in London?"

"Not far from Somerset House." His sharp glance in her direction belied his civil answer.

"What are they like?" she persisted.

"So many questions, so suddenly," he mused softly. "Not thinking of changing your mind, are you?" He grasped her jaw and forced her to look into his furious green eyes.

"As if that would do any good now," she gasped. "It's too late to turn back."

"Aye. You'd do well to remember that." As his gaze flickered over her face and down her body, she realized he was not referring to the distance they had traveled. She supposed she should feel threatened, but another violent bump in the road caused her stomach to reel in misery.

After pausing for another sniff at the vinaigrette, she asked, "My lord, do you think we might start looking for a place to stay soon?"

"Now you're eager to stop? You're rushing your fences, my girl. Few men are stupid enough to think even a woman can change her mind that quickly." His handsome features contorted into a sneer.

"I am not changing my mind, sir," she said stiffly, trying to hang on to what dignity she could. "But I feel most unwell and would be grateful not be shaken about like dice in a box."

"Unwell? You can't be trying to gammon me with that excuse."

"It is not an excuse," Bethany stated in between deep breaths. "And if you do not stop this horrible contraption very soon, the consequences will be unpleasant." She put her hand to her mouth. "Exceedingly so."

"Oh my God." Lord Harcourt immediately opened his window and shouted wildly for Lane to stop the coach.

Bethany did not wait for it to come to a complete halt. As soon as possible, she wrestled the door open and jumped onto the ground. Desperate for privacy, she headed toward a line of trees several paces from the road. But before she took ten steps, she doubled over, stomach heaving.

As she finished retching, she became aware of two arms firmly supporting her. Lord Harcourt murmured into her ear as she tried to compose herself. "Shhh, there now. There's a girl." The stream of phrases meant nothing, but his deep voice soothed her so that she ceased shaking. A folded square of clean linen was pressed into her fingers. He helped her straighten up, holding her against his chest until she could stand on her own. Even then, he kept a steadying hand at her elbow.

Humiliated, Bethany could not bring herself to look anywhere but at the dead leaves around her feet as she wiped her mouth with Lord Harcourt's kerchief. One of his elegantly shaped hands slid into her line of sight, holding a small flask.

"Drink," he ordered. Too ashamed of her weakness to argue, she opened it. The pungent odor of strong spirits nearly gagged her and the fumes brought tears to her eyes. She took a swallow, swirled it around in her mouth, and spit it out.

"God's teeth, woman! That's French brandy," he exclaimed.

"It wouldn't have stayed down," she said weakly. "I'm sorry. It did help get the taste out of my mouth. Thank you, my lord." She still could not bear to raise her head.

She felt him shake with repressed laughter. "Considering that we are betrothed and have just shared a highly intimate experience, I think it's time you called me Richard."

Bethany looked at him for a long minute. Then she bent over and retched at his feet.

His lordship scrambled out of the way, mindful of his boots, but slipped a supporting arm about her waist once her stomach had emptied itself. He sighed and offered the brandy flask once more, wincing when she spit a second mouthful on the ground.

He peered down at her quizzically. "Under the circumstances, I shan't complain, but I am curious. Do you often become violently unwell on long journeys?"

Her stiffening spine assured him of her recovery. When she pulled away, he let her go easily and stood, waiting for her answer.

"Only in badly sprung vehicles." Her frosty stare swept over him. "Where did you unearth such a monstrosity?"

"Simply by telling the livery stable what I could afford, love." The sun had dipped lower in the west while his unwilling betrothed dealt with her indisposition. Bandits and worse haunted the roads after dark, and Richard wanted to find a place for the night before much more time passed. He bowed and indicated the coach. "Your monstrosity awaits."

She did not argue, although neither did she appear remotely enthusiastic about resuming their drive. He watched her square her shoulders and walk to the vehicle. Hiding a smile, he followed.

As they approached, the patient driver greeted them affably. "Mistress done casting up her accounts?" He climbed down from the box and opened the door. "Here you go, my lady. We'll take it a bit slower now."

Bethany could not meet the man's eyes despite his kindly meant words. Richard took pity on his companion's obvious embarrassment and assisted her into the carriage before addressing his servant in a low voice. "We'll stop at the Bell and Moon. We can reach it before sundown."

"Should we take the lady there, milord?" Lane scratched his graying head. "It ain't a place what gets much of the Quality."

"It's clean and I should be able to afford at least one room for the night."

The rest of the afternoon's drive passed without further disturbances, although by the time they reached their destination, Bethany once again clutched the vinaigrette. Clearly relieved by the end of the day's drive, she assured Richard that she suffered from nothing more than a headache. Eying her pallid face, however, he suspected she deprecated her discomfort. Ordering her to stay in the coach, he entered the building to make arrangements for the evening. Lane remained on the box to ward off strangers.

Bethany had indeed minimized the depths of her discomfort. She rested her head against the squabs, eyes closed. Her head pounded and her empty stomach clenched mercilessly. Past experience informed her that she needed a nap and a light meal, and the wait for them stretched endlessly.

The bustle of the inn yard did little to relieve her throbbing head. Other travelers wishing to find an evening's shelter arrived. Hoofbeats, creaking wheels, and shouts for the ostler combined with barking dogs and the shrills of the barmaid to assault her ears in a painful cacophony. Finally rescue appeared in the creak of the coach door and his lordship's voice.

"I've bespoken a room for the evening and a private parlour for our meal." Bethany raised an eyelid to discover her betrothed holding out a hand to assist her. She accepted his help gratefully, swaying slightly as her feet touched the ground. Instantly his arm slipped round her waist. "Are you able to walk?" His lordship made as if to pick her up but she forestalled him.

"I am somewhat light-headed, sir, but quite capable of remaining on my own feet." She refused to disgrace herself by being carried into a public house. Another wave of dizziness assailed her and she hastened to add, "If you would permit me to lean on your arm."

"Of course." Bethany ignored the laughter behind his polite words. He kept his arm firmly under hers as they crossed the yard and entered the half-timbered building. Once inside, he introduced her to a woman about her mother's age. "This is Mistress Gatwell, the innkeeper's wife.

I've asked her to show you to your chamber while I see to ordering our supper. Mistress Gatwell, my sister."

Concluding that her abductor betrothed had not exposed her real name or their relationship, she bestowed a grateful smile on him. "Thank you—Richard."

As she followed the landlady up a set of dark wooden stairs to the gallery, she became aware that this was not an establishment of the highest quality. The whitewash on the walls covered wattle and daub instead of solid wood, and the customers arriving in the yard below consisted largely of farmers and carters. However, the landlady escorted her to a clean, if small, bedchamber. There, she curtsied and told Bethany that the gentleman said she was feeling poorly, and would she like some lavender water and a cloth for her head?

The girl accepted the offer with profuse thanks, and Mistress Gatwell whisked out of the room, shutting the door behind her. The furnishings consisted of a wide bed and a washstand. A square mirror hung above the stand. One window overlooked the road below. Bethany noted the spotless diamond panes favorably, and a closer inspection of the bed disclosed that the sheets smelled of soap rather than mildew.

After a serving girl delivered the promised water and cloth, she removed her white cap and the hairpins holding her braid in a heavy coil at the back of her head. As she undid her hair, she sighed in relief. Dipping the cloth into the pitcher and wringing it out, she then sank blissfully onto the bed's woolen coverlet and placed the cool length of linen over her forehead.

She awoke with a start at the sound of knocking. Disoriented, she clambered to the floor and stood looking about the room in confusion. Judging from the early evening light shining in through the window, she had not slept long.

"Mistress? 'Tis nearly time for supper, if you're of a mind to eat." After a moment's thought, she recognized the voice as belonging to the landlady. "Shall I tell your brother to expect you?"

Her brother! The day's events rushed back to Bethany, along with the realization that the last thing she had eaten was part of a Shrewsbury cake in her mother's library that afternoon. Homesickness battled with her rumbling stomach. By now, her mother had probably visited every home in the neighborhood searching for her. Practicality won out over conscience. "Please tell"—she stumbled over the words—"my brother that I shall join him," she called through the door. "And would you be so kind as to bring paper, ink, and a quill to my room?" She could at least write to assure her mother of her well-being.

Relieved that Mistress Gatwell had not entered to see her mussed hair, Bethany went over to the mirror. As she suspected, she would have to rebraid it before replacing her cap. Freeing the mass, she finger-combed it until it lay smooth enough to manage.

Concentrating on taming the fine strands, she did not hear the well-oiled door open.

"*Jesu.*" She whirled around at the soft expletive. Richard Harcourt's cloaked form stood in the doorway, staring at her. Horrified, she grabbed the cap to cover her head.

He put out his hand to stop her. "No." He shut the door and stalked toward her. She instinctively backed up until the wall stopped her retreat. He stared at her with smoky eyes, then reached out to wind a strand around his fingers.

"I had no idea you were a redhead," he murmured, watching sunlight from the window gleam across the fiery tendril.

She closed her eyes in humiliation. Her wretched hair had been the bane of her existence as long as she could remember. "Please let me put my cap on."

"Why? 'Tis too beautiful to be bound up and hidden." His hand slid into the silky mass, further entangling his fingers.

She jerked her head away. "I'm sure *you* find it most pleasing, but rest assured, sir, that despite my hair I am no wanton." To her concern, a wicked smile spread across milord's face.

"Oh? Let's find out. I already know you've the temper that matches Judas hair." Mesmerized by his gravelly murmur, she froze, heart pounding, as he placed his forearms against the wall on either side of her head. Trapped, she could only watch his face descending to hers.

When their mouths met, she gasped at the unexpected jolt of pleasure that lanced through her. Taking advantage, he swept his tongue between her lips. She shivered at the sensation of warmth in the pit of her stomach.

Her upbringing reasserted itself. Pushing him away, she managed to slip beneath his arms and away from him. He made as if to follow her, but she held up her shaking hands to fend him off.

"Please, no! I have no idea what possessed me, just—leave me at once." Irritated at her betrothed's ability to disconcert her, she wanted nothing more than to be rid of his presence.

He smiled sweetly, clearly amused by her discomfort. "But I've come to escort you to supper." With a slight bow, he gestured to the doorway.

She fixed him with an icy stare, but the effect was ruined when her stomach rumbled loudly. Ignoring his quivering lips, she announced, "Then I shall sup in here, thank you."

He straightened and crossed his arms. "That you won't, Mistress Dallison. I can afford one meal this evening and 'tis laid out in the parlour below. You either join me or go hungry."

Bethany capitulated to her betrothed and her growling stomach. "Oh, very well! I shall join you, but not until I've made myself presentable." She opened the door. "If you would be so kind?"

"Of course, *dear sister*." With a mocking laugh, he left Bethany alone to reorder herself. As she knotted the cap's muslin ties firmly under her chin, a startling reflection entered her mind.

Lord Harcourt—Richard—had called her hair beautiful.

On the balcony surrounding the inn yard, Richard's thoughts ran along similar lines as he pulled his cloak closer against the winter afternoon. He had thought Bethany a pretty girl, but opening the door to see that cascade of golden red glowing in the sunset light had stolen his breath. His first impulse had been to bury his face in it, to discover its scent and softness. The rules of polite society precluded such outrageous behavior, but he'd had no scruples about stroking his hands into those bright strands.

Her initial response to his kiss had matched that fiery hair, warm and soft. He turned his head to consider her still-closed door. He'd told her he would not touch her during this journey, but he had not expected to find his Puritan bride so very pleasing. Strictly speaking, his intentions were honorable. They had to be in order for him to keep his promise to his father. But he now found little inclination to wait for the pleasures of the marriage bed.

He loosened his cloak to allow the chill breeze to cool his heated body while he pondered how he might join his betrothed in her bed after supper.

When Bethany emerged from her room, cap and hair firmly in place, she took Richard's proffered arm with some nervousness. To her immense relief, he made no mention of their embrace. Instead, he spoke lightly of the meal awaiting them as he led her down the steps, apologizing in advance for its plainness.

The unexceptional conversation settled her, although apprehension fluttered through her when he opened the door and waited for her to enter the private room. Her heart pounded as she transgressed one of her mother's cardinal rules: Never be alone with a single man. Following her, he shut the door on the roar of the customers in the common room beyond.

"Have a seat by the fire for a few minutes, dear girl. You looked somewhat pale." She glanced sharply at him, expecting to see mockery in those green eyes. He only waved a hand toward the small settles on either side of the hearth before picking up the crockery pitcher of ale and pouring out some for each of them.

Trying to match his casual manner, she removed her woolen cloak and draped it over the back of a chair. Her hands felt unaccountably cold. She walked over and held them out to the fire. Richard spoke to her from his place by the table.

"Once you're warmed, we had best enjoy our meal. I find cold mutton most unappetizing." Bethany managed a strangled assent. To calm her jangling nerves, she looked about the room.

Light came from the fireplace and from several candles in wrought iron sticks on the table and on a plain sideboard at the room's far end. It gleamed softly off the pewter dishes and tankards. Linsey-woolsey curtains in the shade of amber obtained from onionskin dye hung in the window frames. The inn's goodwife had placed a matching runner down the middle of the dark wood tabletop before setting out their food.

Certainly he had not exaggerated the meal's simplicity. A saddle of mutton sat on a platter among dishes holding bread, cheese, and dried apples. The earthy scent of ale reached Bethany's nose as Richard held out her tankard.

"I ordered this instead of wine this evening. I doubt Master Gatwell carries a potable vintage, but his homebrewed is quite palatable. The only other alternative here would be water and I doubt you'd care to risk that."

Bethany agreed, well aware of the dangers of drinking plain water. She approached him with all the care of a horse skirting a dangerous precipice. Gingerly taking the mug from him, she sipped carefully. The frothy liquid flowed over her tongue, leaving a pleasant tang of yeast and anise. "Most palatable! My mother's brewmaster does not do so well."

His eyes glinted. "You have a brewery on your estate?"

She met his look, seeing the greed behind the question. "I regret disappointing your lordship, but we don't sell any. 'Tis only for use in our household."

He bowed slightly, hand to heart. "A hit indeed, madam. I admit to a flash of hope that I might become possessor of a thriving alehouse upon our marriage. A number of noble houses have magically revived their fortunes by alliances with daughters of the Brewer's Guild."

"Feel free to join them!" Stung, Bethany retorted before thinking. She stopped short. Spending this night at the Bell and Moon made marriage imperative. Besides, she had an excellent reason to wed, if she could keep Richard at arm's length.

He chuckled. "Vigilant fathers take care to keep their daughters away from me." His gravelly voice lowered. "Happily, I found a most gratifying alternative."

Although he made no attempt to touch her, she stepped away, placing the table between them. He followed. Alarm pulsed through her. His smile flashed as he pulled out her chair with a flourish.

Torn between nervousness and laughter, she allowed him to seat her. He did not discomfit her again as they dined. His charm of manner relieved her as he recounted amusing stories about his boyhood in Yorkshire. Chuckling at a particularly funny episode about Gloriana getting stuck in a tree, she watched him finish a second helping of meat. His pleasure in such a plain meal surprised her into commenting upon it.

"I've spent too many days hungry to complain about a full stomach, my dear." He raised his tankard to her. "I may not be able to command the elegancies of life, but my expectations improve daily."

"When does a lord go to bed hungry?" She bit

into a dried apple, enjoying its sweetness. "Gloriana never mentioned any such thing."

"When he's living in exile. Glory was the youngest; we made certain to fill her plate first with whatever food we could afford." He leaned back in his chair, brooding. "Our years in France were—challenging."

An instant later he smiled at her, his easy mood returning. "Good preparation for life at Court, I daresay. You'll be presented, you know."

"What?" She nearly choked on her apple. "At Court? To the King?" Her voice subsided to a squeak. "Unthinkable! I have nothing to wear."

He threw his head back and roared with laughter. "The first concern of every woman since Eve! Faith, I should have known you'd say that."

She watched him, concerned. Both her mother and Mr. Ilkston disapproved of females who spent excessive time considering their appearance. Miss Gloriana Harcourt's elaborate toilettes, for example, often aroused their ire.

To her relief, Richard's eyes twinkled at her from across the table. "I expect you wish to refurbish your wardrobe at the first opportunity, my dear. Once we're settled in town, I'll whisk you off to the shops." He raised his eyebrows. "I can recommend some very fine mantua makers."

"Oh!" Bethany gasped as she realized the implication of his words. "Forgive me, your lordship, but I would prefer not to patronize the same shops as those who provide for your—your women." She pushed her chair back and marched to the closed door. "I think it best to return to my chamber."

He stood, too, but remained by the table. "I fear you must wait until I am finished. Unless you care to traipse through a public house unescorted." Raucous laughter burst from the common room beyond as if to punctuate his remark, followed by a bawdy song.

She halted, one hand on the handle, debating whether it would be more tolerable inside the parlour or outside. Before she resolved the matter, her betrothed crossed to her side.

"Stubborn girl. Did that stiff-necked pride get you in trouble often?" He lifted her hand in his warm one. Ignoring the pleasant flutter of her heart, she pulled it out of his grasp. He let her go but leaned one shoulder against the door and crossed his arms, blocking escape.

"You'll do well in London." His green eyes softened as he murmured the words. She swallowed nervously, but his intense gaze hypnotized her into immobility. "You shall wear the finest silks and velvets, not dull wool. And in colors to show off that lovely skin."

She started at the touch of his fingertips against her cheek. He continued speaking softly, his eyes locked on hers. "I'll be the envy of every man at Court with you on my arm. They'll wonder what your beautiful hair looks like unpinned and falling over your shoulders." His hand slid around to the back of her neck and the other grasped her waist, holding her to him.

He did not let her escape from this kiss. She found herself wrapped in his arms while his mouth played over hers. Her lips opened of their own volition to admit his searching tongue. He tasted of ale and sweet apple. When she shyly touched it with hers, he growled and delved farther into her mouth.

She tried to protest when he lifted her and moved toward the fireplace, but she could not form the words. Instead her arm slid to his chest, feeling the heartbeat pounding beneath her palm. She gulped for air against his neck, inhaling the faint lavender scent of his shirt and neck cloth.

Moments later, he reached the settle, pulling her onto his lap. Before she could utter a word, he bent to her lips again, this time merely brushing them before moving on to whisper her name against her cheek.

When he nuzzled his way to an exquisitely sensitive place on her neck, she gasped and dropped her head back over his arm to allow greater access. Heat gathered in her stomach at his groan of pleasure.

Overwhelmed by the new sensations coursing through her, she stroked his hair, marveling at the softness of the dark gold strands. Only when his hand slipped beneath the kerchief shielding her breasts did she struggle to push him away.

"Enough!" She looked into his darkened green eyes inches from hers. Horrified, she realized that her kerchief was nearly undone while Richard's neck cloth hung loose. His chest rose and fell in rhythm with her pounding heart. His arms tightened around her, pulling her more firmly onto the ridge of flesh pressed up against her bottom.

"Sweet Bethany." He rocked his hips under her, and her breath caught. "Let me come to you tonight, lovely girl." His free hand stroked her neck. "We can be wed as soon as we get to London tomorrow."

"No! We can't." She scrambled to her feet despite the fear that her shaking knees would not support her. She did not know if the angry cast of his face resulted from a trick of the firelight or his own feelings. In any case, she did not dare give in to the carnal urges sweeping over her. Despite the evidence of his need for her money, she would be at a disadvantage until he placed a wedding ring on her finger. She seized on their earlier conversation.

"I won't be married in rags." Cringing inwardly at the incredulity gathering on his features, she tossed her head. "As you said, a woman's first concern is dressing well. I shan't marry you until I can do so in something other a travel-stained dress and an old cloak."

"I wholeheartedly approve your plans, madam, but that has nothing to do with our more private relations." He unfolded himself from the settle. Although her height prevented him from towering over her, she had to look up a few inches to meet his glare. Unnerved, she stepped back a few paces.

"Tell me you don't enjoy my touch." She dropped her eyes at his taunt. "Or that you don't wish to

explore my body the way I want to discover yours."
Bethany stared at the floor.

"Please don't make me do this yet." She raised
her head and entreated him. With an exasperated sigh, he grabbed her cloak from the back of
the settle and tossed it at her. Mechanically she
caught it.

"Cover yourself. I'll take you back to your bedchamber." She nodded at the curt order, not trust-
ing herself to reply as she wrapped the faded wool
around her.

He strode to the door and wrenched it open.
Tight-lipped, he awaited her approach. Grasping
her arm painfully, he accompanied her past the
cheerful crowd in the taproom.

At her chamber, he unexpectedly pushed her
back against the door. The night hid his face, but
Bethany could feel every inch of his body as he
leaned into her, pressing her to the hard wood.

"Tell me you won't dream of this, little Puritan."
His whisper warmed her cheek before he ravaged
her mouth. She felt his triumphant smile as she
instinctively softened beneath him. She heard him
fumble with the door handle. Before she knew it,
she stumbled backward into the room.

His eyes blazed in the light of a single candle, but
he did not follow her inside. "I bid you good night,
madam." With those cold words, he slammed the
door shut, leaving Bethany alone with her jumbled
thoughts.

Trembling, she hastily undressed down to her shift
and climbed between the sheets of the feather bed.

Blowing out the candle, she tried unsuccessfully to convince herself that she shook from cold and fear.

One story below, Richard crossed the inn yard to the stables. He swore under his breath as he stumbled over a stray piece of firewood. Carefully easing the door open, he slipped inside. A horse whickered, reminding him to stop at the stalls where his hired animals rested. He trusted Lane's report that they had been fed, watered, and groomed, but they had served him well this day. Depositing a dried apple from supper in each manger, he made his way to the hewn bars of wood that served as a ladder into the loft.

His sour mood worsened when a splinter jammed its way into his forefinger halfway up. Damning his lean purse, his debts, and his stubborn fiancée, he heaved himself up and made a place in the clean hay. A few yards away, Lane snored blissfully.

Wrapping himself in his cloak, he stretched out on his back, hands behind his head. Thinking of Bethany only worsened his temper. Visions of her fair skin and coppery hair vied with that of her curled up on a soft mattress. He knew not which he desired more, the girl or the bed.

"Curst virgin!" With that final imprecation, he rolled over and tried to sleep.

Chapter 3

Bethany arose heavy-eyed and guilt-ridden the next morning. She had tossed and turned all night even on Mistress Gatwell's comfortable bed as she recalled her shameless behavior. In the normal way of things, she would give thanks to marry a man whose touch pleased her so. Certainly Mr. Ilkston's had brought her no pleasure.

She could not help but wonder what Lord Harcourt thought of a woman who gave in to a few kisses so easily. Her reluctance to face him caused her to linger in her room after she had dressed and penned a note to her mother.

Eventually she forced herself to descend to the yard. Her betrothed stood in the chill winter air speaking to the landlord. He threw her a lowering glance and told her to break her fast so they could leave.

Inside the now empty common room, Mistress Gatwell handed her a trencher of day-old bread and a bit of cheese. After requesting the obliging soul to post her letter, she nibbled her food by the window, observing her betrothed as he tossed off the last of a tankard of ale. She wondered if he had eaten anything with it.

They surely made a fine pair this morning, she reflected. Her skirts fell limply to her feet after yesterday's travel. His rumpled clothing looked as if he'd slept in it, and there were smudges under his eyes to match her own.

Lane guided the creaky old coach up to the pathway leading to the door. Richard exchanged a few words with him and turned to pay the innkeeper. Bethany hastily backed away from the window, hoping he had not caught her watching him.

Almost immediately she careened into a solid mass. Two hands grasped her elbows to steady her, and she found herself looking into the brown eyes of a man nearly a hand span taller than Richard. The thick brown curls of a periwig cascaded over his shoulders, and the fine muslin shirt under the voluminous black coat with green silk facings bespoke a man of substance.

"Pray, madam, forgive my clumsiness!" The gentleman bowed from the waist and swept his feathered hat over the green ribbons and silver buckles decorating his shoes. The country-bred girl stifled a giggle at the sight of matching ribbons adorning his knees. "I thought I saw a dear friend of mine in the yard, and crowded too close to the window trying to see if I was correct. Are you unhurt?"

Distracted by his sartorial grandeur, she scrambled to remember her manners. "Entirely unhurt, sir. I fear it is I who must apologize for not watching where I stepped. I must have been wool-gathering not to have noticed you."

Apparently taking the words as a compliment, he bowed once more. "You are too kind, dear lady. I should have made my presence known to you. My acquaintances often accuse me of being so quiet I nearly sneak up on them." As he said the last words, an unexpected gleam of amusement lit the dark eyes.

"Mistress Bethany!" Mistress Gatwell bustled up to say that her brother awaited her in the yard. Exchanging a last nod with the beribboned gentleman, she left the inn's warmth for the cold winter air.

She sighed at the old vehicle and faced Richard. "Is it a very long way to London?"

To her annoyance, he chuckled at her wistful question. "That depends on your stomach, my dear."

Offended at his amusement, she permitted him to hand her into the rattletrap and place a hot brick at her feet, but refused to speak to him further after he took his place on the seat opposite. Richard knocked on the roof and with a violent lurch the day's journey began.

Inside the Bell and Moon's common room, the large gentleman watched their departure with great interest. He had not set eyes on Richard Harcourt or his family for some time, but he very much doubted that his sister would have grown so many inches since then. Or changed from a blonde to a redhead.

Although the distance to London was longer by several miles than the previous day's travels, the smoother roads prevented another episode of Bethany's illness. After a number of stops to rest the horses and give her a chance to get down from the coach, it was midafternoon before they arrived.

Richard watched her wide-eyed gaze take in the noise and bustle of the capitol, hiding his amusement. For all his twenty-eight years, he had gawked much the same way when he arrived for the King's coronation last spring.

A night in the hayloft left him in no fine mood that morning, and his irritation increased when he realized that the day would see the last of his ready cash gone. Thankfully, his little Puritan had eaten lightly at dinnertime, and he could delay supper until their arrival in town.

His back and posterior ached from the bouncing on the thinly padded seats all day. Despite her fascination with the sights outside the coach's window, she looked pale. Noticing that she rubbed the back of her neck every once in a while, he surmised that she had a headache. He assured her that they would arrive at their destination shortly. Her grateful smile told him he guessed right.

A shout from outside the carriage startled both of them. He sprang to a half crouch between the seats, his sword drawn instinctively. He glanced at Bethany and put a finger to his lips. She nodded, gray eyes wide with fear. Straightening as much as possible in the cramped vehicle, he flung the door open.

Torchlight danced along his naked blade as a couple of soldiers confronted him.

"Where be you going after sundown, sir?"

Richard lowered his weapon a few inches. "I am attempting to return to my lodgings. And what business is that of His Majesty's army, pray tell?"

"Never tell me you don't know anyone abroad after dark is to be stopped and questioned!" The older man, a sergeant, regarded him indignantly.

"Certainly such was not the custom when I left London four days past." Richard assumed the brisk air he'd used during his days in the French army. "Who is your commander?"

The guard scratched his head. "I can't rightly say, sir. A fellow named Venner sent some Puritans on a rampage against the King two days ago, and then again last night. We were called out and told what to do, but we ain't seen an officer all day."

"No officers and you're still on duty? Well done!" Under his calculated praise, the men straightened and puffed out their chests. After giving them his name, they saluted smartly and waved the coach along.

Shortly after that, Lane set them down before the old building containing his lodgings. Richard assisted Bethany out and escorted her to the door. She stopped short as she gazed up at the building.

"What is this place?" She faced him, realization gathering in her gray eyes. "Do not tell me you expect me to share your lodgings."

"I do expect just that." They had not argued excessively, but two days of sitting in that miserable coach, a night in a hayloft, and short rations had exhausted his patience. "Now, please be so good as to go inside and not pick a quarrel on the street."

"I do not normally indulge in such ill-bred behavior, my lord, but no gentleman installs an unmarried lady in his lodgings." His companion's pretty face looked downright mulish as she stood her ground. "I insist that you find a decent place for me to stay. At once."

He reminded himself of his desperate straits and her fortune in order to restrain himself from pulling her inside like a small child. "This, madam, is London. You will find a good number of females living with gentlemen to whom they are not married."

"Those are not ladies." She crossed her arms, daring him to deny her demand. He took a deep breath. Gloriana at her most spoiled did not exasperate him like this chit.

He turned to the grinning coachman. "Lane, return the coach to the Mermaid at once." The grizzled driver barely suppressed a snort of laughter before climbing back on the box and slapping the reins against the horses' backs.

Returning his attention to his outraged fiancée, he grasped her arm and tried to escort her inside. She did not budge.

"Your choice, my girl. Either spend the night in my rooms or on the street. I haven't the silver to buy you a room." He stepped over the threshold and looked over his shoulder. "Well?"

She gave him a withering scowl before flouncing through the doorway.

Following him up the stairs, Bethany wrung her hands under her cloak. It never occurred to her that he would bring her to his lodgings. She faced disaster.

"Do you not have any married friends I could stay with?" She would infinitely prefer to stay with strangers instead of a man who turned her to melted wax with one touch.

"No." She flinched at the snapped monosyllable. She tried to think of an alternative, but her pounding head pushed all thought aside. Except for her wish to avoid the all too attractive Richard Harcourt until after they wed.

She had nearly given in to him last night. His mouth ignited her with its touch and honeyed whispers alike. It would have been easy enough to remedy such a lapse. As a peer he could apply for a special license, and her trustees would have paid to prevent a scandal.

A scrabbling in the wall next to her interrupted her musings. She shuddered and hoped this ramshackle building housed nothing larger than mice.

Richard clearly needed her fortune and only by marrying her could he touch a penny of it. Her jaw hardened as she watched his heavy cloak swaying up the stairs ahead of her. She had consented to wed him for a home of her own and a title, but she hardly cherished illusions of matrimonial bliss. Once she provided him with an heir, she expected him to deposit her at his estate while he lived mostly in town.

Compared to this dank-smelling place, the prospect of living in the country sounded downright appealing. She had learned to order a household and run an estate from her mother.

Bethany stifled a sigh. A husband held absolute authority over his wife and her possessions unless her father or guardians bargained for a decent allowance. As she had neither, she must look after her own interests. If she convinced Richard to settle part of her money on her outright, she would gain some measure of security.

Besides which she objected to Richard gambling her father's fortune away and spending it on his mistresses.

But for her to force his hand, he had to need the marriage more than she did. If she allowed him to finish what he had started last night at the inn, she also must marry in order to preserve her reputation.

Despite her bravado in the coach the previous day, she did care about society's opinion. Growing up in her mother's well-run but austere household, Bethany's liking for display and attention had earned her frequent lectures on proper feminine behavior.

Ahead of her, Richard paused in a doorway off the first landing. His rigid posture indicated his lingering animosity. "Madam." He bowed. Swallowing, she entered the den of iniquity awaiting her.

After one horrified look, she turned back to him, pleading. "Are you quite sure you don't know anywhere else I might stay?"

When he had agreed to bring Bethany to London, he had expected to simply bring her to his rooms, find her vicar, wed her, and pay off his debts. The reality looked different as he saw his rooms through her eyes.

"As I had not planned to bring you back here, I did not take time to tidy it before leaving." He followed her in, trying to cover up his discomfort.

"A wise decision. You'd still be here, wouldn't you?" She moved cautiously into the room, stepping delicately around a few empty wine bottles scattered on the floor. He vaguely remembered playing ninepins with them, using an orange for a ball. After a moment's panic, the sight of the dried peel sitting on a table assured him that the fruit was not rotting somewhere along the paneled wall.

He watched her drift through the room, examining a pile of periodicals, wrinkling her nose at some empty wineglasses scattered on a gateleg table. To his relief, she kept her composure. "I gather you have no servants?"

He cleared his throat. "There's Lane, of course.

He's used to the stables more than housekeeping, but he's been with me for years."

"As has this, apparently." She held a worn seat cushion between her thumb and forefinger at arm's length as a thin trail of sawdust dribbled out of one corner. Gingerly replacing it, she surveyed the rest of the room.

"It came this way. The furniture did, at any rate." He crossed his arms. "Coming to London was your idea, not mine."

She ignored him and wandered over to examine a pile of plates. "I collect that Lane at least comprehends the function of a dishcloth and soap. Do you usually keep clean dishes on the window seat?"

He shrugged. "Why not? They're closer to hand."

A pained expression crossed her face and she shut her eyes. "All things considered, Richard, it may be best that you are marrying into money. We are going to hire at least one maidservant as soon as possible. And the first thing we are going to do after we marry is find a decent place to live."

His lips twitched as she removed a few books from a chair and searched for a place to put them, but he said nothing. After last evening, he had his own ideas about the first activities in which they would indulge following the wedding. They did not include house hunting.

Bethany's exploration ended quickly when she discovered that the far door led to his bedchamber. She immediately closed it again, flushing crimson at his unrepentant grin.

"How on earth do you cook in here?" Her perplexed gaze took in the small fireplace.

"We don't. Lane brings hot meals in, or whatever else we need—bread, fruit, wine, that sort of thing. We keep them in the cupboard in the corner." Her brow furrowed. Obviously she wanted to ask him something, but she hesitated.

"What were you going to ask now?" He smiled at her grave face and clasped hands.

"Do you think he'll be much longer?" Her pensive question reminded him that their small dinner on the road had been several hours ago.

"He's likely been delayed at the Mermaid." Richard chuckled. "He's, ah, quite friendly with one of the chambermaids there. I'm famished as well. Shall I go out and see what I can find among the stalls on the street?"

"That would be wonderful, but how will you pay for it?" She cocked her head to one side. "I thought you had no money."

"That's the great advantage of being a peer. Since coming to London, I maintain quite a comfortable living"—he ignored her derisive exclamation—"by the adroit use of my title in the right ears. London merchants have proved more than happy to extend credit to members of His Majesty's Court." He bowed.

"Provided, of course, that they never visit Hampton Palace and discover just how unimportant the peer truly is." He observed her growing indignation as he finished his explanation.

"Good heavens, this is some sort of game for

you." Her eyes flashed. "You do nothing but trade on your name to see what it brings you. First the merchants, then me."

He froze. "Be careful what you accuse me of, madam. My father refused to sully his name and mine with disloyalty when those fat merchants were scrambling for Cromwell's favor. 'Twas no game. His sense of honor cost him his estates and his life."

He fell silent, hands clenched. How dare she judge his actions? She had no grasp of the life he had led.

She stood by the fireplace, shocked at his vehemence, frightened. He realized that despite her practicality, she was only a few years older than his sister, and had grown up in the relative security of the countryside.

He forced himself to speak lightly. "Besides, that is the name that is going to obtain our evening meal." He jammed his black felt hat on his head, but shut the door behind him quietly, careful not to slam it.

"Richard, wait!" He heard her voice through the door, but hurried down the stairs. He needed to calm himself before he faced her again.

"Trading his name," as Bethany called it, took long enough that he walked directly home after his purchases. Only his insistence that he would possess a wealthy bride within the week induced the shop owners to give him their evening meal.

He would have to discover her father's bank and arrange for a letter of credit in order to eat after tomorrow's breakfast.

His full hands prevented him from opening his own door. Bethany answered his knock and took the parcels from him as he shrugged off his cloak and beheld his room. She had rolled up her sleeves to clean, and taken her cap off. Even pinned up, the flaming strands caught his eye.

While much of the chaotic tumble remained, she had dusted off two chairs and a small table. Other piles of clutter had disappeared. He noticed that all the cushions had been removed. When asked, Bethany informed him that she had tossed them onto the midden heap in the alley behind.

She sniffed a smallish parcel. "What is this?"

"Eel pie. I fear 'twas the best I could coax from the pie man." She eyed it doubtfully but said nothing and proceeded to put away the remaining foodstuffs before setting the pies out, along with bread and wine.

They supped heartily as dusk gathered outside the windows. After her initial cautious taste, she devoured her pie. Richard coaxed her to join him in a second glass of wine as they ate their bread and cheese.

Afterward, Bethany replaced the supper dishes with a candelabrum while Richard prowled the room restlessly. He seldom dined in his rooms, spending most evenings with his cronies at the theater, or visiting the numerous gambling dens and public houses catering to gentlemen. Occasionally he patronized a bawdy house, but he found women of his own social standing more attractive. And for him, their favors were usually free.

Mentally, he shrugged. For the fortune that Bethany brought, he would willingly pay the price of a few nights' boredom. Once his ring was safely on her finger, he could do what he wished wherever he wanted.

The girl sat at the table before a piece of paper, writing steadily with a quill and ink unearthed from somewhere in the mess. Candlelight danced off her blazing hair, and he had a sudden urge to unpin it. What he wanted just now, he decided, was a bit of sport.

With a sly glance at her bent head, he selected a copy of Shakespeare's sonnets. He'd rushed his fences with her last evening. He would take slower steps now.

"Would you care to have me read to you?"

Bethany looked up from her work. He supposed it was a trick of the candlelight, but her bright gray eyes looked almost silver, a most attractive effect. "I'm sorry, I was not attending."

He bestowed upon her his most disarming smile. "I wondered if you would care to have me read aloud."

"That would be delightful." She colored slightly. "If you really wish to, of course. As you can see, I have found a way to occupy myself."

"You put me to shame with your industry, to be

sure." He seated himself opposite her. "Whatever are you working so hard on?"

"Lists, sir. One for immediate household needs, one for errands that must be run, another of questions I have." She flexed her fingers. "Before you begin, shall I pour you a drink? I believe I saw a jug of cider among all your bottles of wine."

"Thank you, yes, but another glass from the open bottle if you please. Pour one for yourself." When she eyed him doubtfully, he dismissed her unspoken concern. "Claret, my dear, the feeblest stuff imaginable."

Once they both settled back down, he thumbed through the book.

"'Shall I compare thee to a summer's day? Thou art more lovely and more temperate . . .'" As he read sonnet after sonnet, he watched her reaction from the corner of his eye. As the quill moved slower and slower over the sheets in front of her, he lowered his voice, forcing her to concentrate in order to hear him.

The quill stopped completely. She sat across from him, unmoving, as he wove his spell. Seeing the kerchief over her breasts moving rapidly with each breath she took, he felt his own body tighten in response.

He closed the book with a soft smack. She raised her eyes then. Looking into their glittering silver depths, he felt himself drawn in, wanting her. He set the book down and rose to his feet, stretching slightly. "Did you enjoy that?"

She nodded, silent.

"I shall take you to the theater. You've never seen a play, have you?" He smiled faintly as she shook her head. "But first the shops. As Lady Harcourt, you'll need fine dresses of velvet or silk. Perhaps in green to show off your hair."

She touched the coil at her neck. "I despise it!"

"Why? It's beautiful." She stood up and backed away as he approached her. He chuckled. "'Tis a small room, you've nowhere to go." Proving his point, he cornered her by the door. She averted her head, eyes closed, her breath coming in soft puffs. "I told you I wouldn't hurt you." With those soft words, he gave in to the itch to unpin her burnished copper locks.

The thick braid unfurled down her back. She did not move as he combed his fingers through it, except to lick her lips. He bent to nuzzle her soft cheek, exulting in the shudder he elicited from her. His lips moved over the silken skin, easing toward her mouth, but not taking it.

She rewarded him by turning her head to him, opening herself to him with a soft moan. He embraced her gently as his tongue swept into her accepting mouth, twining with hers.

As their kiss deepened and roughened, his arms tightened, holding her to him. Her body nearly matched his for height, fitting perfectly against him. He left her mouth, searching for the sensitive point on her throat as she gasped and threw her head back.

It smacked painfully against the wall.

"Bethany! Are you all right?" He stepped back

to avoid a bloody nose when she doubled over in pain, but stayed by her side. "I've never known such a dangerous female." He drew her to a hard-backed bench and sat her down.

"If you'd stop trying to maul me, these things wouldn't happen." She grimaced, rubbing the back of her head.

Still unable to keep his hands out of the soft strands, he carefully stroked over the sore area. He felt heat in the injured spot, but no swelling. Relieved, he let his fingers slide to the base of her neck, circling and pressing.

She shut her eyes once more, sighing in pleasure as he worked the stiffness out of her tense muscles. When he finished, she sighed. "Much better."

"Indeed." He kissed her again, stroking her cheek with his thumb. In her relaxed state, Bethany responded ardently, placing one hand on his chest while the other moved to cup the back of his head.

He emitted a guttural moan as his hand stroked down her satiny throat to the top of her breast. Seeking beneath her kerchief and the edge of the wool bodice, his fingers found a sensitive peak. As they rolled and pinched it to stiffness, her back arched and her breathing grew ragged. Egged on by the sound, he followed with his mouth. Grasping the edge of the kerchief with his teeth, he eased it aside while working the bodice lower with his hands.

Bethany mewled at the pleasurable friction of soft muslin against her straining nipples. She knew she should tell Richard to stop, but thought fled as he freed her breasts from her stays and began to suckle. A trail of fire coursed its way down to the apex of her thighs and nestled there, burning. Her restless fingers tangled in Richard's honey-colored strands as he cupped the creamy mounds in his hands, sucking and nibbling at each coral tip in turn.

A protest left her mouth when he abandoned them, but his mouth fastened over hers before she could complete it. Her hand stroked over his cheek and down to his cravat, loosening the snowy folds. He whispered his desire in her ear before nipping lightly at her earlobe and licking the tender skin below.

She reciprocated, shyly pressing kisses along his skin just below his jaw. At his growl of pleasure, she became bolder, moving her mouth down his muscular throat. Sitting up against him, she buried her face in the base of his throat, kissing and stroking.

She started as she felt her bodice loosen. Richard was untying it with one hand while his other slipped beneath her skirt and petticoat. His arousal pressed against her thigh.

"Shall we finish this in the bedchamber, my lovely girl?" The husky murmur meant nothing to her for a few seconds. When the meaning sank in, she choked and struggled to her feet. Looking down at herself, a wave of shame enveloped her.

"Dear God, what am I doing?" With an agonized cry, she turned away, trying to put her clothes in place. Her hands shook so severely she could barely manage the task.

From behind her, she heard the soft creak of the bench as Richard stood. She forced herself to face him. He stood only a few paces away, arms at his sides. His rough exhalations and the bulge in his pantaloons indicated his clear state of arousal.

She could see the fury in his darkened eyes at being denied for a second night running. They rested pointedly on her breasts where they threatened to spill out of her bodice. Unable to find her kerchief, she drew her hair over her shoulders.

"A trifle late for modesty, little Puritan." He bit the words out.

She choked back a sob. "I'm sorry. I am so very sorry, Richard. I have no notion what possessed me to misbehave so badly these two nights." To her horror, another sob escaped, and tears blurred her vision. She dropped her gaze to the floor, struggling with her chaotic emotions.

He ran a hand through his hair. "Oh, Jesu, don't cry." Frustration descended on his face. "And don't pretend to coy virtue. Your zest for the exercise betrays your eagerness." The lips that had just reduced her to the veriest jade pressed into a tight line as he tugged his own clothing to rights. "God's teeth, we're to be married as soon as we find your minister! What difference does it make to start the honeymoon a night or two before?"

"You said you would not harm me!" Her temper rising, she stepped toward him with the accusation.

"Those were cries of pain, were they?" The last

shreds of shame disappeared at his mocking tone.
"You did not appear to be suffering unduly under
my attentions, madam!"

Unable to deny the truth of his statements,
Bethany floundered for a reply. In the end, she
could only sputter, "Go to your bed alone." Which,
with a deafening slam of the door, his lordship did.

She glowered after him, then proceeded to
make up a bed on the settle by rolling up her cloak
for a pillow and curling up under his. Waiting for
sleep to take her, she stared at the fire. The journey to London must have disordered her senses,
she reflected. She had never experienced the least
urge to behave so badly with Mr. Ilkston. Her last
thought before drifting to sleep was the sincere
hope that they would find Mr. Barker before she
abandoned all her morals.

Chapter 4

Bethany roused intermittently through the night to shift from one awkward position to another, scolding herself for letting her temper get the better of her. She disliked the idea of sleeping on the floor before properly cleaning it, but doubted she would catch more than a few minutes of sleep on the unyielding settle. Her eyes drooped as she wondered how soon she could find a reputable maidservant.

Only a few moments later, it seemed, she scrambled to sit up, awakened by a loud crash and angry voices. Her pounding heart slowed as the dim light of predawn revealed an empty room. She must have slept for a few hours at any rate.

Following the noise of the disturbance, she half stumbled to the window. On the street below, she discerned a dray tilting to one side. Its canvas-covered load looked to be in danger of falling off as the driver castigated another man standing behind a pushcart. They shouted in a cant she understood only a few words of, but she gathered the cart had swerved to avoid hitting the peddler and had gotten stuck as a result. A deep hole in the cobbles held one wheel fast, and the cart now blocked not only the pushcart owner, but a gaggle of other pedestrians.

Some of them put their shoulders to the vehicle as the driver climbed aboard and cracked his whip over his horses' heads. Bethany's eyes narrowed. One big fellow reminded her of Lane.

The dray lurched forward with a wall-shaking jolt and huzzahs from the onlookers. It left a dark pile of something on the street, which a number of them instantly fell upon. She realized the canvas covered a load of coal.

The driver, distracted by hearty congratulations from a couple of men, waved a hand in thanks and proceeded down the street, oblivious of the theft.

The knot of bystanders smoothed itself into a trickle of pedestrians going their own ways as if nothing had happened. Indeed, as far as Bethany could tell, no one else even bothered to look out of their windows.

A nervous peep into the bedchamber revealed Richard snoring blissfully under the coverlets. Shaking her head, Bethany wondered how he had slept through the uproar, and hoped such tumults did not occur daily.

She had washed and put her clothes and hair to rights before Lane knocked softly on the door. She ignored his obvious surprise at finding her awake and raised an eyebrow at the small bucket of coal he carried. "Out getting supplies early? I am surprised you found a merchant willing to give Lord Harcourt credit."

The coachman's grizzled face assumed an exaggerated expression of innocence. "You might say as how a bit of luck fell my way, mistress."

"A bit of coal, like as not." Bethany sighed. They had no other fuel. Indeed, she had clasped her cloak around her to ward off the room's winter chill.

After he made up the fire, she handed him a portion of their remaining bread and cheese, along with a tankard of small beer. "What time does his lordship normally arise?"

The servant considered, head to one side. "That's hard to say, mistress. After a late night, he may not awaken till midafternoon." Hastily he added, "No doubt he'll want to be up bright and early today. No later than noon, never fret." Before she could exclaim at such laxness, he thanked her for breakfast and promised to return the tankard after he had finished.

In his wake, Bethany looked around, at a loss. Normally she spent time in prayer and devotions after dressing. She repeated her prayers from memory, but missed her daily reading. Remembering a battered volume she had come across the day before, she located it. After a deep breath, she opened it to the title page.

The Book of Common Prayer and Administration of the Sacraments. Opposite, a well-schooled hand had written, "To our greatly beloved son Richard upon the occasion of his confirmation." The signatures of both his mother and his father followed. Naturally the Harcourts would cling to a prayer book banned under the Protectorate.

She leafed through the pages, glancing at unfamiliar liturgies to sacraments she had scarcely heard of. She read a psalm aloud, marveling that it sounded nearly identical to those she'd learned in her church. Many of the prayers held little of the papistry she had been taught to expect in the Church of England.

By the time Richard opened the door to the bedroom, yawning hugely, she had replaced the book. She had also washed Lane's tankard, dusted, set the table, swept the floor, and cleaned the window.

"How kind of you to join me for breakfast, sir."

"Breakfast?" He regarded the plate of golden cheddar and the small hard loaves of bread with revulsion. "Never touch the stuff." He poured himself a tankard from the pitcher of beer sitting beside them. "I'll just have a drink, and then we can go find your father's banker."

Bethany's determination to maintain a charitable outlook disappeared. "My back aches from that abominable settle, the sun has been up for over an hour, and out of good manners I have waited even longer than that to eat. Therefore I suggest you do me the courtesy of joining me at the table!"

"You do, do you?" Beer sloshed over the edge of the tankard as he slammed it down. "In the normal way of things, a wife defers to her husband."

"Fortunately for me, I am not your wife yet. And

if you do not sit down this instant, I am not like ever to be." She realized she had said the worst possible thing as soon as the words left her mouth.

Richard's eyes narrowed and his face went blank. "Are you threatening me?" For the first time, Bethany caught a glimpse of steel behind his charming façade.

She gulped, but took her place. Slowly, he seated himself opposite, cutting off a wedge of cheese. She moderated her voice. "You did say you would take me to the shops first thing."

He flicked a cold glance at her. "Ah. So I did. Of course the fact that I have no way to pay for your finery without a letter of credit has conveniently escaped your mind."

"You got this last night." She indicated their meal.

"This may come as a shock to you, madam, but women's clothes are often a great deal more expensive than day-old bread." Richard smiled condescendingly. "Particularly at the town's better mantua makers."

"And I am sure you are most familiar with the cost of female attire." She gave him a look as she ripped apart a piece of bread.

His smiled disappeared. "I wonder if you haven't been cozening me all along."

Her heart nearly failed. Surely she had not given herself away! His gaze bored into her. "I doubt you even know the name of the bank, much less the banker."

Relief swept through Bethany. "Of course I do!

'Tis Mr. Armitage of—" She gasped. "You wretch! You only said that to trick me."

A grin flashed across his face. "Well, I couldn't get it out of you any other way."

She could not repress a chuckle at his frankness. Some of the tension in the room abated. She sobered. "Please believe that I wish to move the matter of our marriage forward. I hope we might visit Mr. and Mrs. Barker as well as the bank today. After a visit to the shops."

She held up the travel-stained gray wool of her skirt. "The future Lady Harcourt can hardly appear wearing this."

Her desire to find Mr. Barker and proceed with their nuptials heartened him but did not ameliorate his impatience to visit the bank. However, guilt at his shabby behavior combined with Bethany's earlier stubborn refusal to render up the name of the banker induced him to allow her to have her way.

He escorted her to the establishment of a mantua maker patronized by several aristocratic ladies of his acquaintance. To his surprise, Bethany hesitated to enter.

Fingering the skirt and the shabby cloak that attracted the scorn of the ladies going in and out of the shop, she cast a nervous glance up at him.

Teasing her that her feisty nature must be reserved only for his benefit, he ruthlessly opened the door and shoved her in ahead of him. Her inherent pride quickly reasserted itself when the proprietor tried to ignore her. His lips twitched in amusement when she wasted no time in announcing herself as Lord Harcourt's betrothed, in want of a trousseau.

She was shortly borne off by the owner's wife, a plump woman with a businesslike air who quickly ferreted out of Bethany the information that Lord Harcourt would be wealthier by several thousand pounds as soon as he wed.

While lacking the fascination in feminine kickshaws that characterized the Court dandies, Richard owed no money at this particular shop and was inclined to linger. However, after seeing no sign of the future Lady Harcourt after three quarters of an hour, he left a message asking her to await his return and departed for a nearby coffeehouse after adding a few items to the account he had just opened.

An hour later, having engaged in a friendly discussion of the King's latest dispute with Parliament, he returned to find his fiancée just emerging from the back of the shop.

He stopped short. She wore a dress of vivid green velvet ornamented by a lace-edged cambric kerchief and cuffs. Its modest cut resembled the discarded gray wool, but the rich material and color flattered her infinitely more. The addition of a wide-brimmed black hat simply trimmed with matching ribbons gave the ensemble an air of elegance. Her hair remained in its braided coil under a frilled cap, but he heard her asking for the name of a reputable hairdresser as she wrapped herself in a new black cloak lined with tawny satin.

She caught sight of him and flushed under his keen regard. He bowed, hand over heart. Her blush deepened at the loverlike display, although she made him a small curtsey in return.

"You're making a spectacle of yourself." She indicated the owner's wife sighing sentimentally behind the counter. Ignoring his unrepentant grin, she continued on a lighter note.

"'Tis the most fortunate thing! The lady who commissioned this dress never paid for it, and it fits me quite closely, except for the length. They pinned a flounce to the bottom and assure me that under my cloak it will not show. They sent a boy to the milliner's across the street for my hat and trimmed it themselves."

To Richard's vast amusement, his little Puritan prattled on about satin, laces, and velvets in a most worldly manner. However, when she expanded on the subject and stated a desire to visit other shops selling such necessities as hats, gloves, fans, embroidered stockings, shoes, and shoe buckles, he balked.

"Since you have an unaccountable longing to pay the bills from all these tradesmen, I must first wait upon your father's banker. His name and direction, if you please." Bethany provided them, albeit with a sigh. Guessing the cause, her betrothed cheerfully informed her the shops would doubtless be in the same places tomorrow morning.

He tucked her hand a little deeper into his elbow as they walked. The girl turned her head this way and that so much that she scarcely attended to where she stepped. If he did not take care, she would end up in front of a dray-cart. He smiled as she craned her head to watch an orange-girl stroll the opposite way, her wares displayed in a basket held on top of her head.

"However does she keep them in a perfect pyramid? I should have dropped them all over the street." He guided her around a mud puddle.

"Practice." Seeing the orange-girl stop to proposition two gentlemen blatantly ogling her, he drew Bethany's attention away by pointing to a set of stocks used by the magistrates to punish local miscreants. Although empty at the moment, he assured her that they were a great source of entertainment to the local populace.

She looked at them for a moment until recognition dawned. In a gesture he started to recognize, she stopped walking. Praying for patience, he asked the reason.

"You shall not take me back to your lodgings!" She looked over at him. The familiar storm gathered in her eyes under the brim of her hat.

"Of course I'm taking you back to my lodgings. Ladies of breeding do not wander the streets unaccompanied." He spoke in the firm voice that usually cowed his sister. His fiancée remained unimpressed. To his astonishment, she stated her intention to accompany him to the banker.

To her astonishment, he flatly refused. No female

ever appeared in the precincts of a financial institution, he assured her. Over her protestations, he informed her that she could return to his rooms either at his side or over his shoulder.

On the verge of daring him to pick her up in the middle of the street, she caught the icy expression in his green eyes and stopped. Bethany realized with a shock that he was completely serious. Distracted by the memory of his solidly muscled arms holding her to him, she shook her head, trying to think clearly.

She capitulated, and he uncrossed his arms to walk beside her, offering her his arm. It might be possible to follow him, she decided.

To her dismay, he suavely ushered her to his rooms, then promptly shouted for Lane. As soon as the good man stumped down from an upper floor, Richard bade him keep watch in the front hall in case Mistress Dallison attempted to leave on her own.

"She is naturally anxious to call upon a number of shops," he explained blandly to the coachman, "but I fear the chill weather may be injurious to her health."

Lane looked at her from his place on the landing and nervously observed the lady's mutinous expression. Nevertheless, he assured Master Richard that he would take care not to let her endanger herself.

At that, milord smiled sweetly over at her and

bade her enjoy the afternoon. Indignantly she watched him clap his hat on his head and make his way back down the stairs. Lane shrugged his shoulders apologetically at her and followed him.

Uttering a wordless cry of frustration, she left the landing and shut the door behind her.

Looking about the still cluttered room, she supposed she might as well finish cleaning it up. Hanging up her hat and cloak, she started in, careful not to muss her new, and currently only, dress.

Not long afterward, she stood in the center of the room, pleased. The last piles of trash lay outside on the landing. Lane, citing his orders to watch the front door, had regretfully declined to carry them outside the building. He promised to do so the instant his lordship returned, however.

With the main room clean, she considered starting on the bedchamber. Remembering her body's reaction to Richard's lovemaking, she decided instead to go through the papers covering a table in the corner.

Before long, she learned why he had been driven to kidnap her. Besides hundreds of pounds' worth of bills, she found lists of gambling losses and thousands of pounds' worth of repairs to his Yorkshire estate. He had not paid Lane in seven months, nor his rent for the last two. He had avoided debtors' prison only by frequently changing addresses.

She shook her head. This would not do at all. Finding a piece of clean paper, she dipped a quill into the inkstand. Midday came and went as she patiently wrote out columns of figures and added them up.

When her belly growled for the third time in as many minutes, she stretched and got up for a dinner of bread and cold meat. Remembering Lane patiently sitting below, she carried some down to him.

When she returned, she eyed the paper-covered writing table with distaste. She had not fully assessed the entire amount of Richard's debts, but she knew not whether to feel relieved or discouraged. He undoubtedly needed to marry her to save himself from ruin, but she wondered if the man knew the value of a shilling.

Thinking to ponder the quandary while keeping her hands busy, she hesitantly entered Richard's bedchamber. She scarcely remembered her father, and had no memory of his masculine haunts.

She need not have been intimidated. The furniture was as rundown as that in the outer room. A sturdy four-poster bed dominated the room, festooned with dusty hangings of an indeterminate design. Along one wall stood a clothes press, partially open. Inside she saw his store of clothing, neatly arranged. A small table sat by the bed. The handsomest piece in the room was a chest of modern design, with two drawers under the main compartment.

However, the rest of the room looked as chaotic as the outer one had been. She tsked at the unmade bed, the empty wineglasses and papers strewn about.

Bethany sorted through the litter and piled it in the doorway for washing or removal. In the smaller room, she finished easily. Thinking next to change the bed linens, she lifted the lid of the chest, hoping to find clean sheets and pillowcases. She remembered reading a note of money owed to a laundress for washing some. To her relief, a clean set lay folded inside. Scooping them out, she closed the lid and examined the bed once more.

A shove on the mattress proved it to be heavy and stiff. Changing the sheets on such an ungainly piece of furniture would challenge two women. By herself, Bethany knew she would be covered in sweat before the job was done.

After a long moment, she furtively undressed down to her shift, carefully folding the new dress and placing it in the clothes press. Just in case, she shut the door to the front room before commencing her struggle with the cumbersome mattress.

The old sheets came off reasonably easily, and she bundled them up and put them outside the bedchamber's door before closing it again. Perhaps she could coax the laundress to wash them by promising payment upon her marriage. Placing the clean ones on in their stead proved as difficult as she had expected. In the end, with much grunting and grumbling, she succeeded.

Blowing several escaped strands of hair from her face with a loud "Whuff!," she flopped back on the bed to catch her breath before smoothing the coverlet back up.

She considered it a matter of most unfortunate

timing that Richard chose that moment to open the door.

He had spent a difficult hour with the trustee of the Dallison fortune. Mr. George Armitage turned out to have known the late Mr. Dallison. He possessed a suspicious nature and a dislike of moral depravity. He expressed doubt when Lord Harcourt informed him of the young lady's presence in London and outrage at his claim to have spent two nights alone with her.

In the face of such disbelief, Richard invited the gaunt banker to accompany him back to his rooms and speak to Mistress Dallison himself.

Mr. Armitage accepted the young nobleman's implicit dare, his supercilious air proclaiming that he was about to unmasque a hoax. The two tromped along in cold silence. The presence of the large and rough-looking Lane in the hallway shook the man's assurance. Richard sailed up to his lodgings with the banker in his wake.

Bowing the man in before him, he followed, only to experience his own momentary shock at finding the room empty. Perceiving the litter and the bundle of sheets by the door to the bedchamber, he languidly stepped over them and opened it. As he hoped, Mr. Armitage's eyes widened at the linens.

"Bethany?" He stopped short at the sight of her lying nearly naked in his unmade bed. 'Twas one he quite fancied, having imagined something similar over the last two nights. Although in his visions she did not gape at him in shock. He could not keep the grin off his face. "What an enchanting surprise!"

She scrambled to her knees and grabbed the coverlet to shield herself from his appreciative view. With a shriek of outrage, she dove toward the small table beside his bed.

Before he knew it, his heavy shaving mug whistled past his ears, followed by a volume of Ovid. Hastily backing out, he slammed the door behind him. He looked sheepishly at Mr. Armitage. "I don't believe Mistress Dallison is receiving visitors just at this time."

Just behind him, the scrawny banker stood holding his hand to his chest in the manner of one suffering from severe heart palpitations. His appalled gaze took in the shaving mug and the book.

"You, sir, are an unmitigated scoundrel," he puffed. He looked so agitated that Richard nearly offered him Bethany's vinaigrette.

The worthy man staggered past Richard and knocked on the door, only to hear Bethany furiously castigate him.

"Madam, my name is George Armitage. I am known in the City as a decent man, and I am prepared to offer you whatever aid you need to escape the hands of this reprobate."

The flow of invective stopped. Richard felt faint at the prospect of the wretched girl taking advantage of the offer and slipping through his fingers.

"I shall be out directly." Bethany's voice sounded

unexpectedly composed. Richard braced himself and waited. She was going to do something.

The door opened wide a few minutes later, providing a full view of the disheveled bed. Bethany had dressed but could not fasten the laces on the back of her bodice tightly. Her kerchief was nowhere to be found. Tendrils of hair flew about her face as she threw herself on the banker's bony chest.

Her fiancé wanted to shake her until her teeth rattled.

"Thank goodness you're here, sir! Lord Harcourt is the most vile beast!" She buried her head on his shoulder. He bade her calm herself, gingerly patting her back.

Richard gritted his teeth at the girl's playacting, but the other man appeared to be completely taken in. A blast of anger erupted when she raised her head once more, begging the other man to rescue her. "Have done, you stupid chit! You've hardly suffered any lasting harm at my hands."

His lack of remorse nearly sent the banker into an apoplexy. Struggling for breath, he looked pointedly from the bed to the half-dressed girl before returning his gaze to Richard's face. "No harm, sir? Mistress Dallison is nearly in hysterics from your brutality."

He turned to Bethany. "I recognized you at once, my child. You bear a strong resemblance to your father." He held her away from him to look her in the face. "Now, you must tell me the truth. Has this man . . ." He swallowed once or twice before he forced out the question. "Has this man defiled you?"

Her wail drowned out Richard's protests. "I cannot speak of it, sir! Abducted from my home and forced to spend two nights in his company— it was horrible."

Mr. Armitage staggered to the high-backed bench and collapsed. "The worst news possible. There's no hope for it, then. You must marry him unless the man your mother chose will take you in your ruined state."

"No, absolutely not." She spoke quickly. "I—I could not foist myself on a decent man like Mr. Ilkston in these circumstances." Richard looked at her sharply as she continued. "But Lord Harcourt only marries me for my money! He has barely been able to feed me these last two days."

"A bad business all the way around." Mr. Armitage's mournful tones indicated his sympathy. "This miscreant could be arraigned for his crime, yes. But you would still spend the rest of your life outside the bounds of decent society, dear child." He shook his head. "Repugnant as it must be, marriage to Lord Harcourt is your only choice."

With a great sigh, he announced that he would send a letter of credit that very day and, recalling Bethany's comments on Richard's poverty, even pressed upon her his own purse for their immediate use.

Contemptuously declining Richard's offer to see him down to the hallway below, he took his leave, shaking his head sadly.

Richard and Bethany looked at the closed door for several seconds before he turned to her. "My father brought me up never to lay a hand on a woman for any reason, Mistress Dallison." He spoke in measured tones. "But after this episode I do not think he would blame me if I took you over my knee. I shall have to marry you to save my own reputation."

"Pish. You shall have your letter of credit and we have coin enough to last us a few days." Bethany dismissed his comment while counting out the contents of the leather purse. "Why, he's given us several pounds. How kind of him—we should invite him to the wedding."

"Which, to preserve both our reputations, should take place at the earliest opportunity." Despite himself, Richard burst out laughing. "Have you always been this duplicitous?"

"I merely stated the facts, sir! 'Twas not my fault Mr. Armitage leaped to conclusions." Her lofty tone could not hide the laughter in her own voice.

"'Horrible'?" Richard's voice lowered to velvet softness.

He watched her face flame with embarrassment, but she rallied and retorted, "I referred to the coach." She cleared her throat. "My own behavior was disgraceful."

Looking down at herself, she realized her state of undress and bolted into the bedchamber.

He watched her flee. He pointed out that she might need help lacing up her bodice, chuckling again when she responded with an outraged, "Oh!"

* * *

Later that afternoon, Bethany walked on Richard's arm toward Saint Bride's parish in search of Mr. Jeremiah Barker, late of Stanworth. Although she had his direction, she had no idea how they would ever find his house in the city's congestion. Unlike the newer district of shops they had visited that morning, the streets they now traversed crossed each other in a meaningless jumble of alleys and odd corners. Overhangs from the upper stories of the houses on either side cut off the winter sun, adding a gloomy atmosphere to the chill afternoon.

She clung to him in the crowd of passersby, while trying to keep the skirts of her new dress out of the dirt. To her relief, he walked steadily along, unfazed by the confusion. His upright bearing as well as the rapier at his side intimidated the less desirable elements of the crowd.

She noted his dress with approval. Unlike the beribboned gentlemen she had seen mincing along with the assistance of their tall walking sticks, his coat and waistcoat were simply cut from a handsome woolen cloth. A fashionable lawn cravat falling in snowy folds ornamented the front of his coat under the black cape fastened over his shoulders. He wore jackboots instead of shoes to protect his feet from the unpaved streets, the supple leather hugging his long legs.

Used to strolling along country lanes to the village, Bethany thought the way to Saint Bride's everlasting. She had not thought a city could sprawl as London did. Finally, Richard spied the church itself. After making enquiries at a bookseller's, they learned the exact route to Mr. Barker's house.

Soon she stood before the painted door of a half-timbered house a few blocks from the church while Richard waited behind her. She gave their names to the maid who answered her knock, and they were ushered into a small paneled parlour. She had scarcely removed her cape before Mr. Barker hurried into the room, closely followed by his wife.

A smallish older couple, dressed in plain gray, they beamed with delight at seeing her. Mr. Barker's bright blue eyes gave the impression that he missed very little going on around him despite his years. His wife, more placid in manner, appeared to be equally alert.

"Bethany!" He greeted her warmly, taking in her appearance from head to toe. "I could scarce believe my ears when our Jane said you were here. What brings you? And in the company of a peer, no less." Those shrewd eyes rested on Richard appraisingly as he turned to make him welcome.

His wife stepped forward to embrace her. "First things first, dearest. We should allow our guests to sit down while Jane brings in some refreshment." She seated herself on the plain settle by the fire and drew her husband down to sit beside her. Richard gallantly offered a dark oak chair to Bethany and seated himself in its mate.

The Barkers made small talk for a time, asking after families in the Stanworth neighborhood and speaking of their life in London. Presently the maid entered, bearing a large charger holding tankards and a pitcher along with some mincemeat pies. She served them and left. The old couple now focused their sharp gazes on their guests, giving the impression of two sparrows about to commence an inquisition.

"Now Bethany, you've gone and gotten yourself into a scrape again, haven't you?" Mr. Barker spoke sternly, but not unkindly. "Suppose you tell me what it is, and how it involves this young man."

The girl took a breath, considering how best to answer. She had spent no little time pondering how she would explain her sudden wish to marry a man her mother obviously had not approved. Before she could speak, Richard jumped in.

"I had the pleasure of meeting Mistress Dallison while visiting my relatives in Stanworth last summer," he replied smoothly. "I found myself drawn to her at the time, but did not realize until recently how very important she has become to my continued happiness. Thus I recently returned to the village in hopes of procuring her hand in marriage."

Bethany stared into her tankard of ale, torn between amusement and indignation at Richard's glib interpretation of his actions.

"I think it must be an elopement, Jeremiah." Mistress Barker offered the mince pies. "Deborah Dallison was determined to gain Ilkston as a son-in-law." A few more wrinkles creased her forehead. "I never liked him."

"Certainly he always struck me as a most self-important young man." Her husband helped himself to a pie then addressed the girl. "The main point, however, is that you must have spent a night unattended during the journey to town." He pierced her with a stern look. "I trust you are visiting us to introduce your husband."

She took a deep breath. "No." Before her host and hostess could protest, she hurried on. "Lord Harcourt expressed his—honorable—intentions to me in Stanworth. I asked him to bring me to London in hopes that you would marry us, sir."

"Ah." The older man set his tankard aside. "You have committed a serious act of disobedience against your mother, Bethany. I cannot overlook that." He frowned until his wife patted his hand. "On the other hand, Eliza and I often wondered if Mr. Ilkston was a compatible match for you. Further, there is the matter of spending a night alone without an attendant. Most reprehensible."

Bethany leaned forward in her chair, concerned at his hesitation. After some consideration, the minister requested an interview alone with Lord Harcourt.

Richard came to attention with an alarmed expression and glared at her accusingly. She returned it with a wide-eyed shake of her head to signify that she had not expected this development. A soft choking noise interrupted this silent exchange.

They turned their heads to observe Mistress Barker's shoulders shaking while she regarded the hands clasped in her lap. Mr. Barker drained his tankard and blandly complimented his wife on her ale, but his eyes twinkled suspiciously.

"Come, Bethany. We shall take the dishes back to the kitchen, and then I must show you over the house." His wife stood to collect the plates, handing the remaining pies to Bethany before gently but firmly shooing her out of the room. Her husband requested that she leave the pitcher behind.

Making sure the door shut firmly behind the ladies, Mr. Barker affably poured out another cider for himself and Richard. The younger man accepted with thanks. His host nodded in a kindly manner. "So. Are you very much in debt?"

Richard nearly dropped his tankard as the minister regarded him. "No need to look so surprised. Here you are, a lord, and the Dallisons no more than gentry. You'd never consider marriage outside your own order without a pressing cause. As Bethany is a great heiress, it stands to reason you want her money."

The aristocrat made a quick retort. "I assure you that my intentions toward Mistress Dallison have always been honorable."

"That is the only way to get her money, isn't it?" Mr. Barker's pointed comment stopped Richard full spate. "I don't suppose that makes you any worse than the fellow Bethany's mother chose."

"She did agree to the marriage of her own free will." Richard looked the old man in the eye. "Ask her yourself if you don't believe me."

Mr. Barker stared into the distance. Richard had to strain to hear his quiet voice. "I've known that girl since she was a child. Her father, a most Christian man, died when she was scarce four years old. Her mother is suspicious of even the most innocent pleasures, and chose a man of similar temperament for Bethany to marry." The balding minister shook his head. "Mr. Ilkston is a proper match, but hardly a suitable one."

He regarded Richard over his steepled fingers. "A title would be grand attainment for Bethany Dallison of Stanworth. But I must ask: What price will she have to pay for it, my lord? Will she suffer contempt for her lower birth while you spend her family's money?"

Richard drew himself up to his near six-foot height and looked down at the little minister coldly. "I beg your pardon, but it is not my intention to misuse my wife."

He paced away before turning back, narrowing his eyes. "She will be presented to His Majesty after our marriage, and appear on my arm in polite society. The rest of the time she shall live on my family estate. I have no desire to curtail her enjoyment of any respectable amusement available to women of her station. Certainly I shall insist that she be treated with the honor due her position as Lady Harcourt and, God willing, as the mother of my heir."

"All well and good, my boy." Mr. Barker sipped his ale again, unperturbed. "But how will she be treated at the hands of her husband?"

Richard stared at him. The memory of his father, lying in a mire of his own blood, rose before him, along with the promise he'd made to give the dying man peace in his last minutes of life. He had already failed Father twice. The Dallison fortune held the key to keeping the rest of his oath.

"No gentleman insults his own wife." A curt answer, but after searching his face intently, the clergyman nodded.

"In that case, I shall be pleased to join you in matrimony."

Bethany looked over her shoulder at the closed study doors before Mistress Barker nudged her back toward the kitchen. There, the capable Jane relieved them of their burdens and her hostess escorted her out.

"You can see all there is from the doorway. And I'd hate to have you ruin such a lovely dress if something spilled. I think Mr. Barker raised his eyebrows at the shade, but 'tis vastly becoming." She prattled on as she led Bethany around the house.

They ended in a small chamber upstairs in the south corner. Sunlight cast shadows of the diamond windowpanes on the darkly gleaming walnut furniture. Bethany exclaimed over Mistress Barker's latest needlework project, a set of curtains worked in amethyst, dark green, and rose on linen.

"Thank you, dear. My daughter comes by often each week and we work on it together. It's a joy being so close to her and the grandchildren." She cocked her head at Bethany. "Now, tell me where you met such a handsome young man."

Bethany floundered before telling the good woman that she met Richard while visiting Gloriana at their aunt's home. After a few more questions, the older woman brought up her greatest concern.

Coughing delicately, she said, "You were brought up as a virtuous girl, but his lordship does have a great deal of, well, personal charm. It would take great strength of mind to resist him if he should try coaxing a young lady into misbehaving. Although forgiveness could be readily granted a female he intends to marry."

Bethany stood up and went to the windows. She doubted she fooled Mistress Barker one whit, but she could not bear for her to see her burning cheeks. "Lord Harcourt has behaved in a manner expected of one in his station." She did not dare let the truth of her own behavior come out.

She heard the rustling of a skirt behind her. "My dear child, if Lord Harcourt compels you in any way to wed him, you are welcome to take shelter with us."

"No!" Her reply escaped before she thought. "It may be a sin against my mother, but I find Lord Harcourt a far more attractive prospect than Mr. Ilkston. Oh!" Her hand flew to her mouth. "That is, I mean to say . . ."

"There, there, I quite understand."

Bethany doubted that the saintly woman did, but chose not to enlighten her. Forcing a smile as Mistress Barker patted her hand sympathetically, she allowed herself to be guided out of the room and down the stairs.

Chapter 5

Two days later, Bethany paced the same upper chamber waiting to be summoned to her wedding. The Barkers had insisted that she remain with them instead of returning to Richard's rooms. She had agreed for the sake of her unraveling morals, but remembered the stab of regret she felt at the realization that she would not see him till the point of their nuptials.

Richard had rejected the idea out of hand until she asked to speak to him in private. While the minister and his wife would not leave them alone together, he agreed to absent himself while Mistress Barker stayed on the far side of the downstairs parlour. In a whispered confrontation, her betrothed accused the good couple of planning to spirit her away despite Mr. Barker's agreement to perform the ceremony.

She had shaken her head then, assuring him that the old man would not have agreed to perform the ceremony if he objected to the union.

His long fingers grasped her chin until she looked into his eyes. "Unless you asked them to help you escape."

The touch made her heart pound so that she could barely reply. "I have no reason to do so. I shall have a title and an estate, remember? And you promised to present me to the King." When his thumb brushed her lips, she swallowed.

"I recall making no promise. Besides, I may have to reconsider." His eyelids dropped, as did his voice. "His majesty has a weakness for beautiful women." He leaned into her for a kiss, only to stop when Mistress Barker loudly cleared her throat from the chair where she sat stitching.

They stepped apart, Bethany unaware that she echoed his exasperated sigh. Unnoticed by their chaperone, he slid his other hand down to clasp hers. She returned the warm pressure without thinking.

"Dusk is falling, my lord. You should be on your way. 'Tis not safe on the streets after dark." The older woman rolled up her needlework and rose to her feet. Her brisk manner made very clear that she was more concerned for Bethany's safety than Richard's.

She had not seen him since, although he sent messages through the offices of Lane, who had taken on the role of an unlikely Cupid.

He had arrived the following day laden with a few parcels for Bethany that had arrived at Richard's lodgings. Recognizing her clothing purchases at once, she had eagerly borne them upstairs for inspection, followed by her hostess. The good woman enjoyed opening the parcels quite as much as she did, confiding to Bethany that she liked bright colors. She had smiled in relief at avoiding a lecture on the evils of personal display.

This pleasant diversion came to an end when Lane brought word that Lord Harcourt had obtained a special license that very day and desired the wedding to take place the following afternoon. Faced with the inevitable consequence of her decision, she had paled, but agreed to the arrangements in a steady voice.

Now she restlessly prowled the chamber waiting for Mistress Barker to fetch her to the parlour, where the ceremony would take place. Earlier, she had helped Bethany into her wedding clothes. The choices had been limited to the dresses delivered from the draper's, as both women rejected the green velvet out of hand on the grounds that she had already worn it.

In the end, Bethany selected a dress of apricot twill that displayed her fair skin and bright hair to advantage. Even though her hostess had insisted on a whisk for modesty, it still became her more than anything else she had ever worn. A small cap perched on the crown of her head over her neatly brushed and coiled hair, letting the afternoon sunlight shine across it.

Unable to stand her own restlessness any longer, she sat down and folded her hands in her lap. Her life had changed drastically in five days. She would become Lady Harcourt in a matter of hours. Wife to a man who tolerated her for her money. That at least was no different, she reflected grimly, then corrected herself. Mr. Ilkston tolerated her. Richard at least found her physically pleasing. She refused to think about her body's heated response to his touch.

Only one piece of business remained for her to deal with. She licked her lips, hoping she guessed Richard's poverty correctly.

The door opened to admit Mistress Barker, dressed in her most formal black and best cobweb lace. She kissed Bethany's cheek, asking if she was ready.

Completely overtaken by nerves, she managed a brief nod. Sympathetically squeezing her hand, the old woman took Bethany's arm and led her down to the closed door to the parlour. There she twitched a fold into a more becoming fall and smoothed a slightly loose strand of hair into place. She stood back with an air of approval.

"You look lovely, dear." Her keen eyes examined Bethany's face. "Are you quite sure you don't want to change your mind?"

She jerked her head "No." Her only alternative was returning to her mother's house, and she shuddered to think of the reception awaiting her.

Satisfied, the other woman opened the parlour door with a flourish and escorted her inside.

In accordance with their beliefs, only the wedding party and witnesses awaited her. Richard looked over at her from his place at Mr. Barker's side, ill at ease. He had dressed with great care in a buff brocade coat and trousers over polished boots. Thin bands of lace adorned his cravat and the shirt-sleeves exposed by his buttoned-back cuffs. His fair hair lay in neat waves on his shoulders.

Such grandeur looked out of place next to the minister's severe black. She supposed this wedding differed from his expectations considerably. She had heard of the elaborate wedding ceremonies of the traditional church, with the bride and groom surrounded by friends and relatives.

Mother said feasting, dancing, and other licentious behavior followed them, but Bethany thought it sounded most agreeable. Aside from herself, Richard, and the Barkers, only Mr. Armitage attended them, along with his clerk. That man, a mousy little fellow, contemplated the street outside the window with disinterest.

She took her place beside Richard. The minister began by asking if there were any impediments to the marriage.

"Yes." Bethany's heart pounded, but she forced her voice to remain calm as she spoke. Richard whipped his head around to gape at her. Mr. Armitage uttered a startled exclamation while his clerk turned from the window with a curious expression. Mr. Barker cleared his throat.

"Please tell us what that impediment might be." He spoke calmly despite his raised eyebrows.

"There is no settlement." Bethany waited for her words to sink in. Richard's eyebrows snapped together and he scowled at her. The clerk brightened at the disruption while the banker babbled.

"Dear child, under the circumstances, a settlement prior to the ceremony is simply not feasible. It can take weeks, and it is imperative that you marry now to protect your good name! As well as account for any"—he coughed delicately and glanced at her slim waist—"unforeseen circumstances."

The clerk beamed at them as if in gratitude for such an unexpected diversion but quickly stopped at Mistress Barker's outraged mutterings.

"Mr. Armitage is correct, Bethany. Normally a signed contract would be a prerequisite to the marriage." Mr. Barker fixed a look of mild reproof on her. "In your case, however, that is a luxury."

Her heart sank. She had hoped he at least might support her. Hoping her fear did not show, she took a deep breath. "No settlement, no marriage."

Varying degrees of shock registered on the faces around her. After a moment of silence, both the banker and the minister explained why the ceremony must proceed without the usual financial arrangements.

On her left, Mr. Armitage pointed out that no one was present who could negotiate on her behalf. On her right, Mr. Barker reiterated that her precarious moral standing made it imperative for her to marry Richard at once.

She looked past them to her groom. He stood frozen in place, incredulity warring with anger in his features. Guilt for deceiving him washed over her until she recalled the lists of gambling debts and unpaid bills.

"My mother does not need to negotiate for me if Lord Harcourt signs an agreement with you, Mr. Armitage."

"Oh?" Richard spoke for the first time since her announcement, his voice soft but his eyes glittering dangerously.

"I want ten thousand pounds signed into a trust in my name only, to be directed by me and administered by Mr. Armitage." She turned to the stunned banker. "If the most recent statements sent to my mother are accurate, that will leave another ten thousand pounds in Lord Harcourt's possession when we are married, would it not?"

The man stammered that she had indeed read the statements correctly.

Looking at Richard's reddening face, she continued, "You said you thought my fortune more than enough to meet your needs when you believed it to be fifteen thousand, sir. Will ten thousand still suffice?"

In response, he grabbed at her so quickly that she scurried to place a chair between them. "You—lying—*jade*!"

She swallowed at the snarled accusation. Her hands clenched the back of the chair to help keep her shaking knees from buckling during his tirade.

"You deceived me from the first, didn't you!" His fury forced the other men into silence as he paced back and forth. "The only reason you agreed to marry me was to get hold of that money."

The utter unjustness of his remark brought her back to her senses. "And why not? You did the same!"

"At least I was honest about my intentions and reasons. My God, to think I was prepared to put you in my mother's place."

An alarmed Dr. Barker intervened. "Do I understand that you are withdrawing your offer of marriage after ruining this young lady?"

Bethany spoke up before Richard could reply. "Indeed, my lord, have you found another accessible heiress?"

His mouth snapped shut. Shaking with anger, he ground out, "No. I have not, madam. So it would appear that I am stuck fast with you." With an obvious effort he moderated his voice as he addressed the minister.

"It would appear, sir, that we shall have to delay this event until the contract can be drawn up."

"I could do it." The clerk spoke for the first time. Everyone in the room turned to the little man, whose earlier boredom had given way to delighted animation. "Give me but paper, quill, and ink, and I shall have it completed directly."

"Very well!" Richard and Bethany spoke at once, and then looked daggers at each other.

Mr. Barker, demonstrating as much wrath as one of his tranquil disposition could, entered the lists.

"This is most untoward, and I cannot approve

of it." Despite this statement, the indignant bridal couple urged the clerk to finish his work.

Just over twenty minutes later, he handed it to Richard. He furiously scribbled his name at the bottom and tossed it on the table in front of Bethany. "Are you satisfied, madam?"

Her heart hammering, Bethany carefully read the document twice through. In plain English it meant that upon her marriage she would have the sole use of half of her father's money. She nodded.

"Very well, then." White-faced, tight-lipped, her groom gestured for her to come stand in front of Mr. Barker. "Marry us."

The divine crossed his arms. "I could not possibly join together in matrimony two persons in your state of inflamed passions."

Richard threw up his hands. "I'm not like to attain a more tranquil state of mind if you refuse me, sir. You agreed to perform the ceremony."

"Aye, you did." Bethany spoke up firmly at his side. "And I consent to the marriage willingly."

After further insistence Mr. Barker conducted the ceremony, albeit in tones of stern reproof. For their part, the bride and groom exchanged vows with an air of distinct hostility and the following homily sounded more like a scold to two squabbling children. Finally, the old man snapped that Richard and Bethany were husband and wife.

Mr. Armitage wiped his face with a kerchief and exhaled in relief. Mistress Barker nervously invited him to join them for the early supper she had ordered, but he hastily declined, citing a need to return to his bank.

Only the drab little clerk wished the newly married couple well with any enthusiasm, pumping my lord's hand. "Most amusing wedding I've ever seen, sir! My felicitations to you and your lovely bride." He left them with a bow. "Edmund Leafley, at your service. If I can ever be of assistance to either of you, do not hesitate to ask." He departed with his master, chortling under his breath. "Never saw anything half so good at the theater."

After sharing a meal of Jane's excellent roast chicken, Richard arose from the table. His temper appeared outwardly restored, but his eyes hardened when they rested on his bride. "'Tis dusk, and past time we returned to our lodgings."

Bethany's heart quailed at his curt manner. Her relief at gaining a modicum of security and independence within her marriage had dwindled with Mistress Barker's toast to "Lady Harcourt" at the start of the meal.

It evaporated completely when he bundled her into her cloak and out of the house, grasping her elbow as he strode through the shadowy streets. A winter night's breeze blew up, chilling her outside as well as in.

Richard barely noticed the cold. He walked mechanically, pulling the girl along beside him. No, not the girl. His wife. His lovely, deceitful wife. His temper flared again, even as the logical part of his mind whispered that he might have done the same, had he been in her shoes. He pushed the traitorous idea back, dwelling on the thought that this simple girl from the country had made a fool of him.

They had reached paved streets by now. She stumbled on a loose cobblestone and he instinctively steadied her. His jaw clenched at her muted thanks. The wench had used him so cold-bloodedly. Refusing to look at her, he strode on. She would pay. Oh, how she would pay.

Truth to tell, he hardly felt like a married man after the short ceremony. A few sentences and a lecture, he reflected, 'twas nothing more. No blessing, no ceremony, not even a ring for the bride's finger. Barker had rejected that idea completely, informing him that even the plainest band smacked of idolatry.

He frowned. That would have to change. He refused to present his wife at Charles's lax court without making it clear that she was not available for dalliances. She might have her own income, but she was his wife and he'd be damned if he'd tolerate any other man trying to tilt a lance at her.

He marched Bethany up the stairway to the landing and led her inside the rooms. The lock grated behind her and she turned in alarm. Richard's glance flickered over her before he placed the key on the mantel over the fireplace. She relaxed slightly.

Whatever awaited, he had no intention of imprisoning her, at least.

Lane had apparently busied himself in his absence. Firewood lay ready to light in the fireplace and two wineglasses sat next to a bottle on the gateleg table. She swallowed suddenly, reminded of the purpose of a wedding night.

He removed his cloak, hat, and gauntlets. Ignoring her, he flung himself over to the window and stood looking down on the street. Anger still rolled off him in waves. She remained where he left her, immobile in the center of the room, still wearing her cloak.

He turned to her, heat overtaking the coldness in his eyes and face. She dropped her gaze to the floor.

She did not raise her eyes as he deliberately crossed to her. "Look at me."

She lifted her chin. Fear made it hard for her to breathe, but she was determined to accept the consequences of her behavior. He seemed to understand, for he nodded.

"Good." Her heart lurched at the near whisper, but she stood her ground. "You used me." She flinched at the hissed accusation, but did not deny it. She fixed her gaze on the wall opposite as he moved to the table and poured a glass of wine. "You humiliated me in front of a group of strangers."

"Did I?" She turned to look him in the eye as she rallied. "You used me. As you will continue to use me because the law gives you that right. Along with my money." She laughed bitterly.

"Will you think of my shame every time you buy another woman with the money I brought you?" She reached up to untie her cloak but Richard grabbed her wrist.

"No, *dear wife*. What did your Master Barker say in his little homily? 'A faithful wife is her husband's treasure . . .'?" He circled her as he spoke, still angry but with an underlying growl that vibrated along her skin. He came to rest behind her.

"Let me see this treasure I've married." His breath puffed against her neck as he reached around to untie her cloak and pull it from her shoulders. "Let me discover how best to use her."

As he grated out the last words, Bethany's heart pounded and her stomach knotted. She had known he would be furious, but it never occurred to her just how he might react. She forced her legs to step away from him, but he caught her back against him with an arm around her waist. She froze as she felt herself pulled against his entire length from shoulders to feet.

She inhaled sharply as he slowly removed the whisk covering the neckline of the dress and let it slip to the floor. His warm mouth pressed against the back of her neck as his fingertips lightly brushed the creamy tops of her breasts. As always, her body betrayed her at his merest touch. She shut her eyes, her skin tingling under the deft onslaught.

"Yes," he murmured in her ear, igniting a darker heat deep within her. "My wife. Mine. To do with as I wish."

She gasped, half in pleasure at his touch and half in annoyance at his arrogance. Trying to escape the intoxicating sensations he aroused in her, she stepped away.

He did not stop her, only permitting his hands to run over her shoulders as she moved. Her relief turned to alarm when she felt a tugging at her back.

"Thank you, my dear." He laughed softly as he unlaced her bodice.

"Stop that!" She glared at him over her shoulder but he ignored her at first, focusing instead on her rapidly loosening dress. When he raised his eyes to hers, Bethany sucked in her breath and her mouth went dry. No one had ever looked at her with that kind of hunger.

"We're man and wife now." He kept his gaze riveted to hers even as his hands worked her stiff bodice open. "Whatever games you play with me, I still have a husband's rights." He turned her to face him fully. She tried to resist, but he drew her close and cupped her face in his hands.

"More to the point, it allows both of us to fully enjoy the delights of the marriage bed." His lips feathered over her face until they met hers. She sighed as his tongue slid into her mouth and retreated, teasing her to respond. She did, brazenly opening to him in invitation. He deepened his onslaught, his tongue mating with hers again and again.

When they at last broke apart, she rested her forehead on his shoulder, breathing heavily. She had never denied her attraction to Richard. But her mother had drilled into her the precept that all men wanted wives of impeccable morals, even if their own characters lacked the same quality.

She raised her head. "Do you want me to experience these—delights you speak of?"

His eyes gleamed under hooded lids. "Yes, little Puritan, I do." His mouth curled in a small smile as he stroked her arms beneath her chemise. Startled, she looked down to discover that he had coaxed the sleeves of her dress down. His cravat had unaccountably loosened, too.

She stepped back from his wandering hands but he followed and eased the apricot cloth all the way off. Mortified, she stood before him with her bodice bunched around her waist. He took her hands in his to prevent her from covering herself back up.

"Coyness doesn't become you, Bethany. Not the way your body answers my hands and mouth." He swept his gaze over her bosom, still held in place by her stays. Bethany gasped when he followed the direction of his eyes to kiss and nibble her neck. The rustle of cloth formed a background to the feel of his hands stroking over to her waist and hips, unfastening yet more ties. With a jolt, she felt the sudden rush of air when the twill dress and her petticoat slid off her body. Her stays loosened as he worked at their laces.

Richard breathed heavily as he held her at arms' length. His eyes blazed green with desire as he looked at her fully. "No more games. I want you; you want me."

Her knees buckled slightly at his hoarse declaration. As he had at the inn, he easily picked her up. She buried her burning face in his shoulder as he negotiated their way into the bedroom.

To her surprise, he set her carefully on her feet at the foot of the bed. She wondered if he had changed his mind until he tossed his cravat to the floor and unbuckled his belt. He kept his gaze on her face as his coat and waistcoat rapidly followed. Seeing him in only his shirt, breeches, and boots, she swallowed but did not move.

"I just don't know what to do." She feared her agonized confession fell on deaf ears as he drew her stays off without a word. As he stared at her nakedness under the thin cloth, however, he finally spoke.

"Follow me, Bethany. Just follow me." His own chest rapidly rose and fell as he lifted his hands to her hair. She felt the soft strands falling one by one as he freed them from their pins. He stroked through the mass, spreading it down over her breast, then letting his fingers circle the soft peak beneath her chemise.

She gasped as the bud hardened and elongated under his touch. The soft intake of breath seemed to break his control. A moment later, she was caught in a firm embrace, his mouth slanting over hers as he played with her breast, lifting and squeezing it. She clung to his muscular arms, moaning his name as his thumb flicked the peak until it ached.

His other hand rested on the small of her back, pushing her more fully against the hard ridge straining the cloth of his breeches. He delved into the tender cleft of her buttocks to press her against the stiff flesh.

He whispered incoherently as he slid her up onto the bed. His hands dropped to the hem of her chemise and worked it up and off as she lifted her arms to assist him. He sat beside her long enough to jerk his boots off his feet then stood to untie the neck of his cambric shirt.

Suddenly aware of her nakedness, she moved up to slip between the sheets, but he stopped her, placing a hand on her ankle.

"Stay. I've wanted to see you like this, spread out on my bed with naught but that glorious mane to cover you." Mesmerized under his hot-eyed stare, she stayed as he asked, watching her husband's body emerge from his shirt and trousers.

She had never seen anything more beautiful. Muscles bunched and released under the smooth skin of his shoulders and arms as he pulled the fine muslin over his head. She licked her lips at the sight of his chest and flat stomach. A dusting of light brown hair gathered into a furred ridge that led below the waist of his trousers. She knew it was terribly immodest, but she could not take her eyes away from it as he undid the waist of his trousers and kicked them off.

Her mouth went dry as she saw the jutting staff of flesh between his thighs. Her gaze flew to his. She must have looked alarmed because he smiled reassuringly as he hoisted himself onto the bed beside her.

"Aye, this is what all the fuss is about." To her relief, he only propped himself on his elbow as he spoke. Perhaps her hair was the sign of a wanton after all, for she felt no shame knowing what they were about to do. Or perhaps she responded to the desire in his eyes.

"Don't be frightened." He ran a hand down her body, his warm palm stopping on her thigh. She licked her lips and nodded.

"I'm not, very much," she whispered.

"Sweet girl." He brought her to him, kissing and stroking her, whispering his want for her. His hands wandered freely over her skin, setting her blood to rushing. When she hesitantly reciprocated, running her palms over his back and shoulders, he encouraged her, urging her to touch him as she wished.

She shivered when she felt him gently grind his rigid manhood against her belly. The erotic play set a fire in her most secret places. She caught her breath and instinctively rocked against him. At his groan, she froze.

"Did I do something wrong?" She watched as he lifted her hand to kiss her palm.

"No, your touch pleases me, especially there. 'Tis just that I am too ready and you've not been adequately prepared." He rolled her onto her back, and began his onslaught in earnest.

Kissing his way to her breasts, his mouth closed over one stiff peak and suckled her while his fingers rolled the other. Bethany arched her back and cried out at the fiery sensations snaking over her body. He took advantage of it by adjusting his body to lie intimately between her thighs.

Her first impulse was to wriggle out from under him but he tightened his arms so she could not escape. Slipping his hand between their bodies, he slid his fingers into the curls protecting her nether lips. Two long digits caressed the damp slit from bottom to top, coming to rest on a tender nub Bethany had never known existed.

As he alternately circled and stroked it, Bethany could only gasp in pleasure. Embarrassing moisture gathered between her thighs, but Richard used it to help his wicked fingers glide faster against her. She felt as if she was being taken up a cliff, higher and higher. When he thrust his fingers into her most secret mouth, she lost control and leapt off, but instead of falling, she flew. Light exploded inside her head as she cried out and helplessly thrust her hips against his hand.

She had barely come back to earth when he lifted himself over her and positioned his member against her damp opening. Sotted with passion, she looked up at him and nodded.

He eased into her, holding her still against his invasion.

"Be easy, love. Easy. Don't be frightened, 'twill only hurt a little, this one time." His velvety voice soothed her as he entered farther, inexorably opening and widening her. There was some hurt, but not much, and she eventually relaxed to accept him.

Then he pulled back and, with one swift plunge, sheathed himself completely. She cried out at a painful tearing sensation deep within. Tears welled at the shock, and he bent to kiss them away, apologizing for hurting her so.

He stayed still within her for several seconds, panting, while she adjusted to him. He moved very slightly within her and she braced for more pain, but none came, only the same deep ache. She felt him shaking with the effort to hold back.

"Richard?" She pushed against his chest so he would look at her. "It does hurt, but not so very much. Please, take your pleasure."

"Oh God, I shouldn't. But you feel so tight around me, love, I can't resist." He resumed his movements, and to her surprise, the soreness became more tolerable. She relaxed enough to let her hips meet his.

He lost control then, holding her close and thrusting into her at greater speed until he climaxed with a roar of pleasure. She pressed her face into his shoulder at his tremors of release, gasping at the sensation of his hot seed exploding into her.

He collapsed on top of her for several minutes, but she found she relished his weight. When she kissed his shoulder, the salty taste of sweat stayed on her lips. Breathless, she stroked a hand down his damp back and toyed with his hair, running her fingers through the long locks.

"Oh no!" She looked up at the canopy as a thought occurred to her.

"Mmmmmm?" Richard, still unmoving, tickled her ear when he spoke.

"What if we got blood on the coverlet?"

He stretched then and reached behind him to fold it down. He slid between the sheets and pulled her with him until her back cuddled against his front.

"We'll worry about it later." She felt so very comfortable that she decided to do just that.

Chapter 6

Richard floated just below the surface of wake-fulness, lost in his favorite dream. The King had awarded him great honors at Court while a bevy of women vied for his favor. He smiled when he felt a woman's body beside him as he drowsed. Perhaps the female he'd found the night before brought him these visions of plenty.

Since his mistress had given him over for the charms of a wealthy man, he had amused himself by occasional amatory ventures with women in want of a lover for only a night or two. He knew he could enjoy more of his favorite exercise if he cast his net beyond women of his own station, but he had no wish to contract the pox.

Judging from his body's satisfied languor, he'd found a partner who enjoyed sporting in bed as much as he. Wanting to return to his enjoyable dreams, he scooted closer to whoever slept beside him. His hand stroked over a slim waist and rested against her flat stomach.

He sighed happily, enjoying the feel of warm satin skin beneath his palm. A familiar stirring between his legs started as memories of her heated response and fiery hair drifted through his mind.

With a sharp inhalation, he opened his eyes. Even in the dim light of the shuttered chamber, that redgold hair blazed across his pillows. Shocked fully awake, he lifted his head.

He spied no more than her hair and the edge of her cheek, but her deep breathing and utter repose told him she slept on. They had made love again last night after sleeping awhile.

Richard realized he had started playing with the soft tendrils spread before him and stopped. He should not have touched her after that first time. But crawling back into bed after shuttering the window, he had found her sleep-warmed body irresistible.

Rolling to his back, he placed his hands behind his head, away from temptation. Fiery hair and heated kisses ran through his mind as he tried to ignore his increasing arousal. How could such warmth hide so cool a calculating heart, he wondered. God's teeth, he stood rampant yet again at the thought of her. Who would have thought a sheltered virgin would respond so ardently to his caresses? Or that she would stir him so easily.

He needed to get up—or rather out of bed, he thought irritably. A nearby coffeehouse served steak and ale for its customers, even in the morning. Disagreeable for a bride to awake alone after her wedding night, he reflected, then hardened his heart. The sooner the girl accustomed herself to solitude, the better.

He would answer her deception with indifference. Let her enjoy the money she'd maneuvered out of him, he thought savagely. She'd have naught else from him, not his affection or his company.

He now possessed the means to match his breeding. He could afford a London house large enough to prevent them from setting eyes on one another. Not to mention such gentlemanly accoutrements as a fine wardrobe and a well-connected mistress. He would take a box at the theater and gamble in the most exclusive hells while his little Puritan sat home and read sermons. A voice in the back of his head told him he was cruel. He quashed it.

Then it reminded him that he must breed an heir. Myriad carnal visions of his wife presented themselves to him at this thought. Unnerved, he eased out of bed and silently dressed. Certainly he planned to get her with child, after he mastered this overwhelming need of her.

Now, however, he needed to flee before he made yet another attempt to reproduce. He told himself the reason he stood staring down at her so long was to assure himself she would not awaken.

Much later, Bethany opened her eyes. She wriggled her toes and smiled to herself, despite the soreness at the juncture of her thighs. Secretive conversations among married women had taught her that a woman's conjugal duties could hold the miseries of hell or the delights of paradise. Hers, it appeared, fell into the latter category.

She twisted around, surprised to discover Richard's side of the bed deserted. Propping herself on one elbow, she listened for sounds of life from the other room. Only calls from peddlers in the street greeted her ears. She hoped he sought something for their breakfast, as she felt unaccountably hungry this morning.

Cold air hit her body when she threw off the coverlet. Gritting her teeth against the chill on her naked body, she grabbed her chemise on the floor and donned it. She recalled with some embarrassment that her bridal dress had not made it to the bedchamber. Richard had acted most improperly in removing it, but he had taken as much pleasure in her body as she had in his.

Growing up on an estate dependent on animal husbandry for food, she had grasped the mechanics of the marriage act. But learning that the joining of two bodies could produce such delightful sensations proved a revelation to her. He had hurt her no more than necessary the first time, and had shown her only ecstasy the second time he had taken her.

His tenderness relieved her; he had not taken her financial maneuverings well at the Barkers'.

Which reminded her that Mistress Barker had sent a man over yesterday with her clothing after she had selected her wedding dress. Finally able to focus on something beside the bed, she noticed a linen-covered bundle plopped on the chest. Opening it disclosed her still-meager wardrobe and two beautifully embroidered pillowcases. A second look at the linen cloth revealed that it was a bed sheet, a wedding gift from the Barkers.

Humming a country ballad under her breath, Bethany folded and placed them on the bed, along with her dresses and petticoats. She noticed a smaller paper-wrapped package tucked on the floor beside the chest with the name of the linen draper inscribed on it. It contained several necessities she had ordered.

Thankfully, she dressed once more in the green velvet, but with a fresh chemise and a lace kerchief. She brushed out her hair and coiled it under a fetching little cap, warmth suffusing her body at the memory of Richard's face and hands buried in it the night before. She broke into another song as she opened the shutters and straightened the room. She did cringe slightly when she ascertained that they had, in fact, left a small bloodstain on the coverlet.

She had just finished rearranging Richard's clothing to make room for hers in the press when she heard Lane's angry voice rising above a sudden babble on the stairway.

"I've got no orders to let anybody into his lordship's rooms and that's flat." Bethany came to the door between the two rooms as muffled voices argued with the coachman's bellowed protest.

She wondered if a tradesman who did not know of Richard's improved circumstances might be trying to collect money owed him. With her fortune available, they could pay everything off, but going through his piles of bills would take some time.

"Stand aside, fellow. I have a warrant sworn out against Lord Harcourt, and if you don't cooperate with the law, I'll arrest you as well." She muffled her intake of breath with her hand. Someone wanted to arrest Richard for debt!

Lane sounded unimpressed with this threat. "Garn, go on then and look. You'll find that paper of yours useless."

She twitched her cuffs into place. Perhaps if she offered to pay the sum in question that day, the merchant would drop the charges. She did not know whether to be glad Richard was not here to be carried off to prison or vexed because she had to deal with an irate debtor.

She shook her head. Mother certainly commented often enough that men always disappeared when one particularly needed them about. Then she nearly jumped out of her skin.

Her mother's unmistakable voice rang out from outside the front room.

"Useless! I think not, you miserable creature. Sergeant, seize him. He looks to be the sort who would help abduct an innocent maid and steal her money. He shall hang alongside his master."

As the handle on the outer door rattled, Bethany fled into the bedchamber. Wildly, she contemplated diving under the bed before common sense prevailed. That would be the first place Mother would search for her. Contemplating whether she might possibly fit into the chest, she peeped through the cracked open door into the front room to gauge how much time she had to hide.

To her astonishment, her mother had brought reinforcements. Lord Rothley looked on as Mistress Dallison harangued a plump stranger in the uniform of a constable. And to Bethany's rising indignation, there, dressed in his inevitable black, stood Mr. Ilkston!

Lane, the constable, and Lord Rothley exhibited varying degrees of alarm at her mother's tongue-lashing. Mr. Ilkston merely echoed her sentiments, nodding his head judiciously as she spoke.

His lordship, midway between the peace officer's stammered confusion and Lane's phlegmatic scowl, stopped asking her to reconsider her opinion of his nephew and stooped to gather something up from its place on the floor.

He held up the apricot twill gown. Bethany closed her eyes in dread.

"Madam, it may be that your daughter is not here after all." He gazed at the pale orange material. "This garment does not look quite like her normal style."

Mr. Ilkston instantly retreated from its contaminating influence. Her mother shrieked and flew at Lane. The officer, demonstrating unexpected courage, interposed himself before she could harm the coachman.

"You sinful creature, tell me where you and your vile master have secreted my daughter!" She grabbed the offending dress and scolded the sweating official. "Lord Harcourt no sooner absconds with my poor girl and her money than he starts to spend it on harlots, and you protect his servant?"

As her mother poured invective on the head of the quaking man, Bethany swallowed and took a deep breath. She hated her mother's rages, but she could not leave poor Lane and a complete stranger to her mercies. Reminding herself that she was safely married, she pulled open the chamber door.

"Please be so good as to put down my dress, Mama." Regrettably, her voice came out in a breathless squeak instead of the tranquil tones she wished, but it did serve her purpose. Everyone in the room turned to her.

And then they all winced at her mother's outraged screech. "Bethany Dallison, what mean you by that?"

She gripped the doorway for support but stood her ground. "I mean that you are holding my dress, and I should not like it to get wrinkled."

At this evidence of her immorality, Mistress Dallison tottered to the settle and collapsed onto it. Bethany took advantage of the distraction, catching Lane's eye. With a glare and a jerk of her head, she silently ordered him out of the room. He tugged his forelock and winked. Then, moving remarkably quietly for such a large man, he backed out, pulling the door to behind him.

Bethany returned her attention to her unwelcome guests. Her mother sat croaking about the waywardness of daughters while Lord Rothley assured her that he would force his nephew to do the right thing by Bethany. Mr. Ilkston delivered a convoluted speech in which he praised Mistress Dallison's maternal sentiments and expressed concern at her daughter's lack of morals. The constable repeatedly pointed out that he could not arrest a man who was not present.

Like it or not, it was past time to take a hand in the matter. Bethany squared her shoulders.

"Mother!" Her raised voice cut through the din. "I wrote you that I am quite safe." An explanation occurred to her. "Did you not receive my note?"

Ignoring the dismay in her voice, her mother looked her up and down scathingly. "Safe? Is it your idea of safety to parade yourself in this cesspool of depravity dressed like a wanton? And in the company of a rake like Lord Harcourt."

Mistress Dallison's exclamation moved Lord Rothley to defend his family's honor. "I beg your pardon, madam, but that's a harsh thing to say. My nevvy's no worse than most blades in town." He scrutinized Bethany. "Your daughter looks proper enough in that rig. Besides, the letter did say she went with him of her own accord."

She looked at her mother. "If you received it, then why are you here?" Her confusion grew by the minute.

Lord Rothley answered. "Why, to fetch you back home, of course." He frowned grimly. "I shall stay behind to have a few words with that nephew of mine."

She thought she had misheard him until Mistress Dallison spoke with awful dignity. "Despite the shame you have brought on my head with your elopement, I am prepared to shelter you until such time that you can be delivered into the hands of a governor more capable than I of strengthening you in upright and modest behavior."

She shook her head, mystified. "I concede that my behavior did not conform to propriety, but just how do you plan to fetch me home? I do believe Lord Harcourt has a say in that."

Behind her, Mr. Ilkston spoke firmly. "Who knows what lengths a libertine will go to in order to persuade a foolish girl to abandon all moral scruples? Despite that, I have consented to uphold the agreement with your mother to marry you once this unfortunate connection with Harcourt has been severed."

The constable, observing Bethany's dumbfounded expression, helpfully explained that the warrant had been issued on the grounds that she had been taken against her will for the lucre of her substance.

Ignoring the truth of this statement, Bethany crossed her arms and stood her ground. "Whether I was or not, I am pleased with my situation now." A thought occurred to her. "And Lord Harcourt acted no more shamefully than Mr. Ilkston—he just didn't have your permission, and didn't agree to give you any of my inheritance."

Her barb reached its intended targets. Her mother scolded her for pertness. Lord Rothley and the constable both pricked up their ears at this piece of news, while Mr. Ilkston's face flooded red with rage.

"Speak for yourselves, but I'll not be made a fool of by an impudent girl." He grabbed Bethany's arm and yanked the resisting girl toward the doorway. "You shall come back at once while we sort this coil you've dragged us into. My lord, if you would be so good as to inform your coachman that we are coming down?"

Instead, Lord Rothley protested his manhandling her. Disgusted at his poor-spirited response, Bethany's erstwhile betrothed demanded that her mother help remove Bethany from the premises.

She approached reluctantly, but did manage to get hold of her daughter's other arm. They tried to compel her to the door over the objections of the other two men.

Losing patience at her stubbornness, Mr. Ilkston gave her a rough shove. Bethany cried out and nearly lost her footing, but before anyone could intervene, the door flew back on its hinges.

"Get your hands off my wife!"

Richard filled the doorway, sword drawn, taking in the entire tableau through narrowed eyes. His breath came and went heavily, as if he had just run a long way. Behind him stood Lane, also panting. Bethany nearly wept with relief at the sight of them.

She extricated herself from her mother's suddenly flaccid grasp with little effort. Mr. Ilkston was not so easily intimidated, however, and clasped her other arm so tightly she hissed in pain. The rapier's point flicked threateningly close to his throat. He flinched.

In two steps Richard reached forward and disengaged her from his grasp. She wanted to cling to him, but he handed her over to his uncle as he sheathed his weapon.

"To what do I owe the honor of a visit from so many of our relations, my dear?" His mild tone belied the twitching muscle in his jaw as he waited for an answer.

From her place at Lord Rothley's side, Bethany answered him, her voice trembling slightly. "They want to take me away and annul the marriage." She gestured to the constable. "That man is here to arrest you for kidnapping me."

Richard's knuckles whitened on the hilt of his sword and he raised his brows at the constable. The plump fellow hastily assured him that the young lady insisted she had not been forced into anything. Watching the sword warily, he added that there remained the matter of stealing her away for her money.

To the official's relief, his lordship released the hilt and brushed a speck of mud from his cloak. "By now that is a moot point, my good man. I married the lady yesterday at the home of a Mr. Barker, a clergyman known to both Lady Harcourt and her mother." Both men took Mistress Dallison's strangled protestations at this information as agreement. "In fact, you see her bride dress right there." He indicated the dress lying on the back of the settle.

"And what, pray tell, would it be doing on the floor of your parlour?" Bethany prayed for the floor to open up and swallow her whole when Richard answered her mother's question with an apologetic shrug. At her side Lord Rothley shook with suppressed laughter. The constable grinned openly.

The older woman regarded both of them with horror as the truth dawned on her. "Wicked, shameless girl! No thought given to my needs in my old age." She dabbed her eyes. "I shall be alone, with no compensation for my years of caring for you."

The men became restive at the threatened tears, but Bethany's patience ran out. "Nonsense. Father gave you the use of the estate and its income for life." She moved to stand next to Richard. "We were properly wed by Mr. Barker, and I am well pleased to be Lady Harcourt." Her tone changed to cajolery. "Think of telling the neighborhood that you are mother-in-law to a lord."

Struck by this cheerful thought, Mistress Dallison remonstrated a few minutes longer for form's sake before announcing her acceptance of the marriage. Informing Lord Rothley that she would await him in his coach, she swept from the room muttering the names of her acquaintances. By the time she reached the landing, she had already decided who would be the first to hear of Bethany's improved circumstances.

Mr. Ilkston did not take defeat as well. He attempted to force the constable to arrest Richard, but that official declined. He declared the warrant sworn out on shaky evidence and begged that the two noble gentlemen might appear before the Lord Mayor to clarify the matter at their earliest convenience. Richard graciously consented to this, and as a sign that he bore no ill will, tossed a coin to Lane and ordered him to show the constable to the nearest alehouse.

Mr. Ilkston watched this transaction with disgust. Preparing to leave, he paused before Richard and Bethany. "Rob me of the better part of twenty thousand pounds, will you?" She stepped back at his venom.

To her amazement, her husband's hand shot out and grabbed him by his throat. "Be very careful how you speak of my marriage in London or out. Touch my honor or my wife again and I'll spit you where you stand." He released him so quickly that the other man fell back a few paces before he could regain his balance.

Gathering his dignity as best he could, the blackcoated countryman addressed her. "I cannot felicitate you on your choice of Lord Harcourt, madam. However, I shall pray most earnestly that after he has wasted your substance, you may repent of your foolishness from your place in the gutter."

He bowed stiffly and stormed out of the room, followed by Lord Rothley's shout. "You can walk to your quarters and then back to Stanworth, you crow. Damme if I'll give you a place in my coach."

Bethany, shaken by her former betrothed's outburst, held Richard's arm as they listened to him stamp down the stairs. He placed a warm hand over hers and chuckled. "No wonder you chose me." She looked at him numbly for a moment before throwing her arms around his neck.

"I am so glad you came when you did." She burrowed her face into his shoulder as his arms hesitantly closed around her. "I feared I'd end up married to Ilkston after all."

Lord Rothley observed them with a benign smile of his own as Richard released her. "Thought I'd have to pull your head out of the hangman's noose. Very havey-cavey way of going about the business, but all's well enough now. Married her in front of old Barker." He chortled. "'Twas a master stroke, my boy. We didn't think you'd find a parson to marry you so soon, much less one they've known for years. And bedded her as well."

He kissed Bethany's flaming cheek and welcomed her to the family. "Too late for missishness, especially if you agreed to run off with him in the first place, minx. Now you've discovered the best and worst a man can do to a maid, you'll go on very well."

Mercifully leaving the subject, he suggested that he accompany the couple to the Mayor's office to deal with the warrant for Richard's arrest. Between the three of them and Mistress Dallison, he speculated, the matter could be cleared up easily. He added that they should then sojourn to his town house, where he could treat them to dinner.

They agreed with alacrity, although Bethany begged to delay their departure. Picking up the much-maligned apricot twill, she announced her intention to put it away before she had to listen to one more piece of raillery.

Richard watched her carry the dress into the bedchamber. When Lane had burst into the coffeehouse to fetch him, only the old servant's worry about the arrest warrant induced him to return. He had resolved to do no more than clear his own name and leave his calculating wife to her fate.

All intentions of indifference had flown out of his mind when he had heard her frightened cry. He had raced up the stairs, drawing his sword in a soldier's reflex. At the sight of his wife struggling between her mother and Ilkston, a possessive fury had boiled up in him, along with gratification that she did not want to leave him.

Of course, as the scene had played out, he came to understand her reluctance. Seeing what she had to bear from that pair, he knew he had to be a better husband than the one she had expected to marry.

Accordingly, her protestations of satisfaction with their marriage struck him as questionable. With the settlement she had foisted on him, she doubtless meant that she liked the financial terms of their union. His conscience pricked him again. She had said nothing of gold or fortune in his bed last night, and he had found plenty of satisfaction himself there.

A soft cough interrupted his thoughts. Lord

Rothley waved him over to the fireplace in an attempt at secrecy. "Seeing that you've married such an heiress, Rickon, I wonder if I might take back the thousand pounds I promised for Glory's dowry. With the Dallison money at your disposal, you can afford it better than I."

Taken aback at his uncle's request, Richard glanced over at the open bedchamber door. "I had hoped, Uncle, that I might add to your pledge when it comes time for my sister to marry. I feel sure you wish her to obtain the best match possible." He wanted Bethany's inheritance in part to provide a decent dowry for his sister, but that greedy settlement impeded his ability to do so. And he'd be damned if he'd reveal its demeaning terms to his uncle, or anyone else for that matter. He'd be a complete laughingstock if news of it ever got out.

Their low-voiced conversation ended when Bethany reappeared, cheerfully announcing her readiness to depart. He studied her expression as he helped her into her cloak, hoping she had not had to overhear yet one more discussion of her inheritance. She gave no sign of having done so, but a hardness in her gray eyes made him wonder.

The visit to the Lord Mayor's office achieved, Lord Rothley invited the newlyweds and Mistress Dallison to dine at his town house in Saint Clement's Lane. There, over a snug meal of turkey-pie washed down with sack, he toasted their health, even persuading Bethany's mother to join him.

Bethany asked so many questions about various

neighborhoods and available rentals that the old man urged them to set up housekeeping in his own house. Richard regarded her with a jaundiced eye. He had angled for that exact invitation for months without success. Now his uncle sat jovially waving aside her stammered thanks.

"I shall be gratified to leave the place in the hands of one who has had such an excellent guide in the domestic arts." He bowed to Mistress Dallison, who unbent enough to smile at the compliment. He smiled indulgently at Bethany. "Stay until you make suitable arrangements for yourselves."

After dinner, Mistress Dallison expressed a desire to see some of the shops. Her daughter reluctantly took the hint and the two ladies set out, following the housekeeper's directions.

Lord Rothley bluntly informed Richard that he could amuse himself for a few hours and retired to his bed for a nap. Pleased to be on his own, Richard strolled to a favored haunt off nearby Lincoln's Inn Fields.

He entered the smoky tavern to find, as he had expected, several friends present. A familiar pale blond head bent over a dice game in one corner. Richard observed the players until the departure of one of them enabled him to slide into the abandoned seat.

"Rickon! I haven't set eyes on you in nigh a week." Lord Thomas Orsey's deceptively angelic face lit up at him. "Hiding from the duns?"

His lordship grinned at his friend's sympathetic

question. "Just the opposite, Tom. You behold a man who's coming up in the world. I've married an heiress."

"You landed the country chit? Well done!" Lord Thomas called for a round of ale to celebrate his friend's change of fortune. The company bombarded Richard with questions about his venture. Mindful of quick ears and loose tongues, he gave an edited account of his recent activities. He described his wife as a Puritan fond of reading and housekeeping without further details.

"To fifteen thousand!" Richard joined the toast silently, unwilling to disclose the fact his wife had outsmarted him.

"Pho! I think Lord Harcourt must be enjoying a jest at our expense."

He tensed as he recognized the voice of Captain Arthur Loring, an old rival. "Why, I saw him five days ago at a ramshackle inn buried in the country, and with a female claiming to be his sister." The newcomer's dark brows lifted suggestively. "As I've known Miss Harcourt for years, I can assure you she most certainly was not."

Richard leaped to his feet. Only Lord Thomas's firm grip on his wrist prevented him from drawing his sword for the second time that day. His friend did not let go as he chuckled at the captain.

"Faith, Arthur, hold your tongue! You make it sound like a scandal when Richard tells us that he just dined with his uncle and his wife's mother this very afternoon." Steel laced the slim nobleman's voice. "Very likely you mistake the matter completely."

The tall, dark-visaged man bowed, the sneer not leaving his face. "I admit I may have spoken in error. Particularly easy to do with a man of Lord Harcourt's reputation." Twirling his walking stick, he sauntered over to a card game on the far side of the room.

"Easy, Rick." Knowing Harcourt's temper, Lord Thomas stayed on his feet as his friend glared after Loring. "You don't want to start a brawl, and it's not as if he mentioned any names."

"He came close enough." Richard slowly lowered himself to his seat. He kept his ears open for any more untoward comments from across the room, but the captain evidently decided on circumspect behavior. The two men did not acknowledge each other's presence again. To Richard's relief, his rival left first. When he stepped into the street himself, he did not observe any sign of Loring.

Dusk approached already, so he hurried back to Saint Clement's Lane. Bethany and her mother had arrived earlier, and he rescued his uncle from a recitation of their purchases by requesting an interview in his library. As the interview consisted of enjoying a glass of brandy free from feminine chatter, he and his uncle parted on good terms.

After escorting Mistress Dallison to her lodgings, he and Bethany returned to the half-timbered building containing their rooms. He helped her out of her cloak and hat, but did not remove his own.

"Take off your things; I shall have supper laid

out directly." She smiled over her shoulder as she moved to set the table.

"'Twill be unnecessary. I sup with friends tonight." His cronies had urged him to join a convivial gathering at a nearby town house that evening, claiming that Richard could not already be reduced to hanging on his wife's apron strings, and Richard's wounded pride had accepted.

Guilt pricked him at the hurt expression in her eyes. Annoyed at the sensation, he spoke sharply. "You wished for a title and social position, my lady. You now possess them unassailably, having been properly wed." His voice lowered suggestively. "And properly bedded, if I do say so myself."

He ignored her crimson cheeks and snapping eyes. "I bid you joy in your new position, not to mention the unheard-of sum set aside for your own use. In our level of society, married couples do not live in one another's pockets, so I bid you *au revoir* for the evening."

Bethany stared at his back as he left, swallowing tears. She didn't know if they came from hurt or from anger, but the latter quickly won out. The tankard in her hand flew across the room and clanged against the wooden slabs of the door. A sob tore out of her throat, followed by another. Before she knew it, she shook with the strength of her weeping.

Much later, she examined her swollen-eyed reflection in the mirror hanging in her bedchamber with one thought in her head. If Richard Harcourt wanted a fashionable marriage, she vowed, she would give him one. With that, she shoved the chest in front of the chamber door and crawled into bed.

Chapter 7

The next several days passed in a state of armed truce between Lord Harcourt and his new Lady. She gladly took over the details of setting up housekeeping in Saint Clement's Lane. Keeping busy helped her from demonstrating the pain she felt at her husband's rejection.

He seemed satisfied to leave the process of removing from his lodgings to her and even unbent enough to deal with such matters as paying his overdue rent and several other bills. When she asked Lane about wages owed to him, he informed her that "Master Richard" had paid him to date from Mr. Armitage's purse.

Bethany had directed the banker to reimburse himself of the funds owed, which he had done with alacrity. His manner toward her had changed since her unfeminine insistence on gaining the use of her own money before she wed. He now regarded her with as much disapproval as he did her lord, although his naturally scrupulous nature did not permit him to tamper with her funds.

Happily, Mr. Leafley's tone of mind was not so nice. He proved as good as his word when she turned to him for assistance. With his good advice, she drew up a plan for the best use of her funds. She admitted to disappointment that she would not be able to live as extravagantly as she might have liked, but the gratification of making her own decisions for the first time in her life compensated for it.

She discharged some of Richard's bills relating to housekeeping, but left the rest for him. And she refused to touch his gambling debts. She noticed the pile of old notes of hand on the writing table decreasing steadily, although new ones appeared regularly. At least those amounts appeared to be much smaller than the older ones.

While Richard spent most of his time away from their rooms, he did respond to her queries about his preferences for their living arrangements. She refused to ask him more than absolutely necessary, but could not avoid such subjects as his requirements in a valet or his preferences for a cook.

Thanks to Lane, she acquired a maid in the person of his sweetheart from the Mermaid. A plump little creature of thirty years, optimistically named Faith, she took over cleaning and the little cooking done in their rooms as well as fulfilling Bethany's basic needs for a lady's maid. She quickly decided to teach the girl to read in hopes that she might someday prove a valuable housekeeper.

Meanwhile the maid accompanied her to shops for propriety's sake. Lady Harcourt had no intention of hiding at home while her husband roamed all over town, and she took care to select a suitable wardrobe. It also allowed her to avoid the loneliness she felt in his absence.

It struck her the night before they were to settle into Lord Rothley's house that she might suffer from Richard's absence less in a larger house than in the two rooms where reminders of him surrounded her.

The next day her husband acknowledged their marriage long enough to escort her to Saint Clement's Lane. They spoke little during their walk from Henrietta Street, although he treated her with his customary courtesy. Her heart sank lower with every passing step.

He had not come to her since their wedding night. On the rare occasions he had returned home from his carousing before dawn, he had simply rolled up in his cloak before the fireplace. When she began moving about the room, he would awake and move into the bedchamber, there to sleep well into the day.

Even the sight of their new quarters failed to cheer her up. A smooth brick front rose straight up from the walkway, with diamond-paned windows set in whitewashed frames above and on either side of the door. Inside, fireplaces warmed each room on the first two floors, giving it an atmosphere of ease and comfort. Lane and Faith had arrived earlier by wagon with the Harcourts' small store of possessions.

His uncle bade them welcome with tankards of Lady Rothley's best cider, sent down in his returned coach. He also informed Bethany that the coach had delivered her things from Abberley as well. She cheered up slightly at this sign that her mother had acceded to the marriage.

"I have a chest full of bed linens and a few hangings I embroidered, and I'm sure she sent my psalms and books as well. I do hope she remembered to put in my notebook of recipes." Her voiced faded away as she noticed the blank stares on the faces of the two men. She chuckled. "All of which means nothing to either of you. But it means a great deal to me, my lord, and I thank you for your kindness in letting us use your vehicle."

"Doubtless my lady would be all agog to hear about it, my dear, but all this domestic stuff is lost on me." With a wink, Lord Rothley turned to Richard. "Nephew, your bride won't impress anyone chattering about sheets and pillowslips. Take her out and about so she can hear the latest gossip. Tell you what, I leave for home in the morning, but I've a fancy to see a play this afternoon. You two come along."

"In that case, you must allow me to treat you, sir. I have already engaged seats with the King's Men for the rest of the season." Richard fixed his eyes on Bethany as he drawled the invitation. "I do not know if my wife's upbringing will permit her to join us."

She gave him look for look. "I shall accompany you and judge for myself."

A slight flush rose to his cheeks. "How very fortunate you are in not having a husband who dictates your actions, my dear, as I am fully entitled to do."

Before the impending quarrel escalated, Lord Rothley interrupted them. "Nonsense, Rickon, there's no need to worry about Bethany. She's uncommonly level-headed."

"Of that, Uncle, I am fully aware." She drew in an angry breath at his faint sneer. "I trust you have a gown to wear for the occasion, my dear?"

She swallowed her irritation, smiling blandly. "I'm sure I can find something suitable."

After a tasty dinner finished off with bread pudding and apples, Bethany and Richard followed the housekeeper upstairs. There, they made the disagreeable discovery that she had placed them in the same chamber. They hid their vexation until the good soul left the room.

"This was none of my doing." Richard paced the handsomely appointed room.

"Obviously, since my charms have decreased markedly since our marriage." She snapped her mouth shut as soon as she spoke, unwilling to further expose her hurt at his neglect. She appeared to have scored a hit, however, for her husband glowered at her and changed the subject.

"If you do not mind, madam, I should like to change in privacy."

She tittered angrily. "I guessed as much, sir. If you would be so good as to inform me when you are finished? I shall be in the parlour consulting with the housekeeper." She sketched a curtsey and quit the room.

If Mistress Cade found it peculiar that Lady Harcourt wished to discuss menus for the upcoming week instead of dressing for the theater, she said nothing. Bethany asked several redundant questions and gave the appearance of listening attentively as minutes passed. An interminable time later, Richard appeared in the doorway. Declaring their chamber free for her use, he left before she could accuse him of lingering over his ensemble for the sole purpose of exasperating her.

Bethany promptly ended the interview, requesting to have her maid attend her. She rushed to their room to find that Faith stood waiting to help her.

The former chambermaid, enthralled by her elevation to the household of a Peer, had declared her intention to provide full satisfaction in the performance of her duties. She had already unpacked her mistress's wardrobe and stored it in one of the room's two clothes presses. On the bed lay one of Bethany's first purchases, a damask gown of bisque interwoven with amber. She curtsied properly at the younger woman's exclamations of gratitude, then told her they had no time for chatter.

Due to Faith's industriousness, Bethany emerged

only a quarter of an hour past the departure time decreed by the gentlemen. She made her way down the stairs at the back of the long hall and approached them where they stood by the door. She bridled at their disappointed expressions, for she had dressed as well as possible with her still limited wardrobe.

Her gown, adorned only by the richness of the material, was cut in the latest mode with a pointed bodice. The lace edging of her chemise peeped over the low neckline and spilled from under her tucked-up sleeves. In lieu of the jeweled pins or strand of pearls favored as hair ornaments, she had threaded a pale satin ribbon through her curls.

Richard, resplendent in gray-green satin, frowned slightly at her bare neck and ears. "You have no jewelry?"

"Mother did not approve of it."

"That won't do." Without further explanation, he strode down the hall and disappeared up the stairs. Bethany looked at Lord Rothley, who shook his head in mystification. Several minutes later, her husband reappeared with a long gold chain dangling from his hand.

His fingertips brushed her skin as he wound the polished links around her neck. Walking around her, he adjusted them on her bosom. She inhaled softly as his knuckles lightly traced their path over the soft mounds and lifted to stroke her cheek. His lips, inches from hers, parted slightly.

"Come, come, lad! There'll be enough time for that when we return." Lord Rothley swung his black cloak over his shoulders. "We're late enough as is." Not waiting for them, he went out to the street, grumbling about doting newlyweds.

They followed, Bethany's mortification allayed by her husband's red face. She forgot her embarrassment at the sight of the sedan chair awaiting her. At her thanks, he replied in bemusement that his wife could not be seen walking along the streets in her best dress. She allowed him to hand her in and shut the small door.

The porters picked up the poles and the three of them traversed the streets to the theater. As she emerged, she looked about, unsure what to expect. The late afternoon sun shone down on the rectangular theater building. A throng of men and women converged on it by chair and on foot. Despite Lord Rothley's complaint of tardiness, it seemed they were not the latest arrivals.

Porters added to the hubbub as they vied with one another for passage. Sundry individuals called out greetings, and occasionally insults, to one another. Men and women of all ages rubbed shoulders, some dressed in bright velvets and satins, and some in more sober woolens or serge.

Hand at her elbow, Richard guided her through the crowd to the correct entrance. Inside they climbed a stairway leading up to their seats. Once settled, she turned her head one way and another, fascinated. She knew she appeared the veriest bumpkin, but neither of her companions teased her for gawking.

She guessed that the raised platform at one end

of the former tennis court must be the stage. On it, a quartet of musicians had just finished playing. After a brief round of applause from those members of the audience attending to the performance, they bowed and gathered up their instruments and music racks.

Above them, chandeliers set with myriad candles glowed. Their light sparkled off the jewels worn by the privileged ladies and gentlemen in the galleries lining the sides and back of the great room. Below, on the main floor, it glowed off oranges sold by girls of varying states of attractiveness.

Most of their customers appeared to be single men, several dressed as grandly as those in the boxes, and it soon became clear to Bethany that the girls sold more than the wares in their baskets. Other men occupying the backless wooden benches in the pit exhibited more discriminating taste by flirting with ladies in the gallery above. At the plethora of bows, arch glances, and blown kisses exchanged between the two levels, Bethany did not know whether to laugh or leave.

The antics in the pit carried on even after the piece started. The crowd did quiet slightly as the prologue ended, although the continual motion and talk all about them prompted her to whisper to Richard that she could hardly follow the story.

"Faith, no one comes for the play, my dear." He nodded at the busy mass of bodies in the pit. "The most fascinating action is usually off the stage, not on it."

"Shhhh!" Lord Rothley leaned forward, his

intent gaze riveted to the play. Every man present echoed his posture and silence finally fell over the entire audience. It felt as though everyone coalesced into one giant creature waiting for a single event.

And then it happened. The crowd collectively caught its breath as a woman emerged from the wings and declaimed her first lines. Bethany gulped. If her mother found out she had witnessed such an immoral display, she would disavow her utterly.

"An actress," breathed Lord Rothley at her side.

She glanced over at her husband, concerned how he might react to the sight of a female performer. She discovered his amused gaze resting on her rather than the stage, as if he expected her to faint or demand that they leave immediately. Rising to the challenge in his green eyes, she returned her attention to the performance.

"You do not appear to share the general amazement at the sight of a woman acting in public."

She heard the rustle of his satin clothes as he leaned in to answer. "I attended the theater as often as I could in France. Actresses have appeared on the stage there for decades." He paused to observe the entrance of a second female character. "Alas, neither of these two compare well to their French sisters. Nor do I find them exceptionally attractive."

Good, Bethany thought as she watched the plot unfold.

* * *

At the interval, Richard noticed Lord Thomas in the pit with a group of his acquaintances, attempting to gain his attention. Leaving Bethany in the care of his uncle, he excused himself and made his way down the stairs.

The floor hummed with activity as he pushed through the press of bodies. Unaccountably, his companions stood in the same spot, their attention still focused up at the galleries. As he leaned over to speak to the man at his side, Tom noticed him and hastened over.

"Rickon, who is she? Who? You must introduce us, dear boy. I insist upon it!"

"Who is who? God's teeth, Tom, you sound like a madman." Richard laughed, wondering what fair creature had now caught his friend's eye. And those of several of their companions, by the looks of it.

"I should beat you with the flat of my blade for holding out on us, you dog." Lord Thomas shook him playfully. "Who else do I mean but that exquisite female at your side?"

"What?" Richard's head whipped around and he gaped up at the seat he had just vacated.

Bethany sat at the front of the box, properly dividing her attention between the stage and his uncle. In the midst of the vibrantly attired crowd, her light-colored dress stood out like a piece of moonlight. Candlelight picked out golden highlights in her fiery hair. One of the swains nearby sighed and compared her to the goddess of dawn.

Revolted at the sickly comparison, he turned on

the speaker, a pallid young sprig in aquamarine satin. "She is not curst Aurora, sirrah! That happens to be Lady Harcourt." He advanced toward the hapless fellow. "And I am Lord Harcourt." The young man became whiter and immediately begged his pardon, carefully edging away. Richard glared at the circle of men around him.

"Meaning you are just the man to make us known to her." The irrepressible Lord Thomas arranged his cuffs and ribands. A sudden expression of hurt crossed his handsome face. "You owe us that much. I thought you said she was a Puritan, all prayers and psalms."

"She is!" The exclamation no sooner left his mouth than his wife noticed him standing in the crowd. Even at this distance, he caught the mischievous spark in her eye as she nodded to him and then looked away as if uninterested.

"That vixen. She knows exactly what she's about." The words escaped before he could stop them.

Beside him, Tom laughed. "A much better description, in faith. Now, introductions if you please."

In the face of their importunity, Richard grudgingly tromped back up to the gallery, trailed by a gaggle of gallants. Barely concealing his chagrin, he presented them to his wife and watched them crowd around her. To his dismay, she proved adept at listening to all, while making each man feel he had her attention.

She accepted their acclaim without favoring any, except for Lord Thomas, made known to her as a particular friend of his. She engaged him in conversation for several moments until he courteously addressed Lord Rothley. Only then did she speak to anyone else.

When the play resumed, he ruthlessly escorted them all to the stairs, even Lord Thomas. Bethany glanced at him when he returned to her side. "Your companions are very kind to welcome me so." He nearly delivered a sharp retort when he realized she spoke in earnest. She took their attentions as no more than generosity to a friend's wife. He uttered a noncommittal reply and moved his chair to hide her from curious eyes in the pit. He spent the rest of the evening in her company, making an unspoken declaration of possession.

At the performance's end, she placed a hand on his arm as he wrapped her cloak around her shoulders. "That dark gentleman across from us seems to want your attention." He followed the direction of her inclined head. From the gallery opposite, Arthur Loring bowed sardonically.

"An acquaintance, 'tis no one of import." Richard nodded coldly and offered his arm to his wife. As they strolled toward the exit, she wrinkled her nose.

"He was at the Bell and Moon the morning we left. He wore a ridiculous amount of ribbons then, too."

The reappearance of those cavaliers who had earlier met his wife drove all thoughts of the captain from his mind. They exhibited an irritating tendency to crowd around her as they made their way out of the building. It took Richard quite half an hour to escort her to the waiting sedan chair.

Back in Saint Clement's Lane, Lord Rothley complimented her on her conquests. "I shall have quite a tale for my lady and your new sister upon my return." He chuckled at her. "But if you say naught to her about seeing an actress, I shall keep quiet about the same thing to your mother." Bethany hastily agreed to his bargain.

After enjoying a sack posset with them, he picked up his candle. Lighting it from a graceful sconce by the door, he bade them good night. Listening to his steps echo down the wooden floor of the hall beyond, Richard debated with himself.

He had planned to deposit his wife in Saint Clement's Lane and join Lord Thomas and several of their friends in a fashionable gaming hell. After seeing her in public for the first time, it occurred to him he only guessed her nature. Such had never mattered to him before, but then he never intended to marry any of his previous women.

He offered her a glass of wine, which she accepted. Pouring one for himself, he seated himself in a leather-padded chair and asked her opinion of the theater. She sipped thoughtfully before answering.

"I should like to go back. From the sermons I heard condemning plays and playhouses, I expected much worse. I understand they live dissolute lives off the stage, but seeing and hearing the women drew me in to their dilemmas." She grimaced. "You will think me foolish, but it seemed as though I stood beside them at times."

"Not in the least. A good actor makes you believe he speaks from your own heart." He looked into her eyes, marveling at the way they held both silver and smoke. "I shall take you again." He could not explain why her brilliant smile made his pulse leap.

They discussed a number of subjects as both the candles in their holders and the wine in the bottle dipped lower. When Bethany stood up to retire for the night, she wobbled alarmingly. Coming to her aid, Richard found himself a bit tipsy, but otherwise in control of himself. She took his arm with an apology. "I seem to be a bit fuddled, my lord."

He led her down the long paneled hallway to the stairs, one hand guiding her elbow and the other holding a candelabrum. The steps proved more of a challenge. He bit his lip at the contact of her slim body when she missed a step and stumbled into him. The feel of her soft curves against his body contrasted sharply with the chaste image of her sitting above him in the gallery earlier, starting a familiar heat in his loins.

He had not planned to take her again until he could master the desire he felt every time he touched her. To want a woman so constantly made a man desperate. He had lived with desperation from his boyhood and wanted no more of it. To want a woman who had used him so coldly made him weak.

He had avoided her successfully until tonight. Now the wine whispered that she was his wife, his for the taking. Should he feel shame because the bride he had chosen for money proved so eminently beddable?

When they reached their chamber, he set the candles down, although Bethany still needed his assistance. He awakened Faith, who had fallen asleep in one of two chairs before the fireplace. When he dismissed her, she shook her head and chuckled. She stopped long enough to light more candles by the bed table before leaving them.

Bethany twined her arms round his neck and pouted. "I need my maid, sir." Richard took an unsteady breath and placed her arms at her sides, running his hands down them. She felt the heat from his palms through the layers of material, but strangely enough the warmth caused her to shiver. Her breath came faster as they moved up to frame her cheeks. His slightly callused thumb brushed her cheekbone as he angled her to receive his kiss. When he spoke, his voice roughened with want.

"I shall maid my lady tonight."

His mouth ravaged hers, but she opened to him willingly. He tasted of the claret he had imbibed so freely, and when he moved to suck and nip at her earlobe, she inhaled the mingled scents of musk and lavender.

Her head swam, but no longer from wine. Her breasts were crushed against his solid chest as he reached back to untie the laces of her gown. Their peaks tingled against the confines of her stays. His mouth continued to explore her neck, skipping over the gold chain he had given her. Breathing in shallow open-mouthed gasps, she dropped her head back farther to give him the access he wordlessly demanded. Had she not gripped his muscled arms, she would have collapsed.

As her loosened bodice came away from her torso, he stepped back, drawing the heavy material down her arms. He sucked in his breath at the sight of her breasts through the sheer chemise, their coral tips already stiffening. He lifted the soft globes, circling and rolling the taut peaks between his fingers. Heat flamed in the cleft between her thighs. She moaned with pleasure as she felt herself becoming moist at his touch.

The combination of wine and her husband's sensuous onslaught loosened Bethany's inhibitions. As his hands worked their magic on her body, she reached up and pushed his satin coat off his shoulders. He let go of her long enough to shrug it to the floor. Taking advantage, she unknotted the lace at his neck.

As it fluttered to the floor, he stroked his hands down her slim curves. Coming to rest where her waist flared into the chalice of her hips, they tightened and he pulled her into yet another kiss. The feel of the exciting ridge tenting his breeches caused her to rock against him. He growled and slid her gown the rest of the way off. His green eyes darkened to emerald as he gazed her scarcely veiled body. She swallowed thickly in anticipation as he unfastened the chain to let it fall heedlessly into the soft pool of damask.

He planted kisses over the swell of each breast while he coaxed her chemise off. His mouth followed the receding lawn, at last closing over a nipple and suckling fiercely. She gave a hoarse cry as his index finger slid into the brown curls between her legs, teasing more wetness from her as it parted her nether lips to caress and fondle.

He lifted his head, watching her as his finger moved rhythmically inside her. His breath came in gasps as his muscular chest rose and fell. "You want this, Beth. Tell me you want me."

She could barely speak as she writhed in his arms. "Yes, Richard. Oh, yes."

He withdrew his finger suddenly and she cried out in need. Kissing deeply, they staggered to the bed, divesting each other of the rest of their clothes. He pulled the coverlet down and urged her between the sheets.

She gasped at the shock of the cold sheets on her naked body. When Richard joined her a moment later, she burrowed against him as much for body heat as for desire. He rumbled with laughter, knowing full well what she did.

She pulled her head back to frown at him. "I'm cold!"

His laughter died, replaced by an intent expression. "That you are not, my lady. Not in my bed, at least. Why is that?"

She looked at him, puzzled at his unexpected seriousness. "It is a great blessing when man and wife find pleasure in the marriage bed." He said nothing more then, but arched an eyebrow into a wicked leer.

"I'm glad to hear you say so." He rolled her onto her back and covered her with his body, his tongue plunging greedily into her mouth. Hers twined around it, tasting, feeling its texture.

She purred at the feel of his warmth pressing her into the soft feather bed. Her back arched slightly at the feel of the crisp hair of his chest against her sensitive nipples. Her hands stroked down his spine to rest on his firm buttocks. He laughed again and obliged her by rocking his hard shaft against her lower belly.

He rose to his elbows and knees as his mouth left hers to kiss its way down her body. She stretched out beneath him as he scooted his way down, arching her breasts into his hands as his fingers plucked and toyed with her nipples.

When his mouth came to the mound between her legs, however, she froze.

"Richard, what are doing?" She lifted her head to see him resting his chin on the soft curls.

"I'm helping my wife find pleasure in the marriage bed." His virtuous tone belied the wicked smile on his face.

"I already have that, you must know it." Vainly she tried to wiggle out from under him, using her hands for leverage. Instantly he pulled her back down, wrapping his arms around her thighs and holding her hands at her sides. She struggled a little as he kissed each inner thigh in turn, but she could not escape.

His hands and shoulders forced her legs far apart, opening her completely to his gaze and mouth. All thought of protest deserted her when his tongue stroked intimately into her. Her hips lifted helplessly as he flicked her tender nub and circled her intimate opening. Her heart pounded so she thought it would burst from her chest as he buried his tongue into her passage, wringing waves of heat and moisture from her.

The first tremors of her release overcame her. He raised himself up and entered her with a single luscious thrust, smothering her cries with his open kiss that tasted of her own juices. He continued to move within her as her body convulsed around him, his steady strokes prolonging her exquisite tremors.

As she finished, he buried his face against her neck, nearly sobbing as he thrust into her harder and faster. Instinctively she gathered him closer, running her hands over his sweat-covered back. When she grasped his butt and pulled him farther into her, he found his own climax, arching his back as his hot seed spilled into her and overflowed.

He relaxed onto her, whispering her name over and over again between kisses on her mouth, cheeks, and brow. She kissed him back, toying with his sweat-dampened hair until he adjusted himself to one side of her with an apology.

"Forgive me, sweet. I shouldn't have just squashed you like that." She snuggled next to him, her eyes already drifting shut.

"I like the feel of your weight on top of me,"

she confessed. "It makes me feel like I've done something right."

He hugged her closer. "Is that so unusual?"

She shifted slightly to stare up at the wooden canopy. "Mother often found fault with me, true. But I was thinking more that I've given you pleasure, too."

"Aye, sweet Beth." His breath tickled her ear. "You did."

Satisfied, she soon fell fast asleep.

Chapter 8

Young Lady Harcourt's success continued after her appearance at the theater. At first, she did not often go out, for women ruled the realm of society, even where a new King sat at its pinnacle. For the first time in her memory, she had no female companions. Mistress Cade managed the house so well that she had little to do but read, attend to her needlework, and shop for herself.

Luckily for her funds, the latter activity soon palled. So many packages of new gowns, hats, gloves, stockings, fans, and other kickshaws arrived that Richard jested that they had moved to Saint Clement's Lane just in time to avoid running out of room in his old lodgings.

Richard seemed to have reconciled himself to their marriage. He dressed in Lord Rothley's bedchamber, but regularly slept in her bed. To her delight, he did so even when he did not make love to her. Her husband also made a point of accompanying her to the theater again, and to other amusements suitable for a lady. But his attentions, however welcome, did not compensate for his lack of acquaintance with suitable ladies.

Granted, she permitted some of his friends to escort her to the park or the playhouse on occasion, for it did not do for a husband and wife to appear exclusively in one another's company. Fortunately, Lord Thomas offered the solution to her dilemma one night at the theater by introducing her to his mother, the Dowager Countess of Planchard, and his sister, Viscountess Haynes.

Although high in the instep, both ladies prepared to welcome her as Richard's wife. It transpired that he was a favorite of theirs and they soon included her in invitations to walk or dine.

After her initial nervousness in their presence, Bethany cautiously enjoyed their company. The viscountess, only a few years older than she, shared her brother's insouciance. She even coaxed Bethany into letting her pierce her ears. Upon hearing that her husband wished to present her at Court, she immediately offered to assist her in selecting clothes and learning the necessary rules of etiquette.

As he was not a gentleman in waiting to the King, Richard had no need to appear at Court regularly, but it behooved him to present his new wife to his sovereign as soon as possible. The coronation was nearly three months away, but crowds of the noble and the wealthy swarmed to Court to curry favor.

On the day appointed by Richard, Bethany sat patiently under the ministrations of the hairdresser while Faith prepared her bodice and skirt. She already wore her chemise, petticoats, stockings, and shoes under a voluminous robe of blush pink. As soon as he had finished, she examined her appearance in the hand mirror, turning her head from side to side.

Her cropped and curled hair hung on either side of her face in masses of ringlets while the bulk of it had been twisted and wound with the gold chain given to her by Richard.

As soon as he retired from the room, she and Faith finished the tedious task of dressing her in the remaining layers of clothing. Richard entered just as she shook out the last frill of heavy lace falling from her sleeves.

"Are you ready, madam?" He sounded uncharacteristically nervous. He had no need to be; she caught her breath at the sight of him.

The fashionable justacorps of bronze satin fit perfectly across his broad shoulders before flaring out slightly over the matching vest and breeches. As usual, he eschewed the frivolity of excessive ribbons and frills. Most of the decoration consisted of the heavy embroidery in cream and bronze thread on the facings of the jacket, and from the worked scabbard of his sword.

An ivory lace cravat flowing down the open front of the justacorps completed his ensemble. He carried a black beaver hat with a single cream ostrich feather and a pair of wide-cuffed gloves studded with brass suns. She could smell the faint scent of amber emanating from the black leather.

"You look very fine, my lord." She spoke softly, aware of her maid's continued presence.

The rich color of the suit enhanced his eyes. She could not look away from their green depths as they took in her own appearance.

"As do you, my lady." She ducked her head at his approval. While he lay with her often, other nights he came home late after carousing with his friends. She did not know his real feelings toward her.

Trying now to convince herself she did not care as long as he treated her with the respect due a wife, she forced a laugh. "I scarcely know if I can move in all this finery." He took her hand and twirled her in a stately circle. The petticoats under her buff velvet skirt rustled sumptuously and the pale blue ribbons decorating her sleeves and bodice fluttered as she moved.

"You shall do very well." His eyebrows drew together as he looked over her hair. "Is that my father's chain?" Involuntarily, she put her hand to the heavy coil at the back of her head.

"If it displeases you, I shall take it out." His carefully neutral expression alarmed her. Rather to her relief, as it had taken some time to put her hair up, he shook his head.

"No, that would only delay us. I would ask that you not use it as a hair ornament in the future, though." He spoke without heat, but with a hint of sadness. Bethany hastily agreed to his request.

"I am sorry, Richard. I had no idea it was your father's."

He shrugged. "You had no way of knowing." Softly he continued, "My mother had to sell most of her jewelry while we were in exile. Most of what remained when she died I gave to my sister." Bethany nodded, unwilling to interrupt. He had never before mentioned his family's life on the continent. The next moment, his manner lightened.

"Indeed, 'tis partly my own fault you had to resort to such measures." He held up a finger. "Faith, do you have the box I gave to you earlier?"

Grinning from ear to ear, the plump maid brought out a leather-covered box from one of the clothes presses. Taking it from her, Richard opened it. Bethany's eyes widened. Inside, a pair of aquamarine and pearl earrings and a matching necklace rested on the satin lining.

"They're lovely." She touched them hesitantly, almost afraid they would disappear. He gave them to her largely because she would look odd at Court without any jewels; she understood that. But he had obviously taken care to select pieces that matched her dress.

She put the earrings in, replacing the gold drops Richard had purchased for her when they were first pierced. She raised her eyebrows at him. "Will you put the necklace on?"

He complied readily, toying with a tendril of hair on the back of her neck after he fastened the clasp. She pivoted and hugged him. "Thank you so much! I've never had anything so beautiful."

"I'm glad you like them. You've never teased me for jewelry so I wasn't sure what you would care for." He held out his elbow, a sign for them to go downstairs.

She laughed as she tucked her hand into its crook. "Is that why you haven't given me any before now?"

The second King Charles kept a Court far less formal than his father's, but those entering the royal presence were to appear suitably groomed. To prevent untoward particles of dirt from marring their new ensembles, Lady Haynes insisted on escorting them to Whitehall in her lord's town coach.

Bethany remarked on her generous impulse as they awaited her arrival in the library. Their domestic harmony faltered when Richard reminded her that they would own a similar equipage by now had she not raised strenuous objections to its purchase.

"I have no objection to owning a town coach, sir." She held on to her temper with difficulty. "As I have said repeatedly, I question the need for one when we haven't any permanent property in London, but do have an estate in Yorkshire that requires a heavy coach to travel to and from."

"You may recall that I wished to order one of each style." His lordship lowered his brows as he leaned on a heavy walnut reading table, where she sat loosely holding an open book in her lap.

She stood and tossed the book on the table's surface. "How will we afford a place of our own here in town if our money is spent on coaches and the horses to draw them?"

"We? You mean me, do you not? I don't recall hearing you offer to put any of your precious trust toward a house!"

"I offered to apply part of my funds toward the purchase of a berlin for long journeys, and of course I would contribute to the cost of a house." She leaned on the table herself now. "We haven't even found one we like yet!"

He leaned farther toward her. "A fine thing when a man must apply to his wife for monetary aid. God's teeth, if word were to get out that I have only five thousand pounds out of our twenty, I'd be a laughingstock."

"And a woman whose husband controls the entirety of any property she brings to her marriage is not humiliated?" She asked the question in a low voice, looking him in the eye.

He hissed his answer as the door to the library creaked open. "That is entirely different!"

The arrival of Viscountess Haynes on Lord Thomas's arm reduced her retort to a roll of her eyes. Her ladyship entered the library in a flurry of chatter and taffeta. Scrutinizing Bethany's appearance, she admired her new jewelry.

"Faith, Richard, you did very well. Did I not tell you aquamarines would suit this gown to perfection? Lady Harcourt, allow me to view your Court curtsey one last time."

Under the watchful eyes of all three, Bethany sank nearly to the ground as her skirt undulated into a pool around her. After holding the position for several seconds, she rose to her feet.

"You shall be a credit to all of us. Only a month ago you could hardly bend your knees, and now look at you!" She turned to relay a choice bit of gossip to her brother while Lord Thomas helped her into her cloak.

Bethany accepted her wrap from Richard with ill grace. "I feel like a trained monkey." Fortunately, the viscountess's prattle covered her whisper. He turned a laugh into a cough behind his gloved hand.

"If you say that aloud, I'll wring your neck, you wretched woman."

She gawped like a green girl after descending from the coach to the restrained bustle of the palace. Around her the jumble of mismatched structures making up Whitehall seethed with activity. Not only courtiers and ladies in waiting scurried from one building to another; the royal servants had their business to attend to as well. Carpenters, stablemen, laundresses, and scullery maids orbited the uncrowned King.

A few enterprising beggars shivered in a clump near the gatehouse the carriage had just passed. They alternated their pleas to passersby with insults to the guards assigned the task of removing them from the royal grounds.

Lady Haynes led them unhesitatingly across the courtyard and into one of the largest buildings, where they were to collect Lady Planchard. Walking alongside her husband, Bethany soon lost all sense of direction in the maze of halls, stairways, and anterooms. Eventually they stood in front of the countess's apartments, granted to acknowledge the late earl's death in the service of Charles the First.

The gray-haired dowager countess invited them inside to remove their cloaks before entering His Majesty's presence. As she listened to her ladyship speaking with her son and daughter, Bethany looked around the small chamber. A bright tapestry on one wall relieved some of the windowless room's darkness, as did numerous candles. A small fire provided additional light and heat, both welcome this day, although she wondered how stuffy the room became in summer.

The countess had expressed only gratitude in her hearing for the small rooms. Bethany had learned from her daughter that the current earl declined to house her, claiming poverty. Lady Haynes herself wished very much to take her mother under her roof, but Lord Haynes forbade it. Lord Thomas, even poorer than his brother, could do little to provide for her either.

As they left the room, she pretended not to notice Lady Haynes slip a small purse into the countess's hand with a whisper. "Just a bit of my dress allowance, I don't need it and his lordship will never notice." She glanced at Richard. From the sympathetic look on his face, she knew he had witnessed the exchange, too.

Careful not to embarrass his friends, Bethany inclined her head to whisper into his ear. "Why so distressed, dear sir? 'Tis no more than what you would reduce me to."

Looking straight ahead, he replied to her jibe equally quietly. "I would not behave so shamefully to my wife."

"I do not think you would, no. But if I had only what funds you chose to allow me, all you'd have to do is change your mind and I would be as helpless as she." By unspoken agreement, they dropped behind their hosts to continue their whispered argument.

"You must know I would not do so shabby a thing." His protest could barely be heard through his stiff lips.

"I know you abducted me for my money. And tried to ruin me after you said you would not." He flinched slightly at her statement, but recovered quickly.

"Allow me to remind you how willing you were to enjoy a title, my lady, not to mention my embrace. You bargained well enough for yourself in the end."

She ignored his attempt to insult her. "Aye, I did, Richard. I do not live in fear of my husband and have no need to intrigue to get what I want."

"And I did not need to touch you to get your money." He stopped walking and turned to glare at her, although he still spoke the softest whisper.

"Then why did you," she challenged him.

"Because I damned well couldn't keep my hands

off you!" He abruptly cradled her face in his hands and kissed her. She grasped his wrists to pull away, but as he deepened the kiss, her fingers loosened as she responded to him.

"Oh." Dazed, she became aware that they stood in a sumptuously decorated hallway in the better part of the palace. Sunlight entered through windows along one side, shining off elaborately carved and gilded frames surrounding paintings and mirrors. The reflected light enhanced the brilliant colors of an immense Gobelin tapestry dominating the wall opposite.

It also flattered the rich clothing and jewels worn by a knot of courtiers and ladies clustered by the far door. Judging by the titters and smirks only partially hidden behind their hands, they must have arrived in time to observe the unseemly display. Bethany wanted to sink in mortification at their amusement. She glimpsed her crimson face in one of the huge mirrors.

One elegantly dressed man, who towered over the rest, found their predicament particularly amusing, for he laughed heartily as he approached them. Richard and Lord Thomas bowed deeply while Lady Planchard and her daughter immediately curtseyed nearly to the floor. She instantly followed suit, horrified at the realization that she had been caught kissing her husband in public by none other than the King himself.

"It is Lord Harcourt, is it not?" His Majesty's teeth flashed in his olive-complected face. "You requested the return of your family estate upon our return last May?" At Richard's assent, he nodded. "We were forced to refuse you a pension. A bitter decision, for we understand too well the grief of losing a father. Have you procured the funds to restore your estate?"

Bethany, listening with fascination to this disclosure of Richard's past, started when he introduced her.

"Oddsfish, do you mean to say you were kissing your own wife?" Though he was accounted less handsome than his younger brother, the Duke of York, his kind smile lessened her embarrassment. His languid manner did not quite hide the appraisal in his eyes as he measured her responses to his questions, but his very attentiveness lent him a great deal of charm. Even the revelation that her family had supported Parliament during the late wars did not impair his affability.

"Why, 'tis the prettiest Parliamentarian I've ever seen." He actually winked at Richard. "Are you become a Nonconformist?"

She spoke before she thought. "On the contrary, Sire! He's now become a wealthy man."

The King burst out laughing. "Well said, Lady Harcourt, though I expect his lordship is pleased to have found such a pretty solution to his problems. We should be so lucky ourselves."

At her side, Richard bowed. "Merely trying to promote Your Majesty's interests in whatever small way I may, Sire."

"Oho, is that what you were doing when we came in? The lady appeared to find your arguments most convincing." Still chuckling, the King drifted over to slip an arm around the waist of a stunning woman with auburn hair. Dismissing his retinue, he escorted her out under the eyes of everyone in the room.

Lady Planchard, bearing down on the Harcourts, whispered a brief scold to both of them for their shameless display of affection. Glancing after the King and his companion, she sniffed. "Ghastly woman." Even that soft statement caused Lord Thomas, who accompanied her, to squeeze her hand in warning.

"Careful, Mother." His lips barely moved. "His Majesty is too much the gentleman to punish a woman's prating tongue, but Barbara Villiers has no such qualms."

Bethany craned her head to watch the King and his paramour disappear through the doorway. So that was the King's notorious mistress! Even in Stanworth, she had heard tales of her greed and brazenness.

The royal departure allowed an indistinct buzz of conversation to rise in the hallway. Richard and Lord Thomas wandered off to speak to an acquaintance while Lady Haynes rescued Bethany before she could be drawn into a conversation with a group of the countess's elderly friends. She confided her opinion of Richard's behavior as most romantic. Bethany admitted to herself that she liked his kisses very well, but it would serve no purpose to say so.

"If he must misbehave so, I wish he would do so in a secluded place." Unfortunately, the viscountess read an unintended double meaning into her reply, and used it as a way of introducing Bethany into her circle of friends as a wicked wit. Discomfited by the raillery this caused, she contrived to drift away from the chattering group to gaze out of a window into the Privy Garden beyond.

"Lady Haynes means well, but her tongue does run away with her at times."

She jumped a bit at the quiet statement. To her further dismay, she found the speaker to be none other than the dark dandy from the Moon and Bell. He made her a graceful leg. "Captain Arthur Loring at your service, my lady."

She had no choice but to give him her name in return before defending Lord Thomas's sister.

"True, she is talkative. But she has shown me several kindnesses; I am loath to criticize." She hoped he did not recognize her. She and Richard had provided enough grist for the gossip mill already. "Lady Haynes has provided welcome assistance to me at the request of my husband." Disliking the way he ogled her, she emphasized the last two words.

"I knew very well you were not Harcourt's sister. I must say 'tis a surprise to find you're his wife." Bethany gasped at the implied insult. As if realizing what he had said, the dark gentleman hastily tried to repair his breach. "Forgive me, my lady. I merely meant that Richard Harcourt is a poor match for a woman of good character."

Bethany suspected that he meant nothing of the sort, but she had no wish to cause any more talk today. "We discovered that we have mutual interests. I greatly enjoy my position as his wife."

"That much was obvious when we entered." He coughed slightly. "Lord Harcourt never could control himself around beautiful women, even ladies of the highest quality."

Bethany did not know which irritated her more, his fulsome compliment or the implication that Richard was a habitual womanizer. She had no control over her husband's actions, and this man's barbed gallantries held little interest for her.

"I'm sure my lord has introduced me to all his intimate friends, sir. I do not recall meeting you, but perhaps my memory is at fault?"

"You remember meeting me well enough." She looked askance at his flat tone of voice. It changed to a fashionable drawl. "Lady Harcourt, my heart breaks to think you do not recall seeing me at the theater. I spent the entirety of the last act trying to get your attention." His glance slid across the room. "I shall have to introduce myself to you, as your esteemed husband is somewhat occupied at the moment." He coughed slightly as he looked over her shoulder.

She turned to follow his glance. Richard was indeed occupied, but not with the men he and Lord Thomas had originally greeted. Now he bent to hear a dainty woman with lustrous dark hair. She placed her hand intimately on his arm as she made some joke, for he smiled and wagged a teasing finger at her. While not in the first blush of youth, no wrinkle marred the creamy skin of her face and bosom.

"Mistress Shadbourne. She and your husband spent a great deal of time together in the past, although he at least had the decency to break with her before he made his most recent visit to Stanworth."

Bethany stood, her stomach coalesced into a frozen ball as her tormentor murmured into her ear. She had expected when she agreed to marry Richard that he would stray; men often did. But she had not thought she would form an attachment to him herself, or take such delight in her own relations with him.

She had hoped Richard's frequent visits to her bed since their first outing meant he had developed a similar attachment to her. It seemed she was wrong, however, as she watched him murmur something into his companion's ear that made her pout very prettily up at him.

With a shock, it dawned on her that the sick feeling in her stomach was jealousy. On its heels followed the even more depressing knowledge that she loved her husband.

Her stiff-necked pride asserted itself. She might feel physically ill with envy and humiliation, but she would be damned if she would show it in front of a roomful of strangers. Her chin snapped up and she looked around disdainfully.

When Lord Thomas rushed up a few moments later, she greeted him with a semblance of calm. Clearly he had arrived to rescue her, for he immediately announced his mother's need of her presence. He regarded Captain Loring with cold civility as he took Bethany's arm.

"Pay no mind to Arthur, my dear. He's a typical soldier, always looking for something to fight."

The captain bowed. "Old habits die hard. You might remind Harcourt how fond I am of obvious targets."

Not deigning to reply, Lord Thomas led Bethany away. Trying to appear sophisticated, she asked him what he knew about Mistress Shadbourne. He dismissed the woman.

"She's been a fixture in society since the King took his throne back. Widow to a Parliamentarian, but eager to seize the main chance. She married a merchant not long ago, but one with money and influence."

"Did she hope to marry into the nobility at one time?" She ignored Lord Thomas's sharpened glance. She had to know how deeply the woman had been involved with Richard.

"Unlikely, my dear. Most of us haven't enough cash to tempt her." He patted her hand. "Yes, they were involved at one time, but I have reason to believe Richard is contented with his bride. Pay no attention to Loring; he will interfere with Rickon whenever he can."

Before she could grill him further, he launched into enthusiastic praise for the last play presented by the Duke's Men, rivals to Richard's favored theater troupe. Bethany disclosed that she had never seen them, at which point he enlisted his sister, whom they had joined, to back his claim of their superiority.

Before she knew it, she promised herself to join a party of Lady Haynes's devising to attend a performance the following week.

In contrast to the cheerful atmosphere of the drive to the palace, silence filled the coach on the way back home. Lady Haynes valiantly attempted to relieve the strain by discussing plans for her proposed outing to the theater, but only her brother responded to her efforts. Richard sat by Bethany looking straight ahead.

No sooner had he conducted her into the house than he took her by the arm and nearly dragged her into the library.

"What do you mean by spending so long in Arthur Loring's company?" His eyes blazed emerald at her. "The man is nothing but malice."

Outraged at this unexpected attack, she lost her own temper. "So I was told by Lord Thomas! Perhaps if you had not spent so much time with your paramour, you would have informed me yourself!"

"My association with Frances Shadbourne ended well before we married. She tired of me, in fact." That he did not deny his attraction to her devastated Bethany. Unable to face him, she walked over to the bookshelf and pretended to search for a volume. "God's teeth, as close as you stood to Loring, I'm surprised you could see around him."

He accused her of improper behavior after everything he had done that afternoon?

"At least I didn't paw him in full view of the

entire room, like your mistress." As his protest, she sarcastically amended her words. "Forgive me, I meant your former mistress! I suppose I should be thankful you bother to kiss me at all." Heedless of her tears, she stalked past him to the door.

"Please be so good as to tell the cook I am taking a tray in my room." She turned the knob and exited. She nearly reached the stairs when she heard Richard shouting behind her.

"Tell her yourself, madam. I will be out for the rest of the evening." She turned in time to see him clap his hat onto his head.

With a sweep of his cape, he stormed out of the house, her furious "Good!" echoing in his ears.

Without further ado, she ran up the stairs to their room. Shutting the door fast behind her, she burst into tears.

Hours later, Richard stared blearily into a mug of ale. Around him the denizens of a tavern in one of London's questionable neighborhoods caroused, but he wanted none of it. Lord Thomas sat across from him, listening sympathetically.

"What does she want, Tom?" He hunched over the table. "I told her I haven't touched Frances in months. I even told her she left me. Bethany should be relieved that the woman isn't interested in me! And what does she do? Goes cold as snow and marches off to her room."

His friend nodded. "Strange creatures," he confided. "Half the time I don't understand why my mother and sister act the way they do." He took a pull from his tankard. "Your wife spends a lot of time with my sister. I'll put in a good word for you where I can."

Richard's impairment did not prevent him from walking home safely. The cold night air cleared his head somewhat, and he thought he might indulge in nocturnal sporting with Bethany. The memory of her ardent response to his lovemaking cheered him considerably. He reminded himself that she had wanted him even before they were married, when he had no money at all.

After letting himself in, he staggered up the stairs singing one of the merrier ditties he had heard earlier in the evening, "When the Cock Begins to Crow."

Just as he reached the top and took a breath to start the refrain, he heard a small click from the direction of her room. He stopped midnote. Striding over to the door, he rattled the handle. It did not move.

"Beth! Unlock the door."

"You're drunk! Go back to Mistress Shadbourne." The solid wooden barrier muffled her voice, but he understood her clearly enough. His only response was to pound on it, in frustration more than anything else. He tried to sweeten her temper.

"I don't want to go to her bed, I want to go to yours." Even this declaration of fidelity did not appease the vixen. He resorted to his full authority as her husband and ordered her point-blank to unlock the door.

"For the last time, I do not want you in my bed. If this is how you're going to treat me, I shall obtain a house for my own use."

Enraged, he backed up and, with a few well-placed kicks at the small lock, broke the door open. Bethany, her face nearly as white as her nightgown, stood in the center of the room armed with a porcelain pomander. He stood in the doorway, breathing heavily.

"Let us be very clear, madam. We are husband and wife, however much gold you have in your money-grubbing hands. Rest assured I have no desire—or need—to force myself on a woman who doesn't want me," he sneered, "but you shall not lock yourself away from me like you did your thrice-damned fortune!"

Before she could argue with him, he pulled the door to with a deeply satisfying slam. He entered his uncle's chamber and collapsed onto the bed, smiling broadly at his wife's shriek of thwarted anger.

Chapter 9

The following days proved some of the most miserable of Bethany's life. Richard refused to explain his whereabouts for the rest of the night. She refused to abandon pride enough to question him. Certainly she should give thanks that he did not expect her to fulfill her wifely duties while he cavorted with, she assumed, other women. But the thought of him in someone else's arms nearly made her unaccountably miserable.

His manner at home upset her as much. The humorous teasing dissipated, replaced with cold civility. He made no demands on her nor commented on her activities. She shopped. She joined Lady Haynes on her barge for a pleasure trip to Greenwich. He made no demur. She attended a musical entertainment with one of the gallants to whom he had introduced her at the theater. He said nothing.

Even the blatant repair of her door and lock during one of his few periods in the house failed to inspire him to anything more than a frigid objection to the noise. As soon as the workmen cleaned up and left, she shut herself inside and sat before her dressing table, hands clenched in her lap, fighting back tears at his indifference. After a long while, her gaze fell on the small coffer that held the necklace and earrings he had bestowed upon her. She wondered bitterly if he would have given her anything at all had they not gone to Whitehall that day. She sighed miserably.

Through the door, she heard the unmistakable sound of his footfalls on the stair. She looked up hopefully as they paused outside her door. Her heart plummeted to her feet when she heard them move on, followed by the soft closing of his uncle's chamber door.

She wondered if he would ever come to her bed again.

Her low spirits persisted until the day of Lady Haynes's theater party. Predictably, Richard professed no interest in her company. Her ladyship, whose circle included no couple who willingly spent time together, kindly assigned Lord Thomas to collect Bethany for dinner before the play. Even the prospect of such an agreeable companion failed to cheer her.

She felt so melancholy that she pled a sick headache in order to escape the commitment. Only a hastily scrawled note from her hostess begging her attendance if at all possible induced her to change her mind. It seemed the party stood in grave danger of having a mismatched number of ladies and gentlemen.

* * *

Richard, chaffing at his continued desire for his wife, had gone for a ride in Green Park. He returned to find that Lord Thomas had arrived earlier than expected. Glad of the chance to speak to him, he invited his friend to enjoy a glass of claret in the parlour. Tom stretched out his legs, leaned back in a comfortable chair, and took an experimental taste of the wine before complimenting his friend's taste.

"Thank my uncle." Richard sipped at his own glass, relishing the smooth flow of fruit and spice flavors tinged with oak. "The old man may be a bumpkin in most things, but his palate is impeccable."

"Indeed!" Lord Thomas raised his glass to toast the absent Lord Rothley. "Pity you're not joining us; the play is *The Mad Lover*." He laughed as his friend groaned.

"When I want a surfeit of dancing trees, I shall let you know." Richard shuddered. "Give me a play with wit, not a mindless procession of spectacle."

"One masque in the final scene hardly amounts to a procession and even you cannot deny the use of music throughout is charming. Besides, the ladies find the final masque vastly pretty."

"I expect Bethany will be no different." Richard stared into the depths of his wineglass. "Thank you for looking after her in my absence, Tom."

"Don't mention it. Your lady is a lovely creature." Despite the compliment, Richard noticed his friend spoke with an air of forced lightness.

"Is there aught wrong?" A note of anxiety sharpened his voice. "You haven't observed anything amiss, have you?"

"Nothing the presence of her husband wouldn't repair." Lord Thomas rolled his eyes as he brought up an ongoing dispute between the two men. "Rickon, if you could see how unhappy she is when someone asks about you, you would put an end to this stubborn game of yours."

"'Tis no game, Thomas, and well you know it!" He set his glass down with a smothered curse. "She may play the part of an abandoned wife in public, but at home she has not breathed one word of regret for throwing me out of her bed. If that is what she wishes, that she shall have."

"Why are you so determined to win an apology from her? Lord knows I've never heard of one of them admitting they were wrong, unless they had something to gain from it." Richard snorted an assent as his friend went on. "As for playing an abandoned wife, she has too much pride to lower herself so."

Fortunately their conversation had moved to other subjects by the time Bethany entered in a rustle of taffeta and lace. Richard's grip tightened on the stem of his glass. Her vivid curls clustered at the back of her head, inviting his hand to bury itself in the soft ringlets. Her dress of pewter gray only emphasized their blaze of color. The somber material set off her creamy skin so that it seemed to glow, and in comparison to it, her eyes glinted with silver flecks.

The only color she wore came from the aquamarines in the necklace and earring set Richard had given her the day they had visited Whitehall. He swallowed. With the soft mounds of her breasts emphasized by the low neckline and her sparkling eyes, he wanted nothing more than to carry her back upstairs.

Instead, he bowed over her hand as convention dictated. A faint, tantalizing scent of sandalwood arose from her skin.

"You look stunning." The compliment slipped out before he knew what he was saying, and her face echoed his own surprise at the civility.

"Th-thank you, sir." She searched his face as if looking for something lost.

Lord Thomas stepped into the awkward moment.

"Rickon, a pleasure as always. My lady, your cloak. My sister's French chef resents having to put meals back for late guests." Before he could settle the black velvet wrap over her shoulders, Richard stepped forward and did so, inhaling another breath of sandalwood.

Shaking his head at him behind her back, Lord Thomas offered Bethany his arm and escorted her out of the room. Richard watched them leave. The snug dinner he had planned to enjoy with several cronies sounded less appealing now.

Bethany felt much the same as she sat in Lady Haynes's fine box in the Salisbury Court Theater. Her companions were most delightful, several having met her before in her ladyship's company.

However, even the witticisms flying back and forth over the dinner table earlier had failed to amuse her. For the play itself, the music and costumes better diverted her more than the plot.

"'Tis probably best Richard did not accompany us. This stuff is certainly not to his taste at all." Lord Thomas leaned in to speak to her under cover of two actors.

"Indeed, he would not care for it at all. Can you imagine his commentary?" She kept her eyes on the stage as she replied.

Her escort shook with suppressed laughter. "I have already had that pleasure, my lady." The actors left the stage, indicating the start of the interval. "Do you care to walk with me for a few minutes? There is something I should like to discuss with you."

She agreed, and stood to take his arm. However, once they left the confines of the box, his lordship merely promenaded along the hallway outside, as if composing some great speech. Bethany waited for him to speak, contented to squeeze through the brightly dressed crowd.

"Sir, I beg you to tell me whatever it is you wish to." She nodded to a baronet she knew. "You will lose your chance, else, at least until the next interval."

Lord Thomas took a deep breath. "I have been thinking of marrying."

Bethany floundered for a reply to this bald statement. "Ah. What does Richard think of the lady you have in mind?" She glanced up at him. "You do have someone in mind, do you not?"

"Yes! Yes, of course I do." Slightly reassured, she took his arm once more and they resumed their stroll. He coughed. "I haven't told Richard yet, actually."

"Oh?" Bethany drew out the syllable, looking at him suspiciously out of the corner of her eye. If Lord Thomas had not confided in her husband about his choice of bride, it could only be because he feared Richard's disapproval on some reason. "What's wrong with her?"

"Nothing! She possesses fortune, beauty, and a sweet nature." Lord Thomas bowed to a passing pair of older ladies. "Friends of my mother," he murmured.

"But not birth." Bethany guessed from its absence in his list.

"She is the daughter of a Levantine merchant." To her irritation, he sounded downright guilty. "My brother found out about her and recommended I make her acquaintance."

"And why do you tell me about this poor girl instead of his lordship? Surely you cannot believe that my husband, of all men, would object to you marrying for a fortune." She returned the salute of another young matron wearing a startling shade of aubergine.

"Yes, I am a younger son and my brother wants a well-dowered wife in the family. But having met her on various occasions, I find both her person and her spirit so very engaging that I should count it the greatest loss of my life not to marry her." His vehemence startled her.

Bethany stared at him a long moment through narrowed eyes. If he play-acted, he outperformed the actors on the stage. Still, his innate charm and glibness might fool her.

"Are you saying you are in love with this girl?"

"To the depths of my soul." He leaned against the wall and sighed dreamily. Straightening right up, he asked, "You won't tell anyone, will you?"

She shook her head at him but promised to remain silent. "I am touched at your confidence, sir, but why reveal it to me? Is it that the lady will not have you?"

He beamed. "Indeed, she indicates that she returns my sentiments."

"My felicitations." Her dry comment was lost on the moonstruck nobleman. "You love her, she loves you, your brother the earl approves, and all is well."

"That's just it." He lowered his voice confidentially. "All is not well. My brother approves, but my mother and sister are too high in the instep to welcome a city merchant's daughter into the family."

"Are they? I have known nothing but kindness from them." Bethany suddenly wondered if they only feigned affection for her. As if reading her mind, he patted her hand where it rested on his arm.

"For one thing, Richard and his sister are great favorites of my mother, and for another, you are gently bred and your family has land." His bright blue eyes twinkled. "And for a Puritan, you have taken to society remarkably well." His features sobered. "I fear Richard shall raise the same complaint about her background, although I trust he'll change his mind when he comes to know my Rosalind."

Knowing her husband's high opinion of his lordship, Bethany reassured him on this point. "Though I'm not sure what can be done about the Dowager Countess and Lady Haynes." Her brow puckered sympathetically.

"If only that were the end of it. Her father objects to the match, of all things." Indignation swelled his breast. "He seems to think my reputation is unsuitable for his daughter. I believe it would rectify the situation if a woman in society befriended her and put in a good word or three with the merchant." Her escort raised an eyebrow meaningfully.

"I should be delighted to help, but only if 'tis what the girl wishes." Bethany pinned him with a hard stare. "I won't be party to a forced marriage."

"I assure you this is not the case." Lord Thomas kissed her hand in gratitude. "She attends the play this evening. If you permit it, I shall introduce you at the next interval."

The crowded hall had emptied until only a few tardy patrons remained. As Bethany playfully swatted him with her fan for his enthusiastic expression of gratitude, Captain Loring sidled by. Seeing their clasped hands, he said nothing, but raised a sardonic eyebrow and bowed at both of them. Bethany lifted her chin and regarded him blandly even as her other hand tightened on the ostrich feather fan.

"Loring." With a curt nod, his lordship accompanied her back to their seats.

"I do not know why, but that man makes my skin crawl." Careful to keep her voice lowered, she looked about to be sure no one sat close enough to overhear.

"He's a poor piece of work, that's why. We all three served in the French army during the King's exile, but Richard couldn't afford an officer's commission. Even so, he often showed up Loring, and Loring didn't like that. He'll make trouble for him if he can." His lordship's fair head bent close to hers as he assisted her into her chair. He caught his breath. "There she is, across the house from us." He adjusted her chair slightly so that she could look without being seen to, and seated himself beside her.

In a box almost directly across from Lady Haynes's, a very pretty girl sat between a middle-aged man in a vast periwig and another lady of indeterminate age. Pearls ornamented the fashionable arrangement of her hair, winding through the soft brown curls. Bethany could not tell the color of her eyes, but they were large, and widened when they caught sight of her companion. A row of small teeth bit down on the lower lip of her perfect rosebud mouth.

"'Tis her. Rosalind Hunter." He breathed the name as if weaving an enchantment. "Is she not the loveliest creature you have ever beheld?" As the girl's expression struck her as rather bovine,

Bethany chose not to reply, deciding to withhold judgment until she met her.

She spent the second act paying more attention to the besotted Lord Thomas, who with blown kisses, winks, and jerks of his head attempted to communicate with his goddess. The object of these displays very properly kept her eyes on the stage, except for the stolen glances in his direction when her father appeared to be engrossed in the play.

By the time Lord Thomas ushered Bethany to the Hunters, she earnestly desired to meet the object of his affection. According to him, Mr. Hunter owned a prosperous bank and had already settled his eldest daughter upon his intended successor. He now thought to marry his youngest into the aristocracy, but he wanted a peer in his own right for her, not the impecunious younger brother of one.

The nobleman had won the support of Mistress Hunter's maiden aunt, the middle-aged lady Bethany had observed sitting with them. The elder woman, having lived for decades under her brother's overbearing rule, fell under Lord Thomas's sway easily. It was she, in fact, who passed communications between the young pair.

"What's needed is for him to be convinced that an alliance with the Orseys brings more prestige than with a mere baron or viscount." He grinned at her. "Don't tell Richard I said such."

"No, I shall leave that to you, shan't I?" She steadfastly refused to help him until she ascertained that he did not manipulate the girl into the match. Recalling her sense of entrapment when faced with the prospect of life with Mr. Ilkston, her mouth tightened. The heiress's predicament gained more of her sympathy than his lordship's.

Her concern for the girl's well-being disappeared when she perceived the couple together. The girl's eyes, which exactly matched the azure blue silk of her gown, never left Lord Thomas's face, even when he introduced her to Bethany. In turn, he spoke to her with tenderness at odds with his usual lighthearted manner. Bethany received the distinct impression that neither would have noticed if the rest of the audience disappeared altogether. Satisfied, she set herself to draw Mr. Hunter's fire by asking his opinion of this afternoon's play.

"I confess that until recently, I never visited the playhouse in my life! I was raised in the country and never had the opportunity." Her exclamation allowed him to expound upon the respective strengths of the Duke's Company and the King's, while arousing the typical City man's pity for anyone with the ill-luck to have grown up anywhere besides London.

She cemented his approval by requiring an extremely reluctant Lord Thomas to leave them for several minutes, insisting that the ladies all wished for sweetmeats. By the time he returned, winded from the haste with which he had carried out the errand, the interval had nearly ended. Clearly delighted that his cherished offspring had spent only a few minutes' time with her objectionable suitor, Mr. Hunter cordially agreed that she might collect his sister and daughter for a promenade at Gray's Inn Field in three or four days.

Bethany listened to Lord Thomas's whispered protests at her shabby treatment of him for only a few paces as they returned to their party. "Pish! May I remind you of how many fashionable people walk there? One never knows who I shall come upon in company with Mistress Hunter and her aunt." She looked at him meaningfully until enlightenment dawned.

"Oh!" His face cleared. "Doubtless my sister and mother will like to take the air there soon. But what about Rosalind? What if she is previously engaged?"

"My dear sir, I can promise you that if she has any engagements, three days will suffice her to think of a way out of them, and very likely purchase a new walking dress for your benefit as well." Bethany could not help laughing at the startled expression on his face.

So that the groundwork she laid should not be disturbed by further interference, she refused to visit the Hunters in the ensuing intervals. Neither did she permit Lord Thomas to, scolding him for his obtuseness.

Although the play did not entirely suit her taste, she did enjoy the music and final dance, and thanked Lady Haynes sincerely for inviting her at the end of the piece. She noticed Captain Loring's gaze upon her numerous times over the course of the performance, but she merely tossed her head and ignored him.

As it was full dark when the performance ended, she and his lordship first accompanied Lady Haynes to her house in her coach. Seeing his sister safely disposed, he obtained the services of a sedan chair and a linkboy and escorted Bethany to Saint Clement's Lane. In a merry humor at the prospect of meeting Mistress Hunter again soon, he begged Bethany not to disclose his intentions to her husband as they entered the hall.

"Of course I won't tell Richard! That is your task." She laughed and gave her cloak to the waiting footman. "Do you care to stay for a glass of wine or ale?"

To her surprise, the library door stood ajar, allowing light to spill onto the polished wood floor. She peeped in, his lordship behind her. Her husband sat by the light of a candelabrum holding a book. He must have just closed it, for his index finger still marked his place.

"I thought you dined with friends this afternoon." Shadow and brightness played over his face and hair in the flickering candlelight. It only enhanced the green of his eyes under his half-closed eyelids. Against her will, Bethany felt her heart pick up its pace as he gazed up at her.

"I decided instead to join them later. I shall leave shortly." He frowned as he scrutinized her. "You both look as if you enjoyed yourself."

She drew back at his suspicious tone of voice. From behind her, Lord Thomas chuckled.

"You would have been proud of her, Rickon. First thing she did when the masque started was lean over to me and whisper 'Dancing trees?'" He strolled in to warm his hands at the fireplace.

"They did not altogether make sense to me. In the course of the play, I mean." She babbled as he maintained his heavy-lidded stare. "It differed from those you have taken me to."

She waited for him to reply, but he said nothing. After a few heartbeats, she gave a tiny shrug and curtsied. "I believe I shall ask for a supper tray in my room. I wish you a pleasant evening, my lord." Her cool voice warmed considerably. "Lord Thomas, I thank you for a most entertaining afternoon."

Richard watched her leave the room. Her laughter coming from the hall had startled him; he had not heard it for too long. He squelched the irrational stab of jealousy that tore through him. That cool pride of hers might infuriate him, but it also meant Bethany did not stoop so low as to embarrass him in public. And surely he could trust Tom.

Still, he wondered whether she would have entered the house so cheerfully if he had accompanied them. He berated himself for his sentimentalism. The woman wanted mastering, and disliked his lessons in indifference.

That he found himself standing outside her door, tempted to knock and ask for admittance every night when he climbed the stairs to his bedchamber, indicated nothing more than mere physical frustration. Irritated by this train of thought, he frowned at his friend.

"What secret do you ask my wife to keep from me?" He tried to assume a bantering tone, but did not quite succeed. Tom's face froze in an expression of hauteur at the sharp question.

"One you shall discover in due time." He kept his reply neutral, but his tense posture warned Richard that he did not welcome this line of questioning.

Richard leaned back in his chair. Tom's evasiveness stirred his curiosity, but he had no wish to pick a fight with his best friend over his wife. He might be talked into spilling the truth over a few drinks, however.

"Why don't you come along tonight? I'm meeting Hardwick at the Wooden Leg. We can find a fourth for a card game easily enough, or see what trouble we can find to get into."

"Delightful." The other man relaxed, accepting the extended olive branch.

His friend's demeanor over the rest of the evening set Richard's mind largely at ease, although he evaded questions about his great secret. He tried again while he and Tom sat playing cribbage while young Hardwick sought a fourth player to join them.

"Let be, Rickon! You shall discover all, I hope sooner rather than later." A grimace crossed Lord

Thomas's cherubic face as they lay their cards down. "Pox on't, you won again."

"That should even out what you won from me last week." They toasted one another with their tankards, chuckling.

Lord Thomas replaced the long, slender mouthpiece of his white clay pipe between his teeth and drew on it, closing his eyes as he exhaled a thin stream of tobacco smoke. Around them, a blue miasma from a dozen other patrons floated, adding its acrid note to the earthy scent of hops and malt from the house's home-brewed. A hint of roasted meat wafted by as a buxom dark-haired girl passed carrying a tray of victuals to another table.

Richard wrinkled his nose; she also left the odor of sour sweat in her wake. It compared poorly with the sandalwood his fastidious wife used.

Their party had taken a table under a lantern hanging from an iron hook in the wall. The guttering tallow candle emitted its share of smoke as well, which rose to blacken the half-timbered walls and beamed ceiling. Around the room, other lanterns lit and smoked their own sections of wall, while an iron chandelier resembling the rim of a coach wheel hung from a massive beam in the middle of the room, its candles impartially illuminating the patrons and the serving wenches.

Their glow reflected off a number of jewels, for the Wooden Leg lay west of Covent Garden in an area inhabited by nobles who needed to live near Parliament and Court. Richard had pinned up the brim of his plumed beaver hat with a gleaming brooch of gold work. Across from him, a fine amethyst glowed on his friend's hand. He nodded at the stone in its heavy gold setting.

"I see you put my winnings to good use and redeemed your father's ring."

"Thanks to you and my brother, I'm in funds for the time being." Lord Thomas regarded his cards with disgust as he placed them on the scarred wooden table. "Or at least I was."

"No rush, you'll pay when you can." Richard sobered when the other man laughed and waggled his ring finger. "Don't pawn it again! One of these times you won't be able to get it back. Trust me, you'd regret it." His mouth twisted bitterly.

"Your parents would rather you sold their jewels than let you and Glory starve, Rick. Had they lived, they would have done the same." He abandoned this melancholy subject abruptly as his eyes widened.

Richard found his forearm clasped in a warning grip. "Don't turn around, but Hardwick has approached Loring, of all people."

His back tensed. It faced the room, while his vision only included the wall behind them and part of the tables on each side. "Damnation. If he invites that blaggard to join us, he will accept out of sheer maliciousness." The fingers of his sword hand twitched. "Faith, perhaps we shall see if his skills have improved since we all fought the Dutch."

Lord Thomas casually took his pipe from his mouth to allow a long pull of ale. His gaze still rested over Richard's shoulder as he made his observations.

"His fortunes certainly appear to have increased. He wears more silks and jewels than my mother and sister combined." He snorted. "And who told him that apricot ribbons suit burgundy velvet? The man's become a crime against eyesight."

"Probably a scheme of his own devising." Richard kept his voice low. "The Lorings never did have any taste, they just didn't have the cash to indulge their vulgarity." He straightened slightly. "Odd, come to think of it."

"That Hardwick invites him to join us? Not really; most people in England know aught of his history with your family."

"No, that Loring has such wealth. The King granted him an annuity for his father's service, but not a large one."

Tom shrugged. "I have no idea. Winnings? Or a wealthy relative."

"He gambles as badly as he dresses." Richard drummed his fingers on the table. "And his father was the only one in his family who supported the King. 'Tis a complete mystery."

"Belike you can ask him. He's coming over with Hardwick." Both men came to attention, although their faces remained neutral. Sir Harry Hardwick, a portly young man with wavy brown hair, had grown up in England and had not learned of the rivalry between Richard and the captain. His florid face glowed as he proudly presented him as a fourth for their cribbage game.

Ignoring their lukewarm greetings, Loring made a great show of seating himself and adjusting the ribbons and bows covering his shoulders, wrists, and knees. Comfortably settled in place, he affected surprise in seeing Lord Thomas.

"My lord, 'tis delightful seeing you again so soon. So kind of you to amuse both Lady Harcourt and her lord." His dark eyes sparkled with malice. "Whatever were you and her ladyship whispering about in the corridor this afternoon?"

Richard had expected such an obvious attack from his rival and ignored it. But as Sir Harry's plump hands dealt the cards, he happened to glance at Tom. A flush darkened his old friend's cheek at Loring's words.

Unsettled, he gathered his cards, sorting them mechanically. By silent consensus, he and Tom played against Sir Harry and the captain. As no one nibbled at Loring's first bait, he cast out another.

"We have not agreed on points, have we?" He smirked. "With your fortunate marriage, Harcourt, we no longer need to stop at schoolboy wagers. Shall we say half a crown for every point?"

Although much smaller than the thousands of pounds won or lost in the most extravagant circles, a losing streak at that rate could still beggar a man. Tom remained expressionless at the proposed stakes, but Sir Harry's face paled slightly.

"Perhaps something a bit smaller, Arthur. I think two shillings a point is sufficient." Richard smiled gently at his opponent. "As you pointed out,

I am a married man, and wives are remarkably extravagant creatures."

"Particularly when the money is their own." The captain appeared the picture of innocence as he focused on his own hand. Richard regarded him under half-closed eyes as he selected his first discard.

"There is also my estate to consider. The Orsey estate belongs to Tom's brother, and Sir Harry's father enjoys excellent health, does he not?" Young Hardwick nodded, nervous at the hostility vibrating between the two men. "And of course, your father had no claim on his family's property, so you are free of such encumbrances as a country house and estate. I, alas, must consider my responsibilities."

Tom's lip quivered, but he said nothing. Loring's teeth nearly ground audibly at Richard's direct hit, but he did his best to deflect it.

"Faith, I hope to remedy that soon enough. My mother's family had some land I might come into, only a few days from town. In Bedfordshire."

At this point, Sir Harry's nerve gave out and he demanded that the game start in earnest.

Chapter 10

The aftermath of that evening was not immediately evident, but Richard found himself watching both his wife and his best friend closely. It went against the grain to suspect Tom in particular, but he could not help noticing the amount of time they spent together.

A promenade in Gray's Inn, another theater party, a trip to Greenwich to enjoy a meal at an eating house there. Every time he stepped into the hall, it seemed that Tom arrived for yet another outing or Bethany came in from one on his arm.

That both included others in all these schemes, and routinely invited him to join their parties, comforted him not at all. Tom knew as well as he did the art of seducing a woman under the nose of even the most zealous of guardians. Only the admission to himself that his own negligence might play a part in encouraging Bethany to stray kept him from calling his old friend out.

He refused to confront either of them, on the

grounds that doing so might give his wife the mistaken idea that he suffered from jealousy. He assured himself that any heartburnings he felt for the prideful woman stemmed only from his concern that her behavior might reflect poorly on the Harcourt name.

He continued his round as before. He visited his favorite coffeehouses to catch up on the latest Court gossip and dined with friends. Evenings he spent gaming in the most fashionable houses, attending the theater and drinking in low taverns where an aristocrat could get a tankard and a tumble.

His cronies twitted him because he now indulged only in the former. He retorted that even to be fashionable, he could not bring himself to touch the filthy and diseased wenches who plied their trade in the alehouses.

"Pho, Harcourt! I haven't seen you do anything but flirt with a wench since you married." The speaker, deep in his cups, sniggered. "Not that we blame you. Saw the lady in Saint James's Park yesterday with a friend of yours—"

The cold scrape of metal on metal stopped him. Richard stood before him, sword drawn.

"I suggest you not finish that sentence!" The shouted advice came from elsewhere in the room, followed by a burst of laughter. The speaker's gaze went from the blade to Richard's face.

He did not move a muscle until after the sot subsided, sinking into his seat with a muttered apology. After a long silence, he put up his blade and returned to his own drink. Those present conceded that he had behaved correctly in preventing his wife's name to be bandied about in a public house.

Despite the quiet assurances of his friends that no hint of improper behavior attached itself to his wife, doubts lingered. He could not help wondering why she spent such an unaccountable amount of time with Tom and his family when a stream of invitations for her poured into the house in Saint Clement's Lane. That Orsey spent less time in his own company did not escape his notice either.

Bethany's success in bringing his Rosalind into favor with Lord Thomas's mother and sister pleased them both. She discovered a taste for organizing parties herself, and proved a popular hostess. With her own invitations sought after by society, inserting Mistress Hunter and her aunt into her gatherings proved easy.

The girl's modesty prevented accusations of trying to jump herself up, while her aunt's sharp tongue amused the wits. Bethany even managed to introduce Rosalind's father, a great lover of the theater, to a few ladies and gentlemen with similar enthusiasm. This number included Lord Thomas, who impressed the old man with his knowledge of the drama.

Neither the Hunter ladies nor Bethany herself tried to hide their middling backgrounds. This made them unacceptable to the highest sticklers, but those were in a minority. Most of the nobility took its cue from the new King's Court, where anyone suitably dressed could enter Whitehall to watch the uncrowned monarch dine.

Bethany took advantage of this rule to bring Mistress Hunter to Court, and thus to Lady Planchard's attention. Although Lord Thomas's mother did not entirely approve of the girl's mercantile antecedents, she gave her full credit for deportment.

"Indeed, Mistress Hunter could teach manners to a number of ladies at Court." The Dowager Countess delivered that opinion as she sat in the parlour in Saint Clement's Lane enjoying a small cup of tea. Bethany had purchased an exquisite set of porcelain cups made expressly for drinking the beverage, and wanted to show it off. Mistress Hunter and her aunt had just left.

Lady Haynes, who had brought her mother from Whitehall, agreed as she selected a jumble to nibble on. Lady Planchard sniffed at the demoralized manners of the young.

"Only yesterday, I heard quite a young lady from one of the best families in England"—she lowered her voice, causing Bethany and the viscountess to lean forward—"say 'pox on't.'" She shuddered and took a restorative sip of tea. The two young women, familiar with the phrase thanks to its use by their respective spouses, struggled to keep their faces straight.

"Mistress Hunter's dress is pleasingly modest as well, for all everything she wears is of the best quality." A speculative gleam entered the Dowager Countess's eye. "I wonder if Thomas has noticed."

Bethany whispered the entire exchange into the delighted young man's ear during a tedious concert of works by Orlando Gibbons at Mr. Davenant's house. She feared that in a less public place he would have kissed her cheek as soundly as he did her hands. As she regarded him in the light of a brother, she would not find that offensive. But as new as she was in society, she knew that malicious tongues would wag about such a breach of propriety.

When Tom burst into the parlour the following afternoon, interrupting her dinner, he did not stop at merely kissing her on the cheek. She scarcely greeted him before he pulled her out of her seat and swung her around in a rib-crushing embrace.

"Bethany, you shall never guess!" She maneuvered to avoid spilling her tankard of small beer on her empty plate.

"Is this attempt to suffocate me related to Mr. Hunter's acceptance of your suit?" She would have laughed at the crestfallen expression on his face had she not stood gasping for air.

"Yes, but how did you know?" Before she caught her breath enough to deliver a tart estimation of masculine intelligence, he waved his own question aside. "Never mind, it doesn't signify. I requested Rosalind's hand this morning and we had the settlements worked out by the end of dinner."

"Money again!" She pulled away. "'Tis always the same cry for an heiress: How much will she bring?" Lord Thomas snapped his head up.

"You know very well I do not regard Rosalind in that manner." He looked at her with eyes gone as flat as his voice. "I shall marry her if her father loses every penny he owns tomorrow."

"Forgive me, Tom. I had no right to cast aspersions on your feelings." Withdrawing a lace-edged square from her sleeve, she pressed it against the tears threatening to overflow. "I wish you both every blessing."

"You could try an apology." He spoke mildly, but she took offense anyway.

"For giving Richard permission to seek out his mistress? Do be serious, Tom." She paced to the fireplace and stared into the low flames.

"For rejecting him." He followed her. "He lost his father at the Battle of Worcester at eighteen. He got his mother and sister out of England after that, but his mother died in Paris a few years later. Mistress Shadbourne would welcome him back now that he has money enough to afford the expensive kickshaws she's so fond of, but he doesn't forget that she cast him off to marry a wealthy old man."

She traced the carved mantelpiece as she listened.

"Even if I would consider such a thing, how am I supposed to beg forgiveness of someone I scarcely see?" Her face crumpled. "Oh, Tom, he doesn't come home until dawn most nights, and he's away again before dinnertime. I can scarce get him to look at me, much less hold a conversation."

She turned and buried her face in his shoulder. "How did the two of us come to this pass?"

"We'll think of something, my dear." He patted her back. "'Tis not right for you to be so unhappy. Perhaps you should leave town for a time."

"Yes, from the looks of things, that would appear to be an excellent idea."

They froze at Richard's silky voice. Bethany whirled to see her husband placing his gauntlets on the table. In his eagerness to tell her of his betrothal, Lord Thomas had left the door open. Sick with horror, she realized he must have overheard the last of their conversation. Remembering her place in Lord Thomas's arms, she gave a small cry and stepped away from him.

"By all means, continue. Forgive me for interrupting such a touching scene." For all his controlled manner, Richard's eyes glittered dangerously in a face gone white. She eyed him nervously, fearing he would go for his sword in the next instant.

"A scene you misunderstand, Rick." Lord Thomas interposed himself between them.

"Have done, Tom." Richard's harsh bark of laughter echoed from the paneled walls. "I've never hurt a woman in my life. You, however . . ." He picked up a gauntlet and would have thrown it in his friend's face had Bethany not pushed forward to grab his hand.

"Richard, no! You misunderstand completely!" He wrestled his arm from her grip, but did not issue a challenge to the other man. Tom attempted to protect her by pulling her out from between them, only to have Richard lunge at him as soon as she was out of danger. She stepped back in between them, arms outstretched to keep them apart.

"Stop this! You are both to blame!" She glared at each in turn. "Tom, if you had not kept your plans a secret from Richard in the first place, he would not be laboring under a misapprehension now."

"Enough." The blaze of anger left Richard's face. He bowed his head and grasped the back of a chair as if for support. "I know well enough I have a share of blame for this, or so help me God, I would skewer you where you stand."

"Richard, will you please let me explain?" Bethany's exasperation mounted as she listened to him.

"Madam, I cannot conceive of anything you could tell me that will explain away your words and actions." He brushed aside her protest to snarl at his friend.

"Get out. Just because I bear part of the blame for this curst tangle doesn't mean I can forgive you for taking advantage of my wife's weakness."

"What?" Both men ignored her exclamation.

"I'm not leaving until I'm sure your wife is safe with you." Lord Thomas crossed his arms and regarded him steadily.

"By my father's grave, Tom." Richard laughed in bitter jest. The other man seemed to understand it, however, for after a bow to Bethany and a curt nod of the head to Richard, he clapped his hat on his fair head and left.

She tried to speak but he cut her off and strode to the bellpull. He rang so imperiously that the porter, the housekeeper, and even the cook scurried into the room.

"Pack her ladyship's things." She sank into a chair in shock at his order. He stared through her. "She leaves for Yorkshire at first light tomorrow morning."

After they scattered out of the room, Bethany tried once more to tell him the truth.

"I saw you with my own eyes embracing my oldest friend and planning to run off with him!" He did not rant or show her anything but the most frigid courtesy, but he would not allow her to defend herself. "'Tis best to remove you from temptation. You said when you agreed to marry me that you would be content to live on my estate. Very well, madam. You may put your housekeeping skills to good use at Graymoor." He picked up his gauntlets, running the leather fingers through his own.

"I shall order Lane to drive you to Stanworth. You may spend a night there and collect Gloriana. 'Tis high time she returned to her own home as well."

"Tell the cook we shall both be home for supper." He had never looked at her so coldly as he did now. "In the meantime, I have arrangements to make. I trust you will understand and cease to importune me."

Without another word he turned on his heel and left her standing in the middle of the room, stunned.

They scarcely spoke to one another for the rest

of the afternoon and evening. By the time he handed her into the new traveling coach she had authorized Mr. Leafley to pay for, her fury at his refusal to listen to her nearly convinced her that going to Yorkshire was her own wish.

She settled back against the comfortably cushioned seat and regarded Faith, who sat across from her. The little maid's eyes welled with tears at the prospect of separation from her Lane, a sight that irritated Bethany considerably.

"Stop blubbering!" She handed the older woman a lace-edged kerchief. "At least you get another few days with your man."

Mopping at her eyes, she looked up at her. "My lady, do you love him?" Bethany did not pretend to misunderstand her, but dwelling on her husband only led to sensations of deep melancholy. "Why can you not make it up with him?"

"Blow your nose," Bethany replied.

Anger sustained her through the long journey to Yorkshire. As the coach crawled northward each day over ill-kept roads, she mastered the nausea that inevitably afflicted her. In truth, she did not know which was worse, her motion sickness or listening to her sister-in-law's chatter.

Finally losing her temper, she threatened to make the girl get out and walk the rest of the way to the North Riding. Fortunately, this did not occur until the fifth day of their travels. After a dinner characterized by cold silence on the part of both ladies, a night's sleep restored them to the point of civility.

They expected to arrive at Graymoor before sundown that day, and even Bethany's spirits lightened at the prospect of the journey's end. Uncertain of what to expect, she asked Gloriana about the estate. The delicate blonde shook her head.

"I haven't set eyes on Graymoor since I was a small girl. I can't even properly describe what it looked like then." A wistful note entered her voice. "Mostly I remember bits and pieces, like playing with my Noah's ark on a wooden floor or following my mother on her daily round." She leaned back against the buttery soft leather squabs, closing her eyes.

"I would hang on to her gown while she visited the stillroom. I was never allowed to touch a thing in there. Mother said physick taken out of turn—"

"—is as dangerous as an illness." Bethany finished the sentence with her and chuckled for the first time since she left Richard. "It must be something all mothers say. Mine certainly does." Laughing with her, Glory's amusement faded as she viewed the surrounding landscape.

"'Tis odd to return home and not be able to recognize the way."

"Do you still think of Graymoor as home after so many years?" Bethany cocked her head, curious.

"Yes." Her sister-in-law answered instantly and emphatically. "It was the only place my family was ever together. And happy."

Neither spoke for a long time after that. Eventually, Glory dozed off, tucking her feet up under her skirts. Bethany gazed out the window, fascinated by the ever-rising hills spread out on either side of the coach. She fancied that they traveled on a vast green roof mounting higher into the bright blue sky.

Several miles later, the coach heaved over a ridge and stopped. The coach bucked as Lane descended from the box. Knocking on the door, he invited them to view the vista.

Bethany stepped out into the gusty wind that had blown most of the day, followed by Gloriana, rubbing sleep out of her eyes. Lane led them along the road a short way. It clung to a mild downward slope, through a village not a mile away. The narrow way crossed a stream and then wandered along to the far side of the small valley.

She saw a small, light-colored house against the rising wall of the far side of the dale. Even from this distance, it had an air of lifelessness. Lane pointed, but Glory spoke first.

"Graymoor."

The closer they drove, the worse the house looked. Built facing the east, originally with two wings sheltering a courtyard, it appeared completely deserted.

"Richard said the Roundheads tried to pull it down." Glory gazed out the window, her usual merriness extinguished. "I had no idea how close they came." Bethany, peering out of hers, could only nod. A mountain of rubble marked the remains of one wing. The rest of the gray stone facing bore gouges from cannonballs and scorch marks.

To their relief, once the coach had negotiated
its way through the rusted iron gates and around
the rubble, a small welcoming committee waited.
Richard must have informed someone of their
impending arrival. After helping them down,
Lane introduced an anxious old couple.

"This is Mr. Platt, what used to be the head car-
penter, and Mistress Platt, the cook. His lordship
hasn't hired a housekeeper or bailiff yet, so they've
been looking after the place since he came back."
The pair sketched a bow and curtsey.

"We're pleased to meet your ladyship, and I
hope you'll understand if things aren't just so in
the house." Mistress Platt did the talking while her
large husband nodded sagely. "We just got word of
your coming two days ago and there's nobut the
chickens for meat, although Platt did kill a coney
yesterday in the garden." Bethany held up a hand
to cut off the nervous spate.

"Do I understand you have a hot meal prepared
for us?" She beamed at the woman twisting her apron.
"As we did not stop for dinner, anything sounds de-
licious." Behind her, Glory chimed in.

"I don't suppose you made any of the ginger
parkins I remember so well?" The cook sighed.

"Bless me, Mistress Glory, but I did not. Master
Rickon—Lord Harcourt, I mean—sends money
every month, but with so much needed, there's
naught for spices."

Her previously dour spouse smiled. "Unless I be
mistaken, I did see a plate of oatcakes in the

kitchen. We're not likely to forget how you'd gobble down any sweet you could reach."

Torn between jealousy at feeling so obviously a stranger and amusement at her sister-in-law's crimson cheeks, Bethany chuckled. "By all means, let us eat. I should hate to deprive you of your oatcakes."

Following the plain but tasty meal, she asked the cook to show them over the house. While it pained her to see the ruin of so beautiful a house, Glory's face grew paler with every room they entered. She burst into tears at the sight of her mother's bedchamber, with its shredded hangings and half-torn-off paneling.

"I'm glad she died in France. She loved Graymoor almost as much as she loved us!" The cook urged them to come down to the kitchen for a bit of cider.

"'Tis not proper," she whispered as Glory sobbed on Bethany's shoulder, "but she always liked visiting me there."

Upon discovering the state of the kitchen, Bethany's opinion of the cook soared. Mistress Platt kept it remarkably clean, but it, too, suffered from years of abandonment. The woman seemed to grow years younger under her praise and she confidently assured Bethany that she could present a full list of housekeeping needs the next day.

The first Sunday after their arrival, Bethany rousted her sister-in-law out of bed in plenty of time to breakfast and dress for church. Glory complied with relatively little grumbling, but to her dismay, Bethany discovered that the girl had ordered the coach hitched up for the short drive down the road and through Kilpenny.

In her turn, Glory objected to the idea of walking and possibly ruining her azure silk gown.

"Then go and change into something more suitable for church." Bethany unconsciously smoothed her hands over her sensible ensemble of camel serge trimmed with golden pins and ribbons of her favorite bright green.

"This is suitable for church." Gloriana tied the ribbons of her hooded cloak under her chin. "'Tis just not suitable for walking." In the end, both ladies voted for the coach when a soaking rain began.

Bethany found she enjoyed the service more than she had expected. In London, she had attended services with the Barkers as well as at the fashionable churches patronized by the Royalist aristocracy. Neither had quite appealed to her. Even the simplest of her new clothes stood out in the Nonconformist congregations, and they had not welcomed her. The services of the established church, with their altars barred behind a railing and their surpliced ministers, still struck her as alien at times.

This morning, she found the same ceremony, conducted in the confines of the small Norman church, much more comfortable. The vicar's enlivening sermon on the subject of Rebecca at the well pleased her also.

Upon making his acquaintance afterward, she discovered that the Reverend Mr. Coker and his wife were also from outside the district.

"We are both originally from Lancashire, although our youngest two were born in Kilpenny." He indicated a sturdy lad solemnly hanging on to his younger sister's hand. They stood behind the rest of the congregation, which gathered in the doorway before scurrying out into the rain a few at a time.

He recognized their name, of course, and offered to take Bethany around the small church while the crowd thinned.

"Thank you, I would enjoy that, but our coachman will be at the door shortly. If you have time on another day, I would very much like to examine the church. I hope you do not mind, Gloriana?"

When she turned to address the younger girl, she discovered her several paces away, engaged in conversation with an elegantly dressed young man. They stood before a marble plaque in bas-relief, at a proper distance from one another, but Bethany misliked the coy expression on her sister-in-law's face. Happily, the good reverend proved a font of murmured information.

"Sir Fothery Lambert. Twenty-five years of age, inherited the baronetcy from his father two years ago. The Lamberts have been the leading family in the parish since the Harcourts fled. Solid family. Royalist sympathizers, but chose to compound after seeing what happened to Graymoor."

Somewhat grimly, she thanked him for this

worldly assessment and crossed to join the two young people. Gloriana greeted her blithely.

"Bethany, you'll never guess! I have already met an old friend. May I introduce Fothery— forgive me, *Sir* Fothery Lambert. Their estate is in the next dale over. Sir Fothery, my sister, Lady Harcourt."

She accepted his bow with a curtsey, but said no more than manners dictated. She did admit to herself that he possessed a pair of striking brown eyes as well as an easy manner. Glory prattled on.

"He even remembered me! See, he is show-ing me a plaque dedicated to my grandfather's memory."

"Delightful, my dear, but the coach awaits. Come along." She nodded at the young baronet, who tore his attention away from her sister-in-law long enough to beg her to wait upon his mother as soon as may be.

"I regret that she felt too unwell to attend the service this morning, your ladyship, but I am sure she will feel much better on the morrow. Say you shall come to visit?" He coaxed with such charm even she had difficulty resisting.

"I make no promises, Sir Fothery. I am sure we shall meet Lady Lambert at holy services next week if not sooner." He and Glory both resembled small children who had just had a prime treat taken away. Stifling a smile, she relented.

"We are much occupied with rebuilding our house and estate, you know. But I shall dispatch a messenger to your mother to ask when she might find it convenient to receive guests." Fixing her with a stern eye, she addressed the girl. "Make your courtesy, dear. 'Tis time to go."

As she expected, Glory spent the drive home alternately pouting at her hard-heartedness and dreamily describing Sir Fothery's fine eyes and handsome profile. Mercifully, the girl got out of the sulks upon the discovery that Mistress Platt had prepared her favorite meal of fricasseed chicken and asparagus.

Afterward, she sent Glory off to draft a note to Lady Lambert while she took advantage of the blessed silence to review the gigantic task of setting the household and estate to rights.

As days and then weeks passed, she tried to run the household as smoothly as possible in its damaged state. Bethany regularly spent hours poring over columns of figures in the household account books. Her day began simply enough each dawn with prayers, after which she listed each day's tasks.

After she breakfasted, the meetings began. Where Abberly's fields and pastures supplied its needs, Graymoor's ruined state caused endless complications. Mistress Platt often had to wait on the day's deliveries to discuss the day's meals. Linens were so scarce, even she and Gloriana had started out sharing a bed to eke out the sheets.

Besides food and bed linens, the estate had little livestock left. Horses, cattle, and sheep could be bought, but breeders of good stock charged high prices for their animals. And those costs paled beside building materials and labor.

Thanks to Sir Fothery and his mother, she had found a talented builder in York who had agreed to oversee Graymoor's repairs. Mr. Quintan had studied buildings in Italy and France, and presented an attractive design for the house that included a handsome façade for the courtyard and an extended terrace and loggia for the western side of the house.

In a letter to Richard she had detailed his plans and the projected expenses, asking for his yea or nay, but she heard nothing back. When he did not reply even after a month of queries, she engaged Mr. Quintan herself. Feeling obligated to keep her husband informed of the progress of his home's repairs, she wrote him each week, careful to keep the letters as impersonal as possible. He never wrote back.

Meanwhile food, cloth for linens and hangings, animals, and building materials had to be ordered and shipped at tremendous expense. Mr. Leafley proved his usefulness once more by sending a clerk by horseback to her with a pouch of gold and a letter of credit for a bank in York. Thanks to him, Graymoor had a steady supply of cash at hand within a week of their arrival.

Going over the accounts, Bethany came to understand Richard's chagrin at her insistence on keeping half her fortune. Seeing the dilapidated tenant farms, she realized that little income from rents would come in for the foreseeable future.

She asked Richard, in a tentatively worded letter, if he would permit her to forgive the rents for the next six months. Receiving no answer from him, she did so on her own, and expected to extend the grace period through the next twelvemonth.

Chapter 11

Richard crumpled up the most recent letter from his wife. He stopped just short of throwing it onto the fire, pacing the length of the study in the small house he had recently rented. His correspondence still went to Saint Clement's Lane, but he found his uncle's house unbearable without Bethany.

Tossing the wadded-up paper onto a side table, he picked up a bottle of claret and poured a glass. After a muttered curse on wives in general and his own stiff-necked termagant in particular, he resumed pacing.

Harsh yearning suffused his loins. A sensible man would relieve his wants with a clean whore or one of the many unhappily married women in London. Bitterly, he cursed himself as well. A sensible man would not have married a woman with Bethany's hot blood and cool head.

The discarded missive proved his point. Other than a perfunctory wish that he continued in good

health, it contained not one word to indicate
that she missed her life with him. It merely detailed the repairs to Graymoor she had authorized,
with requests for his opinions. His wife apparently
embraced her return to country life.

He saw no point in answering questions he assumed were rhetorical. Her letters bespoke a shrewd
mind for management even in her indifference to
him. The vixen could do as she thought best.

He looked down at the wineglass in his hand,
surprised to find it empty again. Settling himself in
a chair, he filled it once more. He placed it at his
elbow and tried to read a book he had already lost
interest in twice. Normally he joined his friends for
a night's carousing when this kind of restlessness
possessed him, but even that would not ease his
foul mood. Light danced across the book in his lap
as he gazed into the fire.

Lord Thomas showed no sign of a man de-
prived of a lover, which both relieved and irritated
Richard. If he could but be certain he had jumped
to the wrong conclusion about his wife and Tom,
he would apologize immediately. He feared his
own pride had driven Bethany away, however. Envi-
sioning her, eyes closed as Tom pressed kisses onto
her neck, he hurled his book across the room. He
leaned back, fighting the combination of anger
and despair that ate at him.

Did she pine for Tom at Graymoor, while that
gentleman played in London? Only the knowledge
that it would destroy her reputation prevented
Richard from challenging Lord Thomas to a duel.

A fine thing when a husband missed his wife more than her lover did.

Someone pounded heavily on his door, one floor below. Richard laughed mirthlessly. He had dismissed the servants for the night, and he felt no desire for the company of others.

"God's teeth, go away!" His shout would not be heard from up here, but the continued thumps annoyed him mightily. He gave an exclamation of satisfaction when it finally stopped.

A moment later, the unmistakable crack of axes on wood reverberated through the house.

"What the devil!"

Richard pushed himself out of his chair and strode out onto the landing to peer over the banister into the modest entry hall. The remains of his front door burst open. It slammed back on its hinges as several soldiers boiled through. They paused, gripping pikes and halberds, as their officer followed them.

Richard's furious voice filled the lull. "What is the meaning of this?"

Arthur Loring's dark eyes glittered mockingly up at him as he swept his hat from his head and bowed. "What a pleasant greeting, Harcourt." He pointed up the stairs with his drawn sword. "Arrest him."

Unarmed, Richard had no chance against the four men who raced up the steps, but he clipped one behind the jaw and nearly booted another over the railing. Lights burst behind his eyes when one churl hit him alongside his face. Thrown back against two attackers, Richard found his arms pinned to his sides. He tried, unsuccessfully, to brace for the fist he knew would drive into his midsection. Nearly retching from the blow, he found himself dragged down to the hall.

"What are you playing at, Loring?"

"Only a fool jests before God." Loathing distorted his rival's face. "I do no more than arrest a traitor."

Richard tried to lunge at him, but his captors jerked him back. "On what possible trumped-up charge?"

"It seems your absence hard on the heels of Venner's rebellion in January has aroused suspicions at Court." Loring chuckled unpleasantly.

"You know damned well my absence had nothing to do with—" Richard broke off. Loring knew perfectly well that he had done nothing any more treasonous than elope.

"Yes, I know who you kept company with." The malice in the other man's eyes deepened to hatred. "Plead guilty and take your execution, and it may be that no one ever hears of your—accomplice."

Richard's heart froze. Loring implied far worse than social ruin for Bethany. He threatened her very life. His gut clenched at the thought of his wife's broken body dragged to the stake for burning.

Loring stepped close, his voice dropping to a whisper. "I beg you, send word to Yorkshire. If the little jade shows her face in London, believe me, I shall arrest her, too."

Richard swallowed his rage. If he disclosed that

Bethany had been in his company, he had no doubt that Loring would drag her into prison as well. And her Nonconformist upbringing would make her an all too easy target for his accusations.

Neither man nor woman accused of treason had a right to counsel or witnesses in their defense. Unless a miracle occurred, he would face execution within the month. But he had sworn to protect Bethany body and soul when he married her. And so he would.

A few days after his arrest, Richard paced his cell in the Tower. His rank entitled him to await almost certain death in a pleasant, if simple, room. Furnished with a narrow bed, table, and cupboards of dark wood, it surpassed the lodgings he had first brought Bethany to.

The thought of her ached like a sore tooth. Perchance it would prove a blessing in disguise that they had parted in anger. At least this way, she would have no desire to come to his aid and her life would be saved. He wondered what he would write her before his execution.

The rattle of the key interrupted his musings. Custom permitted him to bring in food, wine, clothing, and books, provided he paid for their delivery. Today, he expected a chest of his possessions. A guard opened the door and entered, stepping to one side.

Unable to bear the inevitable stares of the

draymen, Richard moved to stare out the window at the Tower Green. "Put it at the foot of the bed."

"If you insist, but it would make more sense to use the table."

Richard jerked his head around to face the speaker. The guard bowed and reminded him that he would be just outside the door, leaving him alone with the visitor.

Lord Thomas uncorked the bottle of ale and poured out two tankards. "I thought you'd be missing your lady wife by now, but getting yourself arrested seems excessive." He held one out to Richard.

"What are you doing here?" He ignored the proffered drink.

"I had hoped to ask you to stand up for me." Thomas swallowed heavily. "But it seems you may be unable to attend my nuptials."

Richard sank into a chair, rubbing his forehead. "You're to be wed? Oh God, Tom." He lifted his head with a bitter smile. "Unlike my wife, at least I am able to beg your forgiveness in person."

The other man waved his words aside. "We've saved each other's lives too often for either of us to hold a grudge. In your shoes I might well have thought the same."

A breath of laughter escaped Richard. "'Twould be a lie to say I don't wish you could help me with this mess. Never mind that, though. Tell me about your lady."

Thomas did, and his obvious delight in his intended bride amused Richard no end. Eventually, however, his friend leaned forward. "Richard, why do you not send for Bethany? She could clear you."

"No!" The word exploded out of him. He explained Loring's threat. Tom argued that if she arrived in secret, the captain would be unlikely to insist on her arrest during the trial itself. Richard flatly refused to risk her life.

If she had to spend one more minute with these account books, Bethany thought she would go mad. She massaged her neck and closed her eyes for relief. Her dinner tray sat all but ignored on a rickety table under a window.

Mistress Platt's annoyance would set off the entire kitchen if she did not eat something. She wandered over. As usual, the cook had prepared chicken and bread for the midday meal, but she had stewed some rhubarb from the garden for something different. Bethany had a few bites of bread and cold meat and started on the sweet. Her mouth watered as she chewed the tangy rhubarb.

She hoped the kitchen boy would catch a few fish today for their supper. Graymoor's pool of livestock remained too small to provide for the estate's needs, and they ate beef, veal, mutton, or lamb only when the herds needed culling.

Looking out the window, she sighed. This side of the house overlooked the courtyard and gate. The ruined end of the southern wing lay partially hidden by the bulk of the house stretching along her right, while to the left, the newly repaired stables stood with their doors open to catch the afternoon sun.

Surrounding the courtyard and stables, the dale sloped down to Kilpenny in the distance, rising in long slopes crisscrossed with low fences. The green folds and hilltops met the sky in a blurry line of smoky blue. In only a matter of weeks, she had come to love the land and people here.

One of her favorite tasks on the estate was to ride the circuit of tenants, shepherds, and cowherds. She and Glory both owned riding horses now, having commissioned Sir Fothery to obtain them from one of the stud farms along the River Rye.

Riding over the estate gave her a chance to escape the constant noise and dust caused by house repairs. It also enabled her to miss the arguments between the itinerant laborers and the permanent household staff, although she inevitably had to adjudicate them upon her return.

Today, however, she had spent so many hours with the books that she would have to assuage her wanderlust with only a stroll through the flower gardens. She slipped down a narrow stairwell near this end of the house. It ended far below in the cellars, but she only took it as far as the kitchen.

Handing her tray to a kitchen maid, she smiled at Mistress Platt on her way out the door. This wing of the house had suffered nothing but neglect. After the workmen completed the improvements to the kitchen, they had focused on the rest of the edifice.

She turned the corner and mounted the steps

to the new terrace. It extended past the house on
the far end, for Mr. Quintan had pronounced the
damage there irreparable. Workers had to tear
the weakened walls down to the ground before rebuilding them. Crews of men had removed the
rubble already, sorting stones and timbers into
piles for reuse or further destruction.

Replanting the gardens proved far more encouraging. Even after weeding the parterres below
the terrace, the beds remained too overgrown to
discern their patterns. Then Bethany found a thin
leather-bound journal tucked behind the drawer
of one of the writing tables. It had belonged to
Richard's mother, a gifted amateur designer, and
included several sketches of the gardens.

Based on that information, she ordered the gardens planted and trimmed according to her pre-
decessor's plans. As Glory had said, her mother
had loved Graymoor, and Bethany felt somehow
obligated to carry out her wishes.

A few pages of the late Lady Harcourt's journal
held drawings of her family. Richard's father
stared up from one page, darker than his son, but
with similar features. Next to him sat a sprite-like
Glory, whose sunny disposition showed even as a
small girl.

Bethany lingered longest over a page marked
"Richard, age twelve." He still had some of his
sister's elfin charm in his thin face, but the proud
carriage of his head and brilliant eyes had developed as well.

She strolled past the formally clipped hedges

toward a small banqueting house at the end of the main walk. Often she brought a book or some needlework to enjoy a quiet hour in it. Today she would just sit and enjoy the view of Graymoor for a time.

As she approached the small white structure, she heard whispers through its open door. Her lips thinned. She recognized her sister-in-law's voice easily, which meant the low masculine voice answering was Sir Fothery's. The young baronet grasped at any pretext to visit. Her skirts snapped about her feet as she strode up the steps, intending to give both of them the trimming of their lives for meeting clandestinely.

She took one look through the door and nearly fainted with horror.

Mercifully covered with a cloak on the floor, but clearly in a state of complete undress, Fothery propped himself on an elbow, his face serious as he brushed a golden strand from Glory's cheek. She stretched out beside him, her gown and petticoats to one side, neatly folded.

"Dear God in heaven, what have you done?"

Glory squealed and grabbed the cloak more firmly around her, while Fothery put his arms around her protectively. Bethany staggered out to the top step.

A frantic rustling of cloth came from inside, along with a few imprecations, before the guilty couple emerged. By then she had collected herself as well.

"Explain yourselves!" Her thunderous voice

even startled herself. Fothery's normal suaveness deserted him, but Glory's brazenness remained unimpaired.

"Fothery and I are in love and wish to be married." She met Bethany's glare firmly.

"Married! 'Twill be a miracle if Richard doesn't run him through on the spot!" She turned her rage on the pale young man. "And as for you, what kind of man would besmirch a woman he claims to love? Shame on you!"

"I am not besmirched!" Glory grew as angry as she. "I am not even with child!" Bethany had to clench her hands to keep from shaking the foolish chit.

"And how do you know that?"

"Exactly my point, dearest." Fothery found his voice. "Lady Harcourt is right, we don't know. And I am tired of waiting for your brother to arrive. I shall go to London and ask for your hand there."

Bethany regarded him with an icy stare. "Then I suggest you do so at once, sir. For you shall not see Gloriana again without his permission." Another dreadful thought hit her. "What if you are with child? Richard will destroy me for being so careless with you."

The scene ended with Fothery hurrying toward his horse, tied at the bottom of the garden. Meanwhile, Bethany nearly dragged Glory by force back to the house.

"Stop that caterwauling!" She pulled on the loudly resisting girl. She prayed Richard would agree to the match, less for Glory's reputation than her own peace of mind. "You could try the patience of a stone saint."

The following morning a message arrived from Fothery announcing his departure for London. Glory waved it under Bethany's nose gleefully. When she pointed out that Richard had not agreed to the match, the girl retorted quickly.

"He will! We've known the Lamberts this age, and Fothery won't need a great dowry if we live in the country." Bethany gaped at the girl who had spent her time with the Rothleys pining for London.

"Heavens, you do love him."

"Yes," Glory said simply.

They did not expect to hear from Fothery before a fortnight. When a servant announced him during dinner scarcely a week later, the Harcourt ladies looked at one another in surprise. Glory immediately rushed to the Great Hall to greet him, while Bethany followed at a more dignified pace.

She stopped short at his appearance. Although clearly delighted to see Glory, dried mud spattered his clothes under a layer of dust. Red rimmed his eyes, as if he had not slept.

"He agreed to let us marry, my love." His worried expression did not change although he kissed her soundly. She cocked her head in an unspoken question. Keeping an arm around her, he approached Bethany, concern radiating from him.

"I found Lord Harcourt in the Tower." Glory clutched his arm while Bethany grasped the newel post for support. "A Captain Loring accused him of aiding some Fifth Monarchists after the uprising in January. It seems his lordship was gone from town then, so none of his acquaintances can prove his whereabouts or verify his actions. He's to be tried before the King's Bench."

Bethany tried to grasp Fothery's words. "But who would believe Richard disloyal to the King?"

He shook his head. "None of his friends, it seems. But they cannot prevent the trial." Ignoring the watching servants, he turned to comfort his fiancée. His whispers mingled with the girl's sobs.

Meanwhile, Bethany stood, unable to summon action or coherent thought. Weeping and babble rose around her as thoughts raced through her mind. During her exile to Graymoor, the knowledge that her husband would have to break down and visit the estate had sustained her. It might take another tremendous argument, but she had convinced herself she could win his affection back.

She could not grasp the idea that she might never see him again. At the image of Richard hung, then taken down alive to have his bowels cut out, she shuddered. No matter how unjust his accusations of infidelity, he did not deserve a traitor's death.

"I must go to London. I can vouch for his whereabouts."

Glory turned from her fiancé's shoulder with brimming eyes. "Even if you could arrive before his trial, the journey would leave you too ill to help him."

Bethany opened her mouth to argue, but from her side Faith spoke first. "She's right, my lady. I'm not saying you shouldn't try, but 'tis unlikely you'd arrive in time, much less fit to do anything." Her round face puckered thoughtfully. "Unless . . ." She bit her lip.

Bethany waited, but the maid still hesitated. "Unless what? Tell me!"

"Unless you was to ride, not go by coach." Faith twisted hands in her apron.

"On horseback?" Bethany paced a few steps, considering. "'Twould be an invitation for every highwayman in England to accost me."

An uncharacteristic note of exasperation crept into the older woman's voice. "You wouldn't be alone, madam! Take some manservants, armed."

"I've heard too many tales of cutthroats attacking traveling females even when they do have outriders." Only one solution came to mind. "I shall have to travel in men's clothes."

For once even Gloriana looked shocked. Bethany disregarded the girl's expression.

"Horses for three, saddled and waiting as soon as possible. We need men's clothes for the ride, but I can't wear those in London. Faith, can you pack an entire outfit for me if I can find a big enough receptacle?"

The maid nodded. Around her, Bethany's words

seemed to have cut a string holding everyone in place. A boy ran to the stables after Glory volunteered her riding horse for Faith. Two chambermaids scurried upstairs to start packing, while Mistress Platt offered a pair of wicker baskets used to carry goods by horseback.

Bethany's back ached. So did her thighs and posterior after two days on horseback. As a girl, she had first learned to ride horses astride, but that had been years ago. And she had never spent hours on end in a saddle. Their party had stopped to rest the animals for a few minutes. Absently stroking her mount's neck, she looked at the surrounding countryside.

Just now they traveled through an area of rolling hills and hedgerow-lined roads. The sun shone bright, though rain the previous night had left their route a morass in some places. Mud covered her boots and breeches.

"The ostler at the last place said as how we're in Bedfordshire now." The first groom, a weatherbeaten retainer who had grown up with Richard's father, wiped his face with his neck cloth.

"Two days more, then." As she replied, Bethany heard a deep sigh behind her. A corner of her mouth lifted briefly. Faith had insisted on coming along, but the long days daunted even her stout heart. Bethany glanced over her shoulder. The second groom, a lad chosen for his accuracy with a pistol, rolled his eyes as the maid muttered to herself.

Sir Fothery had offered his escort, of course. Fearing she would not arrive in time to testify on Richard's behalf, she had begged him to stay in Yorkshire for Glory's sake.

Ahead of them, a brook had overflowed its bed onto a low place in the road. The first groom splashed through it. The muscles in her back screamed in agony, but Bethany gritted her teeth, gathered her horse, and followed.

As the miles passed, memories ran through her mind. The honeyed gravel of Richard's voice that sweetened so when he made love to her. The feel of his hands and lips on her bare skin. The feel of his body under her hands.

The look in his eyes the first time he had seen her hair.

God's teeth, she even missed arguing with him. Other than their last dreadful encounter, he at least admitted she had a right to her own opinion.

She urged her horse to go a little faster.

Bethany paced the parlour of the Rothleys' house as she awaited Lord Thomas. They had arrived the night before. She had slept while Faith had pressed her gown of sage green and her petticoat into a presentable state. Now the redoubtable maid snored loudly on a pallet in her room with Bethany's strict orders not to awaken her.

To the detriment of her already stretched nerves,

the footman had taken some time to return with a message from Lord Thomas. Placing a note from his lordship in her hand, the servant had accepted her generous tip with a deep bow and disappeared, jingling his newfound fortune in his hand.

The nobleman had written little new information, save that he would escort Bethany to the Court of the King's Bench before dinnertime. The prosecution did depend largely on Arthur Loring's statements, he added, and he feared the trial had not gone in Richard's favor the day previous. It seemed that the captain had prepared his case well.

As soon as she heard the knocking on the hall door, she rushed into the hallway. No sooner had the porter admitted Lord Thomas than she begged him to take her to the trial at once. He barely allowed her to tie her hood over her lace cap before escorting her out the door. She was inclined to refuse the services of the chair he had hired, but he insisted.

"If you're going to testify on Richard's behalf, you cannot afford to appear travel-stained and dowdy." He scanned her appearance in satisfaction as he handed her in. "Thank goodness you didn't dress too plainly."

"As he's on trial for aiding fanatic Nonconformists, I thought it best not to." Bethany had taken pains to appear fashionably turned out. Her hair curled becomingly under her cap, and a matching set of enameled gold earrings and necklet adorned her. She dressed modestly, but no one would mistake her for a Nonconformist.

The fetid smell of the river filled her nostrils well before Lord Thomas opened the door. They stood at the top of the Temple stairs. Below them, wherries and barges waited for multiple passengers, along with several skiffs, small slender boats intended for only one or two passengers at a time.

He escorted her down to one of the latter and greeted the waterman standing beside it.

"Good morning, Jack. My thanks for awaiting my return." Unimpressed with the affable greeting, the wiry little man loosened the mooring rope.

"Cost me a shilling in fares. Let's be off." Inured to the legendary rudeness of London's watermen, they ignored his remark and prepared to board.

As a loaded wherry with its two oarsmen shot past them, Bethany wondered to herself if they should not have taken one of those. Assisting her to the low seat in the stern, Lord Thomas reassured her.

"Jack Taylor is the fastest man on the river. He'll get us to Westminster quicker and dryer than anyone else. Particularly for two shillings." The laconic waterman brightened and plucked the proffered coins out of his lordship's palm.

"Never 'ad a haccident in me life." Once his passengers were settled, he released the ropes completely and they shot out into the current.

Although the waterman, inspired by the additional silver, pulled enthusiastically on the oars, the brief trip lasted too long for Bethany's peace of mind. No one spoke as he expertly guided his small craft around and past slower vessels of all sizes. At last Westminster Palace came into view over the surrounding rooftops. Rowing the skiff toward a wooden jetty thrusting out from the shore, its owner angled it alongside.

Lord Thomas led Bethany out of the boat. Gripping his arm with one hand, she negotiated her way along the craft as it bobbed up and down. With the other, she lifted her skirts away from the water and mud. No sooner did she set foot on the creaking jetty than the skiff shot away in search of other passengers.

Ascending the moss-covered stone steps, they hurried through the crowded courtyard leading to Westminster Hall. She continued to clutch Lord Thomas's arm as they passed through the arched stone doorway, fearing she would lose her way in the horde.

To Bethany's amazement, the hall bustled not only with government officials and clerks, but with stalls of merchandise and their customers. Some, like those selling pens or books, made sense next to a court of law. Many sold luxury goods, however. Pairs of fine embroidered gloves sat on one counter, while next to it an old woman watched over a supply of silk stockings. People wandered from one stall to another comparing goods and prices.

She shuddered. That anyone could buy and sell only feet from where a court decided whether men lived or died appalled her.

In the crowd, she did not mind Lord Thomas's

grip on her elbow. She struggled to hear the soft stream of information he poured into her ear as they walked toward the far end of the immense hall.

"The Lord Chief Justice is Sir Robert Foster. He's been a Royalist since the days of the first King Charles and favors the Crown's witnesses to the point of blindness." They walked on. "You'll have to step carefully with him. Rickon's greatest hope is to discredit Loring's testimony." Dismayed, Bethany shook her head as she trotted beside him.

"But without knowing exactly what the man said about Richard, how can I hope to dispute it?" He stopped beside a gray stone pillar stretching into the vastness of the ceiling above. She faced him anxiously.

"Because you were with him and can vouch for his actions." He placed his hands on her shoulders. "I'm sorry to tell you, but there is talk of your departure from town. The world views you as a wronged wife, and your return to speak in his favor shall give your words greater weight." His sky blue eyes clouded. "Indeed, half of them will expect your testimony to hang him." She blanched at the idea, his next words not registering at first.

"My lady, I love Rickon like a brother, but I know his faults. He can admit when he's in the wrong easily enough, but getting him to ask your pardon is harder than pulling teeth." His gaze bored into hers. "Especially when he must ask one he—he cares for deeply. Please give him time, I beg you."

Bethany's fingers folded and unfolded the

pleats of her gown. She tried to think of her present dilemma.

"Will I even be allowed to testify?"

"Luckily—I hope—His Majesty takes an interest in the case, as you shall see." He smiled cynically and answered her unspoken question. "'Tis most fortunate you chose a flattering gown this day."

"If he's so interested, why does he not intervene?"

"He'll do naught to endanger his crown." Lord Thomas lowered his voice to the lightest thread of sound. "His father tried to interfere with judicial proceedings and suffered the consequences."

Indeed, when he escorted her into the enclosure set aside for the King's Bench, the tall form of the King drew her eye. He lounged comfortably in a cushioned chair set on a wooden dais, surrounded by several courtiers. Not quite a throne, it sat beneath an awning, high up at the back of the room. She curtsied to him, receiving a small nod of recognition in turn.

Bethany swallowed. A sea of masculine faces surrounded her. Some expressed surprise, others looked bored. None appeared to approve of her presence.

As Lord Thomas presented her, she strove to present an image of calm. She glanced at Richard, who stared at her in shock from his place. The men sitting on either side of him acted as the jury, Lord Thomas quickly explained under his breath when he stepped back. She nodded. An unexpected sense of oppression settled on her.

As expected, Captain Loring objected to her presence.

"My Lord, you cannot expect a wife to tell the truth of any matter pertaining to her husband's life or death." He dismissed her with a wave of his hand.

Lord Thomas appealed to the Lord Chief Justice. Sir Robert, along with the other judges of the King's Bench, sat across a narrow aisle from the King, under an awning of their own.

"Beg pardon, my lord, but Lady Harcourt just rode posthaste from the north of Yorkshire to speak on his behalf. 'Twould be cruel to reward such devotion by dismissing her unheard."

"With all due respect, I should prefer also that Lady Harcourt not be subjected to the harsh questions of a trial, your lordship." Richard did not look at her as he made his request.

"After the trouble I took getting here? You arrogant—'twould serve you right if I left this instant." Her eyebrows snapped together as she glowered at him. Sir Robert rebuked her for speaking out of turn. She apologized as prettily as she could, hoping to enlist his sympathies.

Her attempt failed. The Chief Justice regarded her balefully before opening his mouth to speak. Another interruption occurred from an unexpected direction.

"A wife demonstrating such steadfastness to her husband? How diverting!" Heads turned as the King delivered the aside to one of his gentlemen. "A chair must be found for the lady." Sir Robert fumed at the command, but could not bring himself to object.

"Calling a female to testify is most irregular." Reluctantly, he indicated that Bethany should come forward. A guard bowed and handed her up the wooden steps, to stand in the aisle between the two galleries. Another brought a stool for her to sit on.

"I thank Your Majesty." Her voice echoed and drifted to the dark wooden beams high above. Settling herself, she arranged her skirts. Pointedly, she avoided looking at Richard. When asked about it, she replied coldly.

"I dislike having my veracity questioned. If I cannot see Lord Harcourt, he and I can hardly be accused of collusion." Red suffused Captain Loring's sullen face, but he made no reply.

As the defendant in a treason case, Richard was not entitled to counsel. A sergeant-at-law, one of a handful of barristers permitted to practice in this court, came forward to question her. The judges, led by Sir Robert, listened from their seats. Below them, several clerks scribbled notes at a narrow table. The dry scratch of their quills against parchment made a soft counterpoint to the words spoken in the court.

Praying for a cool head, she selected her words with care to assure that the chamber heard her clearly. Sir Robert Foster spoke first.

"Please tell the court what information you could possibly have that may influence this case."

His sarcastic manner startled her. She lifted her chin.

"I can vouch for Lord Harcourt's whereabouts on the days for which he is charged with aiding members of the January uprising." She clasped her hands in front of her to keep from wringing them. "I spent several full days in early January in his company."

Loring made a great show of scribbling his own notes as she made her statement, but she forced her voice to remain serene. The sergeant-at-law, a middle-aged man wearing the gown and hood that indicated his office, asked her for details about the dates and their activities.

"On January seventh, Lord Harcourt and I journeyed by coach from my home near Stanworth, in Bedfordshire, to an inn called the Bell and Moon. On the morning of the eighth, we continued to London, again by coach. We went directly to Lord Harcourt's lodgings for the evening." Confident that no one in the chamber knew of his brief absence to purchase their meal, she chose not to enlighten them.

"Lord Harcourt spoke only of traveling to Bedfordshire in company with his coachman, my lady. If you accompanied him, doubtless you can tell the court exactly where this inn is located?"

Bethany realized that her husband had hidden her presence to protect her from London's gossip-mongers. She could cheerfully have brained him for such misplaced gallantry.

"Doubtless my husband omitted my presence

out of a touching, but remarkably foolish, desire to defend my reputation." Laughter, not all of it smothered, rose from the assembled nobles. "We were eloping," she explained for the benefit of the judges and jury.

"As for the location of the inn, I haven't the least clue. I was overcome with the most wretched headache and cared only that the sheets were clean. If the court wishes to ascertain the location of the place or my presence there, you need only ask Captain Loring." She nodded to him with mock civility. "I conversed with him in the tap-room on the morning of the eighth for several moments."

He turned a face of such hatred on her that she leaned back involuntarily. From the shocked expression on the sergeant's face, he had not known of the captain's presence at the inn. The jurors commented among themselves. From his place below the King's seat, Lord Thomas grinned his approval.

Even the King roused, dropping his languid manner to examine the captain with eyes gone shrewd and hard. He whispered to an aide, this time inaudibly. He listened to the remainder of her testimony resting his chin on his steepled fingertips.

"The whereabouts of the Crown's witness is not being tried, your ladyship." The Lord Chief Justice wasted no time taking control of the proceedings, but Bethany retorted quickly.

"If you wish to get an accurate account, it should

be. Any housewife can tell you that a jealous lackey will babble anything to obtain the downfall of a rival." She sniffed disdainfully. A titter ran through the entire chamber at her indignation.

"Can you swear that you were in the accused's presence every moment?" Sir Robert peered hard at her while his voice insinuated that she had just now made up her story. She heard a sharp hiss from Richard's direction, but did not turn her head.

She pinned the judge with her haughtiest stare as her mind raced to assemble an answer.

"Of course not! There are some activities one does prefer to engage in without the presence of others." A few chuckles came from the crowd, but he ignored them.

"So you do admit that it is possible for the accused to have slipped away and given money or other aid to his fellow rebels!"

"As Lord Harcourt has no 'fellow rebels,' my lord, I am unable to admit anything of the sort." She locked eyes with Sir Robert. This bully would not lay a hand on Richard's head if she had aught to say about it. "Surely you don't suggest he provided aid and comfort to anyone while visiting the necessary, my lord? How revolting! Plain common sense must boggle at the idea."

"Vulgar rustic!" Captain Loring's exclamation rang through the room. There were some mutters of agreement, but a few outright guffaws drowned them out. The King's shoulders shook suspiciously.

"As for giving anyone money, how could he do

that when we neither of us had access to any until we arrived in London?"

At this the captain tore off a sheet of paper from his note-book. Flourishing it, he approached the clerks and handed it to the nearest one, who in turn offered it to the judges. As he returned to his place, he saluted her with a mocking bow.

The justices read his message through once and held a whispered conference. After what appeared to be an agitated debate, they resumed their seats. Sir Robert once more addressed her.

"The court is greatly interested in knowing how a great heiress and her husband could not afford to pay the shot at a second-rate inn. Perhaps you could enlighten us, Lady Harcourt?"

Bethany had once nearly fallen into an old gravel pit when part of the path she walked had given way after a month of rain. Her stomach lurched the same way now as she sought a firm path through this ploy to discredit them both. Her mind went blank as she scrambled to reply.

"I am confused, my lord. Am I on trial for treason or for paying my debts?" In spite of her earlier intention, Bethany peeped over her shoulder at Richard, but so did everyone else in the chamber.

Leaning negligently against the wooden bar, he regarded the row of judges with an air of faint boredom. Only the glitter of his half-closed eyes betrayed any tension. He shot her a warning glance as the furious Chief Justice replied.

"You are charged with aiding and abetting the escape, after its failure, of several participants in the uprising led by Thomas Venner. The timing of your marriage to a young woman of means is far too convenient to such a plan. On what possible grounds can you claim not to have the funds to carry it out?"

Bethany waited for Richard to explain the truth. He looked at her with a half-smile and shrugged.

"Ah." He bowed to Sir Robert. "My thanks for enlightening me on that point."

As he continued silent, it dawned on her that he would not give the court the explanation that might help save his life.

Surely he would not sacrifice his life to his honor. She gazed at him in something like horror at the idea. Only one solution presented itself to her. She took a deep breath, for she feared a misstep would mean Richard's execution.

"Your Lordship asked me to clarify a point, I think?" Bethany waited until she had the attention of the entire room.

"I should think the explanation would leap to the eye, gentlemen." She paused as if waiting for a response. "As I said, Lord Harcourt and I eloped. We married in London. Only then did we have access to my inheritance." Excited whispers broke out at this disclosure of scandal, but she did not wait for them to subside.

"Even in the highly unlikely event he sympathized with the traitors, he would have had no means of supporting them." She finished her statement, watching its effect on the judges. Another point suddenly occurred to her.

"I must congratulate the court on finding so well informed a witness as Captain Loring. For one who says he merely chanced upon this supposed plot, he shows a remarkable grasp of the events surrounding it."

She did not try to hide her scorn, and ripples of agreement swept through the room, but only a few. The King, looking less amused than his wont, nodded as his wide mouth curled cynically.

Sir Robert snapped at her not to speak of Captain Loring again before resuming his examination. Hoping she had scored her point, she listened to his next question.

"Do you seriously expect this court to believe that over the course of three days, you and Lord Harcourt did not spend any significant length of time apart?"

"My lord, I did point out that we were eloping." She raised her eyebrows suggestively. "I have no intention of going into the details of our activities, but I assure you we spent nearly all of our time in the same room. One might say 'twas our honeymoon trip."

The chamber burst into laughter. Two of the judges smiled broadly and she even heard a few bouts of scattered applause. Sir Robert, evidently considering it fruitless to question her further, testily announced that she might step down from the witness stand.

After he dismissed her, Bethany rose from her seat. Uncertain of where to go, she gratefully followed a guard who escorted her to a place on the floor in front of the jury. As she passed Richard, she tried to gauge his state of mind. His impassive face gave no hint of his thoughts.

Studying him up close, he appeared even more drawn. Her heart ached at his humiliation and hurt at the insult to his family's name. She hoped he would not consider her testimony another attempt to discredit him. She simply could not think of another way to save his life.

Sure he would despise her pity, she attempted a smile with trembling lips. He did not react openly as she took her place near him.

She must have been the final witness to speak, for the Chief Justice directed the jury to render its decision. Its members left their seats to huddle in a knot on the floor far enough away from the galleries that their debate could not be heard.

"My Lord, do not allow her to stand so close to the traitor." A sneer cut across Arthur Loring's face as he uttered the last word. A chorus of hisses from Richard's supporters erupted.

Bethany herself stepped forward, ready to confront the captain, until her husband's voice stopped her.

"I should like to request that Lady Harcourt be escorted from the court before the verdict is given." She whipped her head around to face him.

"I beg your pardon?" She and Sir Robert asked the question in unison. He sounded surprised. Bethany's tone indicated a more passionate emotion.

"Given the effort the lady exhibited in her

attempt to save my life, I fear she may be overcome in the event I am convicted." His calm request carried over the chatter of the audience. Her temper, already tried by the grueling ride and her fear for his life, issued forth in a whispered stream of angry words.

"Do you dare to tell me that after I rode from north Yorkshire till I near fainted with exhaustion, and then subjected myself to that dreadful man's questioning, you are throwing me out of the chamber?"

"Madam, you are overwrought, and I wish only to spare you any further pain." His low, measured tones failed to soothe her.

"No, my lord, I am not 'overwrought.' I am livid. What are you going to do next, order me back home?"

"As a matter of fact, yes, I think that might be best under the circumstances."

"Of course, sending me back to Yorkshire proved so helpful to you last time!" She suddenly became aware that they spoke aloud, and that the entire room sat listening to them. Several of the men shook their heads at her in disapproval. A few openly chuckled. The King held a kerchief before his mouth to hide his smile.

"I believe the Chief Justice can dismiss the accusation that she testified out of partiality for her husband." His Majesty addressed his courtiers, but this witticism also carried from one end of the court to the other.

She ignored them all, except for Richard

and the Chief Justice. "I am not leaving unless the guards carry me out."

"Shameless Jezebel!" She could not place the vaguely familiar voice that shouted. When she craned her head toward the part of the crowd it had come from, she saw no one she recognized.

"If the jury might deliver the verdict?" Sir Robert regarded her balefully. She flushed hot at the realization that the jury had finished deliberating. She stood as near Richard as the guards allowed. He did not glance in her direction, but his fingers tightened once more on the bar before him as the Chief Justice read the jury's decision.

"We hereby conclude the accusation against the grand traitor Richard Marcus Harcourt, Baron Harcourt, whose crime was no less than high treason. He was to succor, shelter, and aid the most bloody-handed men acting in the riots of January last, led by the foul murderer Thomas Venner. We contend that he was brought to a fair trial before the Court of the King's Bench at Westminster, where it was proved by good evidence that he abetted those who were to have killed his Benovolent Majesty . . ."

As the meaning sank in, Bethany felt as if a set of invisible fingers choked her. She tried to protest that she had just proved he was innocent, but could not push the words past the suffocating pressure in her throat. Over the roaring in her ears, she could barely hear the sentence handed down by the court.

"He shall be hanged up by the neck, and cut down whilst some life remains in him, afterward his breast to be ripped open, his heart taken out, his body quartered and displayed for the warning and correction of public morals."

Chapter 12

"No." Her knees gave way, try as she might to stay upright. Richard's arms held her up. He had broken away from his guards to come to her. Tears blurred his face in front of hers before she buried her face in his shoulder.

"I am so sorry, Rickon. I failed you, it was all for nothing." He held her close for a moment, his lips brushing her cheek while he stroked her hair, soothing her.

"No, sweet girl, 'twas not wasted. You came for me after all, didn't you?"

She had no idea what he meant. Anguish lanced through her as the guards pulled him away. Ignoring them, she clung to his hand as long as she could before they forced her toward the door. "Please forgive me. I thought if I told them the truth, it would save you."

"And so it has." King Charles rose to his full height, gaining the attention of the entire chamber. "Lord Harcourt, approach."

With a guard on each side, Richard walked over to the King. The clop of his shoes was the only sound in the chamber, until he knelt before him. The King regarded the assemblage sternly and spoke.

"Richard Marcus, Baron Harcourt, is this day graciously granted the benefit of a full and free pardon for the crime of treason against the Crown in relation to the January rebellions, the reason being that we are sufficiently satisfied by the testimony presented by his wife that he never did knowingly associate with any supporter of the rebellion and spent the days in company with her. So ordered by Charles the Second, King of England and Scotland, in the thirteenth year of our reign." He finished and pointed to the Chief Justice's clerk, who bent over his parchment scribbling furiously.

"Write it up and present it for our seal and signature." The crowd roared its approval.

Through her shock, Bethany noticed a number of individuals who had howled earlier for Richard's blood now cheered his freedom, in view of His Majesty's professed belief in his innocence. She shook her head over their shameless reverse of opinion, but in the end, it did not matter. Richard was free.

From her place by the door, she observed Captain Loring. Predictably, he did not rejoice in the King's pardon. His face black with anger, he shouldered his way through the crowd in her direction. Thinking he wished to leave the site of his defeat, she moved out of his way, for the idea of speaking to him revolted her.

The small movement must have caught his eye, for he changed his route to confront her. Although shaky from Richard's brush with death at this man's hands, she lifted her chin. He could hardly harm her in the middle of a crowded courtroom under the King's eye.

"You interfering little bitch." He hissed the words so softly, even the guard could barely hear him. "Why could you not have stayed in Yorkshire where you belonged?"

"Because your lies about my husband endangered his life." She met his eyes steadily as she spoke.

A flash of motion at the corner of her vision caused her to turn her head. With a shock, she recognized Mr. Ilkston as he detached himself from the back of the crowd near the royal party. The captain's glance had followed hers. Now his lip curled.

"Just as well." He reached under his coat. "Mayhap this will hurt that whoreson you married more." Grabbing her wrist with one hand, he pulled the other out, revealing a steel knife.

Bethany screamed and fought to pull her hand free from his grip, but he struck too swiftly for anyone else to react. He stabbed low, aiming beneath her breastbone in a blow so heavy she reeled from it. The blade glanced off the stiff whalebone busk and tore through her quilted and boned stays. By then the guard and several bystanders acted, disarming him and holding him in place.

Kind hands supported Bethany as she held her torn bodice and stays together. As she watched Richard's white face trying to push his way through the crowd, a stinging sensation along her side increased until she could no longer ignore it. Glancing down, she realized blood oozed out of the torn material of her gown and stays.

It did not spread fast enough to indicate a deep wound. She breathed deeply, forcing her heart to stop pounding.

"Bethany!" Richard pushed at the crowd to get to her, but the solid wall of bodies pressing in on her and Loring prevented him. She tried to catch his eye, to assure him she had not been hurt badly, when she cried out again.

"Richard, behind you! The King!" Mr. Ilkston had pulled out a dagger of his own and crept so far into the distracted circle of courtiers that he stood nearest Charles. His Majesty had not armed himself with a sword, but he pulled a dagger of his own and took a defensive stance.

"King Jesus and the heads upon the walls!" To the horror of the assemblage, the countryman shouted the motto of the Fifth Monarchists. Richard wasted no time. Grabbing a rapier from one of the guards, he stepped between Ilkston and the King.

It ended quickly, for Ilkston was no more a swordsman than an assassin. In moments, Richard struck the dagger out of Ilkston's hand and would have run him through save for the intervention of Charles Stuart.

"Stand down, my lord." The King's voice rang out in cold fury. Richard relaxed but rested the point of his blade against the attacker's jugular vein. Two startled courtiers remembered themselves enough to grab Ilkston's arms. "We earnestly desire that this man and Captain Loring stand their trials."

The hum of shouts and cries rose to the ceiling around Bethany and threatened to drown her. Feeling faint, she groped her way through the mass of bodies. She walked, hard, into one.

Familiar arms encircled her as Richard's honey over gravel whisper recited her name repeatedly and added something she could not hear. As she rested her head on his shoulder, the buzz of the crowd merged into a black cloud. It enveloped her without warning, cutting off sight and sound.

She swam back to consciousness slowly. Gaining her senses fully, she found herself staring up at a kindly older man who awaited patiently for her to rouse. She examined his face stupidly for several seconds, wondering where she was and why she did not recognize him.

Suddenly remembering, she struggled to sit up, batting at the hands that urged her to remain still.

"No, milady, you have suffered an injury and great fear on top of a hard journey." The gray-haired man spoke gently but in a manner indicating that most people obeyed his orders. A friendly smile that crinkled the corners of his eyes softened the command.

"I can feel that." She winced as she raised herself on one elbow to look around.

Someone had placed her on a long wooden table in a small chamber with half-paneled walls, lit by two narrow windows. Carved wood covered the ceiling. The floor, she noticed when she sat up, was tiled by small black and white lozenges. She grasped his arm.

"Richard! I beg you, where is Lord Harcourt?" Her heart hammered as she pleaded, fearing he also had suffered an injury.

He patted her hand. "The pardon has been written out and signed by His Majesty, madam, thanks to your determination. And the cowards who attacked you were arrested on the spot." He picked up a folded square of linen. "If you must sit up, I might as well bandage you."

She did, and he pressed the makeshift pad onto her wound. Glancing down, she noticed it still bled a little, but she moved easily, if painfully. Her heavily quilted stays and quick movement had prevented serious damage.

To her alarm, the stays were clearly visible, as her open bodice bunched around her waist.

"Your husband insisted on stopping the proceedings until someone arranged treatment for you." Bethany hissed as he bound the pad firmly in place with a length of batiste heavily edged with lace. "Fortunately I am a doctor and was in attendance this day, although I had to borrow kerchiefs and cravats to use as bandages."

He tied the length of cloth tightly. She gasped in pain, but did not complain. She had no desire for the thing to slip.

"There's only a clean pad on the wound, for I certainly have nothing at hand to make a poultice with. Is there anyone at home who can make one?" At her affirmative answer, he nodded. "Very good, you shall need something to draw out the humors. Do you know what receipt is used?"

Bethany explained that she had an entire book of physic receipts gathered by her mother. The old man listened carefully to her description of the one it recommended for bloody wounds. He nodded again.

"That will do well, but I would recommend using half again as much cobweb to be sure the wound closes." His eyes twinkled. "In the meanwhile, I expect you would like to dress."

Bowing, he excused himself. Bethany wasted no time putting herself to rights, although the ties on the back of her gown proved a challenge. Eventually she managed to tighten them enough to give herself the appearance of respectability.

Exiting the room, she found her companion waiting politely for her. She tamped down her impatience to find Richard and curtsied to him.

"To whom do I owe my thanks, sir?" He bowed over her hand.

"Doctor George Bates at your service, my lady." She thanked him sincerely for his assistance and begged to be allowed to offer him payment. He brushed the request aside. "'Twas an honor to assist so intrepid a woman."

"Truly a credit to her gender." The familiar voice came from behind her. She turned around and instantly curtsied nearly to the floor.

King Charles inclined his head to acknowledge her.

"Please arise, Lady Harcourt." His teeth flashed white in a charming smile. "We should dislike protocol to cause you further pain, particularly when we owe you our life." Having abandoned his attendants, he invited her to walk with him. "Accept our heartfelt personal thanks for proving one man's innocence as well as exposing a pair of traitors to the Crown."

He extended his hand. Giving him a questioning look, she tentatively placed hers in it. To her secret relief, he merely brushed his lips over the back of her hand in a polite salute before releasing it. The King spoke again in a far more businesslike manner.

"At this point, one is permitted to name a reward." He prompted her with a twinkle in his dark eyes and waited for her to speak. Nonplussed, she searched for something to say.

"Sire, you gave me what I most desired when you pardoned my husband." She lifted her eyes to the royal countenance.

"Indeed! No gold, no lands, no title?" The heavy black eyebrows rose. "One does hear fascinating gossip about a trust fund." His voice trailed off suggestively.

"I have learned, Your Majesty, that there are some things far more vital to my happiness than money," Bethany replied firmly, to the King's obvious amusement. "I cannot speak for Lord Harcourt, however. Perhaps there is something he wishes."

He regarded her with uncharacteristic seriousness. "If his lordship is foolish enough to wish for more than a lady of your loyalty and quick wits, he doesn't deserve his pardon." Her fear must have shown on her face, for he hastened to finish.

"Do not fear, Lady Harcourt, we shall not rescind our word." He turned to leave, and she curtsied once more. "Convey our friendship to him, and our felicitations upon his choice of a consort."

She watched him mince away on his heeled shoes before beginning to search for her husband.

She started with the building's entry hall, but Richard did not await her there. The porter assured her Lord Harcourt had not passed that way. Searching the nearly empty maze of hallways, she found no sign of him. A few clerks scuttled about, all assuming an air of importance, but the dramatic end of the trial seemed to have signaled a general exodus.

With mounting frustration, she realized she had gone in circles. The door at her side led to the council chamber. It stood ajar, showing rows of empty seats. Although looking for her husband inside would likely prove fruitless, she supposed she might as well be thorough. She swung the door wide enough to enter, marveling that it moved so silently on its well-oiled hinges.

She paused on the threshold, frozen in horror. At the far end, Richard stood locked in an embrace with Frances Shadbourne.

Under Bethany's stunned gaze, Mistress Shadbourne handed her husband a small package. He held her close and said something; his gravelly voice sounded sad, but she could not catch the words. Possibly the roaring in her ears prevented her from hearing clearly.

Getting stabbed in the side hurt no more than a pinprick compared to this. She wanted to collapse, to lose consciousness and never regain it. Even the fact that she had secured his freedom could not change his feelings for his mistress.

Pressing her full skirts to her sides to prevent them from rustling, she backed out. Her throat closed so tightly with tears she could not have uttered a sound had she wished to. Blindly retracing her steps to the main hall, she stumbled in just as their guards escorted Captain Loring and Mr. Ilkston to Newgate Prison. Loring jeered at her.

"Already sorry you saved your husband's miserable life?" Bethany had no idea how he guessed at Richard's activities, but her fury vented itself on him.

"I have nothing to say to you."

The guards cheered her, but she ignored them.

She had to leave, now, before her composure deteriorated any further. Slipping past them into the street, she found a chair and directed the men to the house in Saint Clement's Lane.

Inside, she drew several shaky breaths and buried her face in her hands. She had to get away, to hide until she could mend the gaping hole Richard had just torn in her heart. Since she had brought only what could be carried on horseback, packing would take a matter of minutes.

She started issuing orders as soon as she entered the hall. Soon a footman scurried to the nearest livery stable to procure a heavy coach while a maid trotted upstairs to fold her few clothes. Bethany commandeered a small chest from the attic for them and instructed the kitchen to send a tray up to her room.

"Bread and cheese will do if naught else is at hand." She shouted the directive after the retreating back of the housekeeper.

Faith proved the greatest impediment to her departure. First no one could find her, until the scullery maid recalled seeing her slip out with Lane. Further questioning disclosed that Richard had rented a small house not far away in Brydges Street.

"Then send the footman to fetch her back!" Exclaiming under her breath at the obtuseness of servants, Bethany retreated to the chamber she had used last night to await her meal and her maid.

The footman caught Faith *in flagrante delicto* and haled her back before she could completely

adjust her appearance. Straightening her dis-
arranged clothes, she begged Bethany to delay
her departure.

"Please, my lady, I haven't had even a full day
with Augustus." Tears rolled down her round
cheeks. "Why must we leave so sudden-like?"

"Oh, do stop blubbering!" The maid's evidence
of a happy reunion with the coachman irritated
Bethany beyond measure. "As for your Augustus—
er, Lane—he probably enjoyed the favors of every
pretty tavern wench he could get his hands on
while you were gone."

She regretted the words as soon as they left her
lips. In the first place, to lay a charge of infidelity
at his door was unjust, and cruel to poor Faith. In
the second, it defeated her intention to leave
London as soon as possible, for the older woman
burst into miserable wails at the idea that her
beloved would so misuse her. She held the weeping servant to her shoulder and patted her back.

"Forgive me, Faith, 'tis not true. We all know he
loves only you. 'Twas cruel of me to say differently."

Several minutes passed before the little maid
lifted her head and hiccoughed.

"It's a terrible hard thing to say, milady, and not
like you." She scrubbed the tears off her face and
blew her nose. "Why must we leave? You were
right terrified for his lordship all the way here, and
Lane says as how you saved his life. You should
be happy now."

Bethany clenched her jaw. She could not trust

herself to speak of the scene she had witnessed without breaking down herself.

"I am sure Lord Harcourt and I shall be quite content, Faith. But I must return home to Yorkshire as soon as possible and his lordship doubtless wishes to remain with his friends in town." Her voice quivered over the last words, but she remained calm under Faith's suddenly sharpened eyes.

"You two are going to have a hard time getting an heir sleeping that far apart," she muttered. Bethany ignored her.

"Off you go to the kitchen. You must eat something before we leave." The maid's eyes filled with tears yet again, and she hastily urged her out the door, shutting it behind her. She fidgeted until a scratching on the wooden panels announced the arrival of her own cloth-covered tray.

Removing the clean napkin, she discovered a pewter plate filled not just with two small loaves of crusty bread and a wedge of golden cheddar, but with sliced cold chicken on one side. In a small dish, fragrant hothouse strawberries rested under a dollop of clotted cream, and a goblet held some of Lord Rothley's favorite sack.

She thought eating any of it would choke her.

The cook, a most expensive employee, took justifiable pride in her craft, but in her misery Bethany might as well have forced down sawdust and vinegar.

A footman arrived to take the small chest downstairs to wait for the coach while she ate. She had just finished when familiar footsteps thudded up the stairway. Richard threw the door open and glared at her.

"Where the hell do you think you're going?"

"I suppose Lane told you my plans. I should have known." She sighed, wiped her hands and mouth, and rose to her feet. Oddly, his wrath inspired a strange calmness in her. "Come in, my lord, and shut the door."

He complied. The concern on his face as he approached nearly undid her, but she stood her ground. The anger faded from his eyes.

"Beth, what is this? Why do you leave before giving me a chance to thank you?" He took her hands in his. Trying to ignore the shiver his touch inspired in her, she pulled away. He reached for them again, but stopped when she backed away from him.

"Please, my lord." She regarded him a trifle unsteadily. "'Tis not necessary for you to bid me stay."

"You save my life, very nearly at the cost of your own, and now you turn around and leave?" He ran his fingers through his honey-colored hair. "At least tell me why."

Bethany swallowed as she remembered the feel of those silky strands. "Does it really matter if I go, my lord?"

"And stop calling me 'my lord' every other sentence!" She jumped and glared as he slapped his hand on the surface of her dressing table.

"You sent me away. You never said you wanted me back." She exhaled, unexpectedly tired.

He dropped his eyes at the implied accusation.

"I did not realize how much I missed you until I was imprisoned." His voice was only a thread; she could scarcely hear it. "All I could think about in prison was that I would never see you again."

She wanted to believe him more than she had ever wanted anything in her life, but she could not. Exhausted by the journey from Yorkshire, and facing the prospect of setting out on the return within the day, she could not find the energy to argue with him over his mistress.

"If you wanted to see me, why did you not even send word to Graymoor when you were arrested?" She searched his face, trying to read his expression. A shadow crossed it and he sighed heavily.

"I expected you to leave me to hang." He could not meet her eyes. Bethany thought she had misheard him for a moment.

"Dear God, can you truly believe that I am such a monster?" She whispered the words through numb lips.

"First you accuse me of infidelity and now this." With such a low opinion of her, no wonder he had turned to his old mistress.

She stepped around him, hastening to the door. He gently grasped her wrist. She pulled, but he did not let her go.

"Under the circumstance, 'tis best I return to Yorkshire, Richard." She averted her head to hide the tears trembling on her lashes.

"Beth, listen to me. I was a great fool to believe that you would betray me, and with Tom, of all men." Richard's shaky breath stirred her dangling earring. "After making such an accusation, I couldn't very well ask you to turn around and save my life. And—and if I was executed, you would be free to enjoy your entire fortune."

"This is worse than accusing me of adultery." A sob ripped through her.

To her shock, Richard cradled her head in his hands. His thumbs brushed the tears from her cheeks.

"Hear me out, sweetheart. The Crown would confiscate Graymoor and my money as the property of a traitor, but not your trust. I told Fothery to petition for the estate after my death so that it would stay with Glory's family." Bethany wept harder and he pulled her against his shoulder. "I ordered Leafley to transfer my funds into your trust. I was going to ask you to provide for Glory out of my share, but all else was—is—yours." He spoke dryly. "I do hope you enjoy the irony of all this, my dear."

She gulped and drew out her handkerchief to blot her wet face. When she stepped back, he regarded her with a puzzled expression.

"I'll tell Leafley to put your share back immediately." She crossed to the door. "Then I'll leave. You'll never have to set eyes on me again if you don't wish to."

He followed her, touching her hand where it rested on the knob. His fingertips traced the fragile bones under her skin. She caught her breath. Even this small caress sent a current of excitement through her body.

"Tell me something before you go, Beth." She waited, unmoving. "Tell me why, if you were so willing to entrust your person to my care, you could not do the same with your fortune."

"The money never mattered, Richard." She left the door and paced back to the center of the room. "I spent my entire life in the shadow of a fortune I would never be allowed to touch.

"I was seven when I became aware of its existence. One of the neighboring families came to visit with their son, a boy my age. We were playing in the garden when I fell and scraped my hand. He bound it up in a kerchief for me. When I thanked him, he told me his father ordered him to be nice to me, for we might suit and I would bring a fortune to him."

"What a disgusting brat! At least I waited to adulthood." She brushed Richard's indignant comment aside.

"'Tis not the point. I was thrilled with the discovery. That night at supper, I started to tell my mother all the things I would do with my money when I grew up." She shrugged.

"Childish stuff, you know. I wanted to build a home for stray dogs and give the poor dinner every day, and buy chapbooks for all their children."

Richard remained by the door, arms crossed, but he listened attentively.

"Mother stopped me short. She told me my husband would decide what to do with my money, for it would all belong to him as soon as I married. I confess I did not believe her, for how could

something so obviously unfair be permitted?" She
smiled bitterly.

"I later learned that my opinion verged on sac-
rilege." She paced. "When Mother announced
that I would wed Mr. Ilkston, I was aghast. He possesses a harsh nature and I loathed his inability
to show kindness or understanding to others."
She turned to her husband.

"Then you came. I knew you were charming
and handsome, but little else. I didn't want the
money so much as I wanted safety, and the use of
my own judgment. I would never wish you dead."

Chapter 13

Richard said nothing for a long while after she had finished. Finally, he nodded. "It does seem strange to hear a woman say so, when I was raised to protect and cherish them. 'Tis something one would expect a man to say," he mused. His glance swept over her figure as he smiled slowly. "But you are most certainly all a woman."

He approached her and caught her hands. Bringing the palms to his lips, he kissed first one, then the other. The warm pressure of his lips set Bethany's pulse beating faster. It had been so long since he had touched her. Nor had she ever seen that expression of longing on his face.

"Could we start again?"

No, her mind screamed, warning her of the disastrous consequences of giving her heart to a rake.

Too late, her heart replied as she stepped into his open arms and gave him a searing kiss.

He responded fervently, searching her mouth as if he would draw out her very soul. She twined her arms around his neck to pull him closer, brokenly whispering his name.

They both jumped when the footman's voice sounded beyond the closed door.

"Milady, the coach is here. Shall I bid it wait for you?"

Richard stepped back a few paces, making it clear that the decision was hers. She looked at him, remembering the scene in the council chamber even as her body hummed from his touch. A sensible woman would ignore the fire running through her veins and leave before she was burnt to a cinder.

"Milady?" As the footman spoke again, her gaze locked on her husband's face. She tried to discern whether the passion he felt for her this moment would last or not. In the end, she pleased herself.

"Dismiss it." Instantly Richard enveloped her in his arms, his hands and mouth moving desperately over her body and face. She prayed she had made the right decision even as her hand caressed the back of his neck.

They undressed one another, taking turns removing articles of clothing, until their clothes surrounded them in a pile. He took great care not to disturb her bandages, asking if they should continue.

"Oh, yes, Rickon." He kissed her mouth, then sank to his knees to carefully brush his lips over the strips of cloth. A smile played over his full lips as he looked up at her. She chuckled even as she blushed a little under his avid inspection.

"What?" Rising smoothly to his feet, he circled behind her and she felt the tug as he removed the first pin holding her hair in place. Others followed quickly, landing on the wooden planks under their feet with light ringing sounds.

"Our clothing does have a habit of ending up in a heap on the floor." A breathy laugh escaped her as Richard buried his face in her newly freed tresses. "What is it about my hair?"

"'Tis like silken fire, warm and soft at the same time." His breath blew hot against her ear. "I love knowing I am the only man to see it flowing down over your breasts and back." He reached around to lift her breasts, rolling the sensitive peaks to stiff attention before grasping her hips and pulling her back against him. She gasped at the feel of his manhood against the small of her back.

"Growing up, most people acted like I had horns when they saw it. Mother forbade me to expose it." She emitted a whimper as he gently took an earlobe in his teeth. "Dear God, that feels good."

With an aroused growl, he turned her to face him and rained kisses across her forehead, eyes, and cheeks. Eyes closed, she ran her hands over his shoulders and down his back, fascinated at the feel of the different muscles as they bunched and relaxed under his smooth skin.

Daring, she grasped his rocklike buttocks and pulled him closer, glorying in the feel of his heated erection against her bare skin. Richard groaned and thrust himself against her as if he could not help himself.

"Wait, sweet. I would love you as gently as you deserve." She touched the side of his face, and he opened his eyes. The green depths glowed, stealing her breath.

"How would you make love to me, Rickon? If 'twas all for your own pleasure?" The arrested look on his face told her no one had asked this of him before. Guilty color flooded his cheeks. Intrigued, she squeezed his hips and rolled her pelvis against him. "Tell me."

"You've been hurt, sweetheart." He sucked in his breath at the feel of her body and rested his forehead against hers, panting as if he had just run a race.

His hesitance to tell her his desire alarmed her a little. But he had come to her arms, not Frances Shadbourne's, and she feared she would be given only this one chance to win him back to her. She framed his face in her hands.

"If I was your mistress, not your wife, what would you have me do now? If I do not wish to, I shall say so."

He swallowed and wet his lips.

"I want you to ride me hard and fast until you scream my name when you climax."

His honeyed voice entered her ear and seemed to flow down to pool between her thighs. Her skin tingled where he stroked over it, alternating his palms and knuckles. She placed her arms around Richard's neck and looked up at him uncertainly.

"Is that even possible?"

"Indeed it is, love." He drew her to the bed and pulled her to sit beside him, nuzzling her neck and caressing her body. Stretching out to his full length on the soft feather mattress, he coaxed her to straddle him, letting his hands slide over her thighs and up her body. Her nipples puckered as he brushed the soft undersides of her breasts. He circled them with his thumbs, then leaned forward to suckle one coral peak. Panting, she raked her hands through his soft hair, gazing at the strands of honey mingled with lighter wheat-colored highlights.

"I'm not hurting you, am I, Beth?"

She could only shake her head breathlessly. He turned his attention to her other breast, while his hand slid to the curls covering the tender mound between her legs. Searching through them, his fingers spread her moist folds open and teased the small nub that controlled her passion. His member pressed intimately against her, hot and hard. Finally she could stand it no longer.

"I want you inside me, Rickon." His hands tightened on her hips as she guided herself onto him. A gasp caught in the back of her throat at the amazing sensation of being filled from below. She rocked against him, sliding up and down on his shaft. He urged her on, praising her beauty as he caressed her with hands and mouth.

They moved together faster and faster as their climax built to dizzying heights. Crying out, she exploded around him, her back arched in ecstasy.

He held her firmly against him as he ground upward, his teeth gritted and eyes shut as he erupted into her.

Sweating, shaking, she collapsed onto him, unable to do anything for long minutes except listen to his heart thundering in rhythm with her own.

"You're all right, sweetheart? I didn't hurt you?" She stirred only when Richard's question vibrated in her ear.

"No, love, I'm not hurt. 'Twas the veriest scratch, I hardly feel it." She raised her head slightly. At her gasp, he opened his eyes. "I fear you must be the one in pain."

Both his shoulders carried red marks where she had dug her nails into his flesh. Horrified, Bethany begged his forgiveness, only to be cut short as he pulled her back into his embrace.

"You didn't mean to, Beth, 'tis no matter." His chest shook with laughter under her. "Besides, 'tis a great satisfaction to know I can induce my lady wife to act the wanton."

"Truly?" Her fingers explored the soft hairs peppering his chest. "I was taught that a wife should display modesty and decorum at all times."

"So you do. Except when you lose that temper of yours." He grinned and caught her hand before she could swat him. He kissed it. "A man likes to feel desired in his bed as much as a woman. And so you do that for me, Beth." He cuddled her close.

Curled up next to him, she considered his words for a long time.

* * *

Bethany jerked awake as the coach hit a pothole. Dreams of her last night with Richard intruded on her peace of mind waking and sleeping.

They had dozed on and off through the rest of the afternoon, rousing only to take the dinner that Bethany ordered brought to their room on a tray. They made love again afterward, leisurely exploring one another. When they fell asleep for the night, Bethany thought her heart overflowed with joy.

She awakened early the next morning. They had not bothered to draw the bed curtains closed, and she watched him as he slept soundly beside her. With his hair falling into his face, smiling a little, he looked younger and somehow more vulnerable.

She slid out of bed and pulled the curtains closed to prevent the growing light from awaking him. Her skin prickled in the chill morning air as she bent to pick up their clothes from where they had fallen the day before. Her spare chemise was packed, but she borrowed one from the store Lady Rothley kept on hand in the house. She could order a replacement from the linen draper's easily enough. She would have to order a few dresses as well, for the saddle packs could hold only one.

She picked up the sage green gown and laid it over a chair before gathering Richard's clothes. As she picked up Richard's coat, she felt a slight weight in one pocket. Biting her lip, she recalled his mistress giving him something the day before. Summoning all her resolution, she placed the embroidered garment over the back of the chair and left it.

Where the coat had lain on the floor, a small piece of paper sat, unsealed. Meaning only to set it on the dressing table, she picked it up as if handling a poisonous snake. It fell open as she grasped it between thumb and forefinger, exposing his handwriting. It fluttered to the floor seconds later, as Bethany doubled over, hands clamped to her mouth.

Clearly written in her husband's flowing hand, it declared in unmistakable terms his devotion to Mistress Shadbourne.

She stared unseeing at the slow-moving scenery beyond the coach window. The fields and hedgerows looked much the same as they had that morning and the day before. She wondered if she would ever travel the long route to Yorkshire in a state of content.

At night, she had taken to ordering a bottle of any available spirits to her chamber so that she could drink her way to oblivion.

His betrayal would not have hurt so much had he not bedded her so passionately the night before. She unsuccessfully fought back a sob. Of course he had come to her; her testimony had convinced the King to pardon him. But 'twas no more than gratitude, however much they pleased each other's bodies. The thought that he aroused so intense a response in her when he felt so little himself nearly made her ill.

The only sop to her pride came from the knowledge that she had not spoken of the letter of apology she had burnt. At least she had not suffered the humiliation of begging forgiveness from a man who thought so little of her.

Where anger had sustained her the first time she left London, now she experienced suffocating grief. She had lost her husband as surely as if the court had found him guilty and executed him.

Her weeping turned to painful laughter in the empty coach. In order to lose Rickon, she would have had to possess him in the first place. As his letter had demonstrated with painful clarity, she had never had a hold on his heart.

Glory alternated between effervescence and moping as the month before the wedding passed. Bethany kept her own misery locked in her breast as she coped with the girl's moods. Mastering her own emotions proved difficult in the face of her sister-in-law's changing sentiments.

She suffered from envy whenever she saw Fothery and Gloriana. Not for the elaborate wedding plans expected by the blissful couple and by Lady Rothley. Richard's aunt responded to the news of the impending nuptials with a letter of epic length detailing a number of traditions and recipes expected at Harcourt marriages.

Bethany, used to the sober weddings of her mother's congregation, thought most of the suggestions shamelessly extravagant, and even Glory vetoed several of them. Both wrote tactful replies citing Graymoor's unfinished state as the reason for declining to follow all of her directives.

Instead, jealousy threatened her equilibrium when she saw the joy the betrothed couple experienced while engaging in activities as simple as walking in the gardens or softly discussing names for their unborn children. At those moments, she reminded herself of the rarity of love matches and tried to join their happy banter.

On the rare days when Fothery did not visit and lift her spirits, Glory fretted for her brother. Bethany comforted the girl as best she could, but as the days passed without any word from him, his sister wondered if Richard had indeed washed his hands of her. She assured the girl that Richard might disapprove of her careless behavior, but he would never cast her off.

Two weeks before the wedding, a rider from London arrived in the courtyard, handing over a brief missive addressed to Glory. The housekeeper brought it to her in the Great Chamber, where she and Bethany stood discussing the number of guests the room might hold.

His Majesty, having pardoned Richard, had requested his presence at the coronation.

"'Tis a great honor, and so public an appearance will restore his name in the eyes of the world. But that is April twenty-third, and we are getting married on the twenty-seventh." Glory's hand trembled as she sought Bethany's eyes. "How can he possibly travel from London in time?" She choked back tears.

Struggling with her own blighted hopes, Bethany looked at the letter longingly. By rights, she should have received the letter from Richard. It was a measure of her husband's disgust with her that he had written to Glory instead.

She drew the sobbing girl to a bench against the wall. As her sister-in-law wept onto her shoulder, she stared unseeing out the windows. Even the sun shining on the burgeoning garden below failed to cheer her. She swallowed a lump in her own throat.

They had parted so badly in London. Despite her fury at his flaunting of his mistress before her very eyes, she had believed his sister's wedding would bring him to Graymoor. And then what, her mind taunted her.

If he wanted a legitimate heir, she knew he would have to return to her bed, but the idea that he would touch her only out of dynastic duty wounded her beyond words. And yet she wanted to show him the improvements she had written of, to show him how well she could care for him and his.

She yearned to start over, to apologize to him and tell him she loved him. Doing so, she feared, would merely earn his contempt. Nay, she had fallen in love with a rakehell and the idea of winning his heart in return would remain no more than a dream.

* * *

She could not bring herself to confide in Glory. To keep her thoughts from eating at her soul, she buried herself in wedding plans and managing the household, supervising all from the dilapidated room near the head of the kitchen stairs. Glory, perhaps for similar reasons, proved more than willing to assist her.

Only in the loneliness of the great bed within the master's chamber did Bethany give in to her despair, weeping bitterly and sleeping fitfully as the nights crawled by.

The days, however, flowed past as rapidly as the freshets springing to life on the green downs beyond the estate. First it was a week before the wedding, then the day before.

The Rothleys, as the only living relatives of Richard and Glory, planned an extended visit. Glory dreaded her aunt's scolding at the circumstances of her marriage, but Bethany welcomed another reason to wall off her emotions. Besides, in Richard's absence, Uncle Rothley could give away the bride. They did not arrive until noon the day before, delayed by muddy roads.

Having given up the master's chamber for them, Bethany urged the older couple to rest until dinner. Lady Rothley accepted with alacrity, complaining of a headache from the rough ride and unseasonable warmth. Although heavy clouds had covered the sun by then, the heat did feel oppressive for spring. Bethany perspired even in her loose muslin gown.

Completely sympathetic to her new aunt's woes, she turned her over to Glory and sent for hartshorn and lavender water. Her sister-in-law descended to the hall shortly afterward, disclosing that her ladyship had fallen asleep.

His lordship's more vigorous constitution needed only a good dinner to restore him, and he took a great interest in the repairs under way in the house. He demonstrated an inclination to ask for detailed information about most of them, nearly driving his niece by marriage to distraction as she tried to supervise the decoration of the Great Hall.

Mr. Quintan, whose workmen received an unexpected holiday when she forbade any activities not directly related to the wedding, rescued her. Offering to provide his lordship with any information he required, he bore the curious peer away.

Lord Rothley had to content himself with examining the interior of the house, for not two hours past dinnertime, a lightning strike and a clap of thunder presaged a steady downpour that bade fair to last into the next day.

Fortunately, the household had kept an eye on the increasing clouds and gotten everything needed for the morrow under cover beforehand. Inside, preparations continued.

Bethany had reserved the best of the remaining hangings for the Great Chamber on the floor above, and set Glory to work arranging them on the walls. That enabled her to oversee the preparation of the Great Hall on the ground floor during the rainy afternoon, while keeping the bride-to-be from mooning about under everyone's feet.

Carpenters working to Mr. Quintan's design erected frames to hold vines of ivy intertwined with flowers, while his masons and the footmen laid out trestle tables along one wall and hoisted barrels of ale onto them. Plenty of space remained for the platters of food for both the Graymoor tenants and the iterant jobbers working on the repairs, who would celebrate in the Hall. The smaller number of friends and relatives would enjoy more refined food and drink in the freshly decorated Great Chamber upstairs.

For once, relative peace ensued between the staff and the workmen, thanks to the assistance rendered by the latter. Mistress Platt contributed to the pleasant atmosphere by sending up plates of dainties that failed to meet her discriminating eye. The savory scent of beef and pork pasties mingled with the woodsy odor of sawdust as maids, footmen, carpenters, lime burners, and masons alike shared the cook's mouthwatering discards.

She even slipped an overbrowned venison pasty to Mr. Quintan, a singular sign of favor, in thanks for the neat array of shelves and the enlarged kitchen fireplace with its new chimney.

Just before suppertime, Bethany stood in the center of the flagstone floor and looked about her. They had finished all that could be completed ahead of the day. After praising everyone lavishly, she added to the festive air by ordering a barrel of ale broached, informing them that they had to ensure Mistress Harcourt's health was toasted with a proper brew.

Afterward, having decreed the Hall and Great Chamber alike off-limits to anyone not actually working in them, she sank onto a cushioned chair in the parlour. Glory sat on one opposite. Between stood a table holding their supper, a simple affair of bread, cheese, and more ale from the newly opened cask.

Truth to tell, the small room felt pleasantly cozy. Bethany had ordered fires lit to keep off the chill and damp, and the dull clouds darkened the skies so, candles burned already to give light. They settled in to make a hearty meal of the crumbly blue-veined cheese and fresh bread when a man's voice sounded from the Hall beyond.

"Is there room for a third place?"

Glory's shriek of joy threatened to shatter the windowpanes as she scrambled to greet the newcomer. Behind her, Bethany jumped to her feet, but remained by her chair, clutching its back for support. Richard stood in the doorway, dripping water from his long cloak and tracking mud from his caked boots all over the floor.

Her heart pounded. At last he had come. Only for Glory's wedding, she supposed, but he would finally see the careful repair work she had written of, and perhaps he would respond to the care she had lavished on the home she wished so desperately to share with him.

He smiled fondly down at his sister as she exclaimed her delight at seeing him. Bethany's feet came unglued from the floor and she moved toward him, a greeting on her own lips. It faded as he stared at her resentfully over Glory's head.

She felt her face fix itself into a neutral mask. Jerking her chin toward the excited girl, she stepped forward.

"Let me take your wet things." Understanding that she did not want to quarrel in front of his sister, he suffered her to remove his sopping cloak and spread it over a chair near the fireplace. He seated himself and tugged at his tight-fitting boots until they came off. By the time he completed the process, she had had time to summon a maid to mop the Hall.

Seeing his valet hovering outside the parlor door, she ordered the man to clean and dry the cloak and boots, and to get himself a hot supper from the kitchen after sending up something for his lordship. When the maid returned with a tankard and a covered dish containing only a helping of roasted fish, more bread and cheese, and some greens, she silently dared Richard to complain.

"With so much to prepare for tomorrow, I told Cook not to bother with anything but the simplest evening meal for us." Richard, inhaling the herb-scented fish with closed eyes, unbent enough to assure her that it suited him well.

"I collect you managed to get the kitchen in order, at any rate." On that querulous note, the two of them finished supper to the sound of Glory's chatter, barely speaking to each other.

Once the covers had been removed, Bethany watched him out of the corner of one eye as she and Gloriana reviewed the morrow's plans. His face remained impassive as he sat and stretched his legs out to warm his feet on the hearth. The bride thought of several details she feared they had overlooked, and Bethany mustered all her patience in replying to her sister-in-law's queries.

Yes, they had hired plenty of extra staff from the village, she informed her. Mistress Pratt had the feast well in hand. And both wine for the honored guests and ale for the tenants had arrived in time, and the stable hands had indeed cleaned and polished the coaches before the rainstorm. At last Gloriana stopped fidgeting and, to Bethany's profound relief, announced she wished to retire early.

"I wish to be in looks tomorrow morning, after all!" The girl kissed Bethany's cheek affectionately. "Forgive me for teasing you so, dearest. Indeed, I am sure all will be perfect. Thank you a thousand times over for arranging everything! You have stood as both sister and mother to me over the last month."

She shifted nervously at Glory's encomium. Richard's face darkened at his sister's words, but he remained silent. The praise did please her, but she sought to lighten his mood in her reply.

"'Twill be perfect if this rain stops. Have no fear, my love, if it does not, we shall manage one way or another."

Glory laughed. "It will be perfect even if we have a veritable gale. I am to marry my Fothery!"

Bethany could not help smiling back. Sure the girl would not settle down easily in her excited state, she offered to send some spiced cider to her room. Accepting thankfully, Gloriana danced over to wish her brother a good night.

Bethany shook her head as she rang the bell-pull. She doubted an entire gallon of the potent stuff would send her volatile sister-in-law off to sleep this eve.

Richard escorted his sister out of the room as Bethany waited for a servant to answer her summons. Through the open door, she heard her thank him rapturously for arriving in time to give her away.

"Faith, Glory, you're all the family I have! Not even the King himself could stop me." Her heart ached as she remembered times early in their marriage when he had spoken so tenderly to her. Glory's reply was lost in the depths of the Hall as they moved away from the study door.

Guiltily, she peeked through the doorway in time to see him kiss her cheek and hand her a candle. Before she could duck back inside, the cook's boy appeared from belowstairs. She softly ordered Glory's cider, unwilling to interrupt the two of them.

Richard waited for the boy to disappear before approaching her. He grimly pointed into the room.

"I would speak with you." She licked her lips. The gentleness left his voice, replaced with steely resolve.

She followed him into the small study, stifling a

sigh. No sooner had the door closed behind her than he whirled to face her.

"What 'improvements,' exactly, have you made, madam?" He paced the floor as he railed at her. "I walked through the entire house before I entered the hall! Even more of the walls are gone than on my last visit, the hallways on the upper floors are nearly untouched by hammer or paint, while my stable—what in God's name have you done to my stable?" He pointed out the window, although this room faced the opposite side of the house from the courtyard. "It looks like it dropped from Covent Garden!"

"Why, my lord, are the repairs not to your liking?" Finding her voice, Bethany planted herself in front of him. "You packed me off from London and asked—nay, ordered—me to repair your house, then refused to answer my letters asking your opinion or instructions. The work I've contracted for is costing three thousand pounds of my half of our money! If you do not like the manner in which it is being rebuilt, I suggest you take some interest in it instead of spending your days fornicating with your mistress!"

"What?" Richard's voice was awful in its anger. Equally horrified, Bethany wanted to sink into the floor at this revelation of her weakness. She tried to distract him.

"I delayed the repairs as long as I could." She spoke airily, trying to sound confident. "If we waited on your instructions, we would have lost the entire spring's work and doubtless the summer's as well! And as long as you were traipsing through the house, you could have had the decency to remove your boots before tracking mud all over."

"My feet were cold and I don't give a damn about the floors!" Richard returned to her last accusation. "For your information, the scene you witnessed after my release was arranged for both our benefits by Arthur Loring." He stood nearly nose to nose with her now, although he continued to shout.

"I had not been involved with Frances for months before we married, nor have I been involved with her or any other woman since." He turned his back to her and flung himself over to the window. Silence fell as he remained there, apparently transfixed by the rain pelting against the panes.

Bethany's mind reeled at the admission. The thought of his infidelity had eaten at her for weeks. She would give her half of their fortune to believe that he might love her, too, and that she had only imagined his concern for Frances Shadbourne.

Common sense raised its head then. However unintentionally, she had read his letter. However much she might try to please him in bed, or by running his household, she remained nothing more than the wife he had married for money.

She drew a shaky breath. She was mistress of Graymoor; she would not break down where any of the servants could see her and gossip the news that Lady Harcourt had fallen in love with its lord.

"You want only to placate me so I do not inconvenience you with jealous scenes." He turned around at her bald words and opened his mouth to refute her, but she would not let him. "I would think, my lord, that you might have written me this explanation of yours weeks ago. But then, the excuse just now occurred to you, did it not?"

He looked taken aback, but recovered quickly. "Do not accuse me of prevaricating. I read enough of your letters to grasp the plans you claimed you would carry out." He smiled contemptuously. "Unfortunately, dear wife, the first thing I did after arriving at Graymoor last year was obtain any number of estimates, which I still have. While they were beyond my means at the time, I assure you they are well below your three thousand pounds." He gave her a hard look.

"You have done nothing but hide the truth from me since we've met, Beth." He no longer shouted, sounding saddened more than anything else. She started to defend herself, but he held up a hand. "I know, I leaped to the wrong conclusion about you and Tom, but my apology was apparently unacceptable to you." He sighed heavily.

"Which brings us back to my point. You've spent three thousand pounds? On what? Not on materials or labor, that I know well." He laughed, a harsh bark of sound in the small room. "Do you support a lover here? Do you avenge yourself on me in that way?"

Chapter 14

His crude suggestion hit her as hard as if he had physically struck her. A wave of cold hard anger such as she had never before experienced enveloped her. A moment before, she had been prepared to justify every penny she'd spent, to plead with him for understanding. Now, she would be damned if she would give him one word of explanation.

As the rushing faded from her ears, she realized he repeated a question.

"Well, madam? What have you to say for yourself?"

"Evidently you are tired after a long and wet ride, my lord." Bethany remained composed, if shaken. "I suggest you sit by the fire and drink a brandy to warm yourself." Her ice-filled gaze swept over him. "One of the servants can take your cloak. I shall send word when the great bed-chamber is prepared. In the meantime, I wish you a good night."

* * *

Without another word, she slammed the door shut behind her. When a maid entered a few minutes later, he heard her in the hall speaking in a voice too low to be heard. He caught only the "Yes, milady" and "No, milady" of the replies.

True to her word, she did not return to the hall that night. After drinking nearly half the brandy bottle, Richard wandered off to bed.

As he had suspected, she'd put him in the second-best bedchamber. His valet dozed in a chair before a small fire, his feet resting comfortably on the hearth. At the sound of the closing door, he sat up and rubbed his eyes blearily. As soon as he realized Richard had entered, the man jumped up, ready to help him out of his clothes.

Waiting for him to gather the damp clothing for cleaning and pressing, along with his muddy boots, Richard prowled the room.

Part of the walls had been stripped of their paneling. The gray stone stood out against the darker wood overlay like light scars on a man's skin.

He held his candle up to inspect a water stain on the ceiling. To his relief, nothing leaked through the roof tonight. He hoped his wife had at least arranged to have the roof repaired. He supposed he should be thankful she had cleaned it and replaced the broken furniture. And the room no longer reeked of must.

The valet bowed and left, expressing his own approval of the clean and dry servants' quarters.

Richard lifted the bed hangings to examine them in the firelight. They looked and smelled cleaner than the last time he'd visited, but several tears marred them.

The sheets felt new as he crawled into bed, and blessedly warm against the chilly night. He made a mental note to tip the servant who had remembered to use a warming pan.

Memories of Bethany's warm body stirred his own. He berated himself for wanting her still. Even if she had not played him false, she had deceived him yet again. He shifted uncomfortably, damning the soft skin and blazing hair that made all other women pale in comparison.

Another blast of wind and rain whistled outside, followed by the blue glare of distant lightning. He jerked the ragged curtains shut and pummeled his pillow in frustration. For a long time, he stared upward as the carved wooden canopy above him flashed dimly in and out of sight as another thunderstorm came through the valley.

Strangely, an unfamiliar silence startled Richard into wakefulness the next morning. Instead of the peddlars' cries and clop of hooves against the cobblestones, only the muffled voices and footfalls of the servants greeted his ears. He opened his eyes as the squeak of his door cut across their muted bustle.

He heard the metallic clatter of pewter against wood, and the fragrance of fresh-brewed coffee seeped through the closed woolen bed hangings. Evidently his wife did not deny herself the small luxuries of life, he thought. No, that was not right. Her preference for chocolate or the newfangled tea sprang to his mind, but he could not believe she kept a store of coffee on hand for his benefit.

A rattling beyond the bed followed by a "whoosh" and a current of cool, earthy air indicated that someone, contrary to all common sense, had opened a window. Sticking his head out of the curtains, he started to upbraid the serving girl. The startled creature told him apologetically that her ladyship ordered them opened every morning.

"I weren't told otherwise, sir." Despite an inclination to wring her raw-boned hands in her apron, the girl looked at him in shy curiosity. "Be ye his lordship, then?" At his grumbled assent, she beamed at him. "Bid ye welcome, sir. I'm Annie Beckins, and my mam were Old Bet what worked in the laundry before. Her ladyship took me into the house for all that—"

Fearing an extended review of Annie's connection with his family, he assured her that he remembered both her mother and her father, who had worked in the stables. Elated at such recognition, she flushed and produced a spasm intended as a curtsey.

"Do you go look about then, me lord. Her ladyship's doing right good putting the hall back together." She crossed to the door, but Richard stopped her.

"Annie, who is the bailiff?" She screwed up her face in thought before she answered.

"Well, her ladyship says as how she don't like to hire one without you knowing him, so she tots up the accounts. By herself!" The amazement in the maid's eyes showed her awe at such cleverness. "But Mr. Quintan overlooks the rebuilding for her."

Asking the maid to give a message to the overseer, he dressed and breakfasted before meeting him in the Great Hall. The builder's cheerful manner wilted under Richard's grim questioning. In the face of his disbelief, the older man finally offered to show him the repairs made on Graymoor.

As he followed the irritated overseer, Richard looked around him, bewildered. He walked through rooms he had last seen littered with debris, some charred by fire. Now new paneling and freshly plastered walls lined them. He listened with growing shame as Quintan described the slowness necessary in rebuilding the ruined southwest corner of the house.

"When Miss Harcourt started planning her wedding, Lady Harcourt directed us to work on the Great Hall and the terrace. But the plans are drawn up for all the repairs." Tipping his hat at him, the overseer left Richard alone with his thoughts.

He frowned. His wife had organized much more work than he had seen the previous evening. But he had learned painfully well how much the materials and wages would cost to repair his home. During their quarrel the night before, she claimed she had spent far more than that amount.

Entering the kitchen in hopes of sneaking up the back staircase only plunged him into the organized madness of wedding preparations. The staff stopped their activity to curtsey as soon as they noticed his presence, and the mistress invited him to take a trencher and enjoy it elsewhere. Interpreting her unenthusiastic offer as a wish for him to get out from underfoot, he refused it and departed upstairs to his room.

His footsteps echoed on the stone steps. This end of the house had suffered depredations as well, and the long hallway on the floor above stretched before him, shabby with neglect. Through the windows on his right, he could see the sharp rise of the downs to the north. Opposite lay a series of doors, closed now, but once leading into the bedchambers he and Glory had used as children.

He had walked through them the first time he had returned, his heart nearly breaking at their ruined state. Curious, he turned the handle to his old room.

To his surprise, it showed signs of habitation. A worn but clean crimson bedcover lay on the old bed, contrasting with the scratches and initials gouged into the carved wooden posts and head. The only other furniture in the room, a writing table and chair, sat near the fireplace.

His footsteps on the wooden floor echoed as he crossed to the table. A pile of account books sat neatly arranged on one corner. Flipping the top one open revealed a column of figures on the right. A corresponding description of each expenditure filled the left side. He stared down at the pages, mentally adding the figures.

They represented a tremendous list of household goods: linens, hangings, pots, roasting spits. He leafed through the slim volume. Page after page of records appeared. One notebook itemized purchases for the house, another for the stables. Others enumerated spending on wages for the house's repairs and other farm labor. With a shock, he recognized the hand as Bethany's.

Why had she not told him of all her work, he wondered. The answer came to him quickly enough. He had misjudged her once again.

He remembered his outburst the night before, accusing her of laziness and greed. How like the prideful vixen to respond by refusing to account for all her work over the last weeks. Sighing heavily, he found he could not blame her.

"What are you doing here?" He whirled to find her standing in the doorway, nearly engulfed by an armful of yellow satin. As she entered, the bright morning light threw her fair skin into delicate relief against the rich material. He was reminded sharply of the first time he had seen her with her hair down at the Bell and Moon. He cleared his throat.

"This is my old room." His eyes soaked in her bright hair as she lay the material down on the bed. He remembered all the times he had buried his face in the silken mass during their lovemaking. She faced him, her gray eyes as cool as her voice.

"Ah. I was not aware of that." She gestured to the bed. "I slept here last night, as most of the chambers are, as you said, uninhabitable."

"Bethany, I spoke out of tiredness last night." He stepped toward her, but her stiffening posture stopped him.

"It is no more than the truth." He hated the dispassionate tones, so unlike her dry wit. "Forgive me, but we must leave soon and neither of us are dressed. If you will excuse me, my lord, Faith will be up to attend to me momentarily."

He tried to speak to her again, but she made a show of spreading the skirts of the gown out and would not look at him. He bowed.

"Very well, Bethany. Until later."

Gloriana and Sir Fothery were married in the square-towered church where she had been christened. The bride wore azure satin and carried a bouquet of lilacs from the Harcourt gardens. She welcomed Bethany's offer of the aquamarine and pearl set until a servant came to her room with a set of pearl necklet, earrings, and bracelets. A tender note from Sir Fothery accompanied his bride gift to her.

Glory did not show anyone the note, but its contents touched her deeply enough that the pearls lay to one side, quite neglected, for near a quarter of an hour. Finally adorning herself with them, the girl insisted Bethany wear her own jewels.

"Richard will be vastly pleased, my love. And

they will look charming with your dress!" Bethany complied rather than admit how little her husband cared for her. Later, watching him walk his sister up the aisle of worn stone, she privately considered the joy shining from the bride's eyes added more to her beauty than any finery.

"You look very pretty this day, wife." The murmured compliment barely reached her ears as he joined her in the front pew. Keeping her composure, she nodded. When she realized he noticed her jewels, she regretted giving in to Glory. Likely he would take it as another attempt to soften his anger toward her, and treat it with the same contempt as her efforts to repair Graymoor.

It did not aid her peace of mind that he looked devastating in the bronze and cream coat and pantaloons he had worn to Whitehall.

To her relief, he held her arm all the way to their coach after the ceremony. At least he did not embarrass her in front of his friends. As Fothery and Gloriana tossed handfuls of coins from the steps of their coach, Richard gave Lane the signal to leave.

The only sounds in the coach were the thud of hooves and an occasional creak until the road crested the rise of the small valley. As the coach slowly descended, she watched Rickon as he looked out the window. She could not see his face, but when he froze and softly inhaled, she winced. She had ruined his home; he would never forgive her.

She opened them again at the touch of his

hand on hers. He had turned back and now struggled for words beside her.

"I am astonished." He drew his hand back as he regarded her soberly. "I had no idea how much you had accomplished, or the care you had taken."

"You should have read my letters." She stared straight ahead, proud that she could remain dry-eyed. The coach lurched over a rough spot; she thought the noise might just cover the crack of her breaking heart.

"I stopped after a while." She had to strain to hear his nearly inaudible voice. "All you ever wrote of was the house, or Gloriana. They sounded as personal as progress reports from my bailiff. They didn't even sound like you."

"Why would I think you wanted to hear aught else from me, my lord?" She pounded her knees in frustration, unable to stifle her bitterness any longer. "You told me to leave you and make myself useful at your estate. I tried to the best of my ability."

"And you've done well. I was wrong. I walked over the house this morning while Quintan told me of the improvements you've made." His voice filled with anguish. "I thought you'd write me an explanation, or a denial. I half expected you to throw something at my head and not leave at all."

"It seems we've been at cross-purposes then." The tears now threatened to spill down her cheeks. To hide them, she looked out her window. Graymoor loomed larger and larger as they drove into the forecourt. "Forgive me for not better grasping your expectations."

The coach finally jerked to a halt. To preserve her calm, she thrust the door open and scrambled down with the assistance of a surprised footman. She thought she heard Richard speak her name as she rushed up the steps into the Great Hall, but she did not wait to find out.

Soon she immersed herself in the role of hostess to the well-wishers invited to celebrate with Glory and Sir Fothery. She pasted a bright smile on her face and bade her guests eat, or drink, or dance. After the toast from a great vat of wine, everyone turned to their own devices and she escaped the mirth and music.

Richard missed his wife among the crowd milling about his restored home. It took several inquiries, but at last he found a servant capable of disclosing her ladyship's whereabouts.

The noise of merrymaking faded behind him as he stole away from the loggia and crossed the terrace. The sun shone warm on his bare head as he looked about. A lump rose in his throat as he took in the repaired walls and the newly planted gardens.

Even their immense fortune could not disguise all the damage caused by so many years of neglect. Bethany had healed the hurts as best she could, but the house would bear visible scars as long as it stood. A sad smile curved his lips as he considered the new wing. He fancied he could hear his parents commenting on it. His mother would approve the updated style, and she would have brought his father around to her view.

A high wall of Elizabethan brick arose before him as he approached the end of the terrace. It, too, showed traces of repair work on its bare surface. Richard ran his fingers along the rough brick, old and new, remembering the thick ivy covering it had borne in his childhood. A soft laugh escaped him as he looked down. There, at his feet, a line of young ivy plants poked up from the soft dark earth, their tendrils reaching up as if to grab hold of the wall.

He walked around two sides of the squared enclosure until he reached the door. The heavy oak planks grated on their hinges as he pushed it open and stopped dead on the threshold.

"My God." He could scarcely breathe the words, so great was his amazement.

The last time he had walked in this spot, its neglected state had overwhelmed him so completely he could not bear to stay.

Now the walls surrounded three tidy concentric rectangles, each with a border of flowers behind a vibrant green strip of turf. A narrow walkway led from where he stood, carried down each level by flagstone steps and widening to form a circle around a small pond in the garden's center. From there, it rose again to a small arbor on the wall opposite the door.

A lump formed in his throat. His parents had

whiled away many an afternoon sitting in that exact spot.

Now the heady fragrance of flowers permeated the still air. Banks of them had been planted against the wall. Other scents floated around him, too. Lavender and sweet pea mixed with the pine-like aroma of rosemary and the earthiness of sage.

Bethany sat on a stone bench to one side of the pond, looking at him apprehensively as he walked down toward her. Her dress shimmered in contrast to her glowing redgold hair. She stood as he neared, twining a stem of lavender in her fingers.

He stopped a few feet away from her, barred from coming closer by the memory of their quarrels. He cleared his throat nervously.

"It's beautiful. All of it." He struggled to say more, desperate to bridge the gulf between them. "How could you tell what it was supposed to look like?" He listened in amazement as she described her discovery of his mother's diary and drawings.

"She spent hours here, especially in the summer. Some of my earliest memories are walking on the grass at her side." He stepped close to her, taking her hands in his and planting a kiss on each palm.

"You have done so much for me, sweet Beth." She would have pulled away then, but he gently drew her to him until his breath stirred the curls over her ears. "You have repaired my home and saved my life and honor." She shrugged, doubtless remembering his harsh treatment of her.

"My home, too." She kept her eyes averted. Unable to bear that she would not look at him, he lifted her chin with his knuckles. He stroked her silky skin, unable to resist its lure.

The small gesture seemed to undo her. A choked sob escaped from her as he enveloped her tenderly in his arms. As she tried unsuccessfully to stop crying, he held her against his shoulder, tears pricking his own eyes.

"Beth. Oh my Beth." His voice cracked as he broke away to graze her cheeks and eyes with his lips before kissing her full mouth. "I was so caught up in my curst pride, I refused to admit how much you mean to me." He rumbled the words between kisses.

Lifting his head to look into her tearstained face, he inhaled shakily as she brushed aside his own tears. "My sweet girl, can you ever forgive me?"

"I can't seem to help myself." She gave a laugh that turned into a hiccup. "How long shall I have you before you leave again?" He winced inwardly at her assumption that he would only stay by her side temporarily.

"If you still want me, you shall have me forever."

Bethany could not believe she heard aright. She forced another sob down. "Rickon, you have no obligation to stay by my side. And I would prefer that you not pretend to love me."

"Look at me." She forced herself to obey the command, praying her pain did not show. As soon as she turned to him, his manner changed to one of pleading.

"I am not trying to wheedle you or play a jest. Frances only ever wanted to use me for her own advantage."

"You said the same of me." She fixed her gaze on his jabot. A small breeze strayed into the garden and played with the lace as she spoke. "Mistress Shadbourne may be out of your favor, but I have no doubt any number of women are vying for her place."

"I already have a woman there. The one who has healed my home and my heart." Her gaze flew to his face at those words. She searched his expression intently, her heart pounding in hope.

"I love you, Bethany." Somehow his hands had found their way around her waist. His brilliant eyes looking down into hers, he said wistfully, "I'd like to believe that you put such care into rebuilding Graymoor because you might love me, too."

Overwhelmed at hearing the words she had longed for, she buried her face in his satin-covered shoulder. He would not have it, however, and held her at arm's length. "Tell me. I need to hear it from your own lips."

The dam holding her emotions back gave way. Tears threatened again as she wound her arms around his neck. "Oh, Rickon, I think I was lost to you by the time we arrived in London." She laughed bitterly. "I wanted the money so I would never have to depend on a man. Then I discovered that the thing I wanted most from you couldn't be bought."

"The words, vixen." He gave her a slight shake even as he smiled at her.

"I love you, Rickon." Then she gasped, for he swung her off her feet and around in a circle. Her feet barely landed on the flagstone path before he kissed her fiercely. She opened to him eagerly, tangling her hands in his honeyed locks to hold him to her.

He eventually lifted his mouth from hers, a grin lighting his face. "Only one thing remains to be done before I have truly fulfilled my father's wishes."

"Oh?" She mistrusted the mischief in his expression. "I rebuilt your home—"

He corrected her. "Our home. And you brought me love."

"I'd like to think we brought each other love." He kissed her again. Resuming the point of their conversation, she looked at him sternly.

"And I helped your sister plan a wedding so elaborate your military campaigns pale in comparison." She regarded him with mock sternness. "Just what have I missed, my lord?"

He crossed his arms and gave her a teasing glare back. "If I am to reestablish my family, I require an heir."

She raised her eyebrows. "The blame for that cannot be laid entirely at my door!"

He cocked his head. "Upon careful consideration, I believe you are correct, your ladyship. But I must insist that we remedy the matter at the earliest opportunity."

Bethany twined her arms around his neck. "Tonight, my love?"

His eyes turned deep green as he toyed with the delicate lace at her neckline. "Sooner, I think." Shivers ran down her spine at his husky whisper, but she drew back in disapproval.

"Richard Harcourt, you are not dragging me upstairs in front of a houseful of guests for a quick tumble!" Her heart turned over in her breast as his eyelids drooped to half-mast.

"As you wish, sweetheart." Despite his smoldering look, he tucked her hand into his elbow and they strolled up the steps toward the wall. His steps became more purposeful as he directed them to a secluded corner. She almost failed to notice the slight jerk when he tweaked her cap to the ground.

"Rickon, what are you about?" He confirmed her suspicions as his cravat followed the cap. She stopped dead. "Have you gone mad? Someone will see us!"

Keeping his gaze on her face, he stripped off his coat and let it fall.

"Are you even listening to me, you wretch?"

"No." The monosyllable was whispered against her neck. He kissed and nibbled until her knees went weak, but she managed to gasp one more protest.

"We shall get grass stains on our clothes."

"Not if we remove them first." He stopped her shriek of protest with his mouth.

"My love, we must get back to our guests." Bethany sighed regretfully from her place atop her husband's naked body. "Besides, I freckle dreadfully in the sun."

He chuckled and caressed her bare backside. "Most of them won't be visible." He rolled her over onto the fresh-smelling grass. "I hope you enjoy spending time here, for I want to see you again like this." His eyes glowed with love. "A beautiful wanton of my very own."

When they returned to the house, most of the merry-makers appeared to have overlooked their absence. Some people raised eyebrows and whispered behind their hands, but others smiled indulgently at them. As she circulated among the crowd on Richard's arm, she surreptitiously examined their appearances in the great mirrors hanging on the walls.

Assured that neither of them looked as if they had just come from a lewd romp in the gardens, she passed among their guests serenely. She and Richard paused briefly in their duties, just in time to overhear two elderly women conversing. One remarked on the happiness radiating from Lord Harcourt. Her companion dismissed such romantical notions.

"If I'd married twenty thousand in cash, I'd jest like that myself."

"Judging from the way he looks at her, I hazard he likes her for more than her money." The first speaker nudged the second. "I heard she's from a Roundhead family, and if you ask me, 'tis a mighty good thing. A sober modest woman will tame that family's wild streak."

Lord Harcourt could not stop laughing, even after his wife elbowed him in the ribs.

Keep reading for an exciting preview of
Ann Stephens's next historical romance,
coming soon from Zebra Books!

Tonight called for some act of rebellion, no matter how insignificant, against the role her family would force her into tomorrow. Diantha Quinn crept across the thick Aubusson carpet, her way lit by the lamp she carried.

The soft wool tickled her bare feet as the dancing light illuminated a room she had come to loathe. Swags of burgundy velvet draped the solid mahogany four-poster bed and the ornately carved mirror over the vanity. Combined with the gilding splashed on furniture and knickknacks, they lent the room an air both sumptuous and oppressive.

She picked up her quilted wrapper, uttering a small noise of distaste. Although her mother adored the garment's vivid apple green color, the shade gave her own skin a sickly cast.

The alternative of stepping out of her bedroom wearing only her nightgown did occur to her. She managed a small smile at the thought of

her family's collective horror should she do so.
However, considerations of modesty and good
breeding aside, chill drafts filled the halls of her
family's New York City mansion even in May. She
sighed and tied the corded sash around her waist.
After sliding her feet into an equally garish pair
of slippers, she approached her door and turned
the handle.

When she cracked it open, the footman drows-
ing against the corridor wall opposite startled to
attention. "Now miss, you know your father's
orders. You're to stay in your room till it's time for
you to dress tomorrow." The sympathy in his voice
did not stop him from taking a purposeful step
toward her.

"Eoghan, I've spent the last week imprisoned in
here. Please, I just want to go the library and
read." She hoped the use of his real name would
soften the young servant's heart.

Eoghan, who had been rechristened "Edward"
because of Mrs. Quinn's fears of appearing too
Irish, crossed his arms. "Like you said you were
going to visit Mrs. Schuyler last month and nearly
got all the way to the railway station before they
caught you?"

Diantha shuddered at the reminder of her
abortive escape attempt and its aftermath. The
servant's voice softened.

"Look, miss, I feel bad for you, I truly do. But
your father says he'll send me back to Ireland if I
let you get away. You know I can't chance that."

"I know." The twenty-year-old footman, older

than she by only a year, had confided that most of his earnings went home to his mother in County Tyrone. Her father ordered his household with the same ruthlessness that characterized his business dealings. It was not an idle threat.

"I promise I'll come back. You have my word." A grimace twisted her face. "Besides, as my parents pointed out last month, I have no other choice."

How odd to see pity in the eyes of a stripling whose yearly wages did not equal the cost of one of her hats. The boy sighed.

"You'd better, or I'll be hauled aboard the next packet to Belfast." He cleared his throat. "You know, miss, Lord Rossburn isn't a bad sort. For a Scot, anyway."

"The difficulty is that I'm going to be his wife, not his maid." She muttered the words to herself as she made her way down the hallway. A flash of bitterness coursed through her. "Servants can give notice if they're unhappy. I'll be tied to him till I die."

She stared moodily ahead of her. Lord Rossburn had been a complete stranger six months ago. Tomorrow she would marry him in a ceremony orchestrated to bring her parents into the inner circle of New York society.

The whisper of her nightclothes echoed ahead of her down the hall to the marble stairway. Unseeing faces painted by European masters gazed out of ornate frames as the glow of her lamp passed. The flicker of light on the statues her father collected lent the impression of movement.

As a girl, the illusion had terrified her, but tonight she kept her eyes fixed straight ahead.

Even the thirteenth-century French gargoyles guarding the top of the Grand Staircase failed to unnerve her now. Her older brothers had named them Buster and Willie. During her childhood, the boys had prevented her from wandering the halls after bedtime by assuring her that the stone carvings came to life and roamed through the mansion.

Her siblings anticipated the prospect of her marriage to a lord as enthusiastically as her parents did. They took no pains to hide their delight at her engagement, and often spoke of the cachet of claiming a British peer as a brother-in-law.

She had tried, cautiously, to correct them once. She recalled the occasion with painful clarity. The Quinns had dined *en famille* that evening, a rare occurrence.

"I don't believe he thinks of himself as British." As she and her fiancé had yet to converse privately during their courtship, she could not be sure of this, but she did notice he bristled slightly when referred to as an Englishman.

They sat in the pool of light shed by a single chandelier over their table. On either side of them, two other tables stretched the length of the immense room, their far ends lost in the shadows. Enormous antique tapestries lined the room, their age-dulled colors enhancing the gloomy atmosphere.

"Of course he does. The British have been united for a hundred years." James, the elder, helped himself to a generous slice of layer cake.

"Besides, he doesn't complain about it." Thomas took a final swallow of vintage Bordeaux and handed his glass to a waiting footman. "Not that he'll dare gripe if he wants to get his hands on any of our money. Right, Father?"

Harold Quinn tore his attention away from his plate long enough to glare at his younger son. "I'm not dead yet, boy. I earned my own fortune and I'll damned well decide who gets it when I'm dead and gone." His jowls quivered. "Not that I can see any business advantage whatever in marrying my daughter off to some overbred dandy."

In all fairness, Diantha did not think his lordship remotely dandified or effeminate, but chose not to venture her opinion.

"Mr. Quinn, we discussed the matter thoroughly when we agreed to Diantha's engagement. Kindly stop speaking in such a vulgar manner, all of you!" Still tall and slim after fifty years and three children, with only a few strands of silver in her honey-colored hair, Amalthea Helford Quinn's fragile beauty belied a will every bit as unyielding as her husband's. Noticing the piece of cake in front of her daughter, she rang the small silver bell at her right hand.

"Edward, Miss Quinn does not care for dessert. Please take it away."

"Mama, I should very much like to have some this evening. Could I not eat just a small piece?"

She gazed longingly at the chocolate-frosted confection Eoghan whisked out from under her fork.

"Do not contradict me, young lady. If I let you eat everything you wanted, you'd swell up like a hot air balloon." The words caused a wave of heat to mount slowly into Diantha's cheeks. No matter how hard she tried, she could never live down her mother's disappointment in having borne a daughter who did not match her own beauty.

"For heaven's sake, Mally, there's nothing wrong with the girl's figure." Her grandmother, the one person in the family unafraid of her daughter's temper, patted her lips with a damask napkin. "I certainly never treated you like that growing up." The old woman winked across the table at Diantha, signifying the arrival of a slice of cake in her room later that evening.

She dared a small smile of thanks while her parents were distracted.

"I never had the opportunity to marry a Peer of the Realm. Although I have had a very satisfactory life with Mr. Quinn." Her mother inclined her head toward her spouse.

As the two regularly engaged in sharp disagreements, she and her brothers glanced at each other and sought another subject to discuss.

Diantha pattered down the steps into the darkened entrance hall. The scent of burning oil drifted from the lamp in her hand as she passed the ballroom, already decorated and set up with tables and chairs for three hundred. She did not bother to look inside. Mama had arranged the decorations without consulting her.

Since that conversation with her family, she had suffered through a series of humiliating meetings with her husband-to-be. Forbidden to utter more than the barest commonplaces, she had listened, eyes downcast, while her mother arranged every detail of the wedding and reception. Her parents had even planned their honeymoon trip aboard the flagship of her father's shipping line.

Worse, Mrs. Quinn, in an attempt to secure attention for the splendid match, had permitted several pieces of the trousseau to be examined by society writers from a popular journal. After exclaiming over the exquisite creations ordered from Worth of Paris, they published descriptions of several items.

Diantha had wanted to sink with shame when she read a detailed account of her embroidered underclothes. The article sparked one of the few times she protested to her parent.

"No one I know has ever had such an intimate intrusion into their wedding!" She had shaken the paper in accusation.

Her mother rebuked her sharply. "Stop crying, you stupid girl! Society has closed its doors to this family for twenty-five years. Well, this will make them sit up and take notice."

"I hardly think they're going to be impressed because my corset covers are embroidered with a flower and leaf pattern." The remark earned her a box on the ear, but in her agitation Diantha had not cared.

She had tried to escape the single time they left her unwatched, but failed. Wedding arrangements continued. To the gratification of her father, Astors, Belmonts, and numerous other names from select clubs accepted their invitations.

Tonight, she engaged in the only act of defiance she could think of. Slipping into her father's darkened study, she retrieved a small key from its place under his inkstand and opened the inlaid wood liquor cabinet. Her brothers had taken Lord Rossburn out for a last spree this evening, so she would have one of her own.

She supposed they were visiting the establishment of a Madam Sweet. From whispered conversations between James and Thomas, she gathered gentlemen obtained the services of loose women there. She occasionally wondered just what those services entailed, but knew better than to ask.

After examining each bottle, she picked up one and read the label aloud.

"Cognac, XO Imperial." She poured the dark amber liquid into a cut crystal snifter and sipped cautiously. It burned going down her throat, but not unpleasantly. In fact, the warmth in her stomach felt very nice indeed in the chilly room. Papa and her brothers often drank more than the small amount swirling in the bottom of her glass.

After a moment's consideration, she filled the bulbous container nearly to the brim. Removing a book on architecture from her father's bookshelf, she settled into an overstuffed wing chair and opened it to a chapter on the Georgian Era.

Then she started to weep softly.

James Quinn needed to go on a slimming regimen. Kieran Rossburn held the portly young man up while his younger brother fumbled to unlock the door. "Why not ring for a servant?" His irritation roused his burden from his stupor.

"Father considers drinking and debauchery a waste of good money. So every single time we go out for a bit of fun"—his future brother-in-law indicated the front door of the Fifth Avenue mansion with a sweeping gesture that nearly pulled Kieran off his feet—"the old goat locks the door on us at midnight. We have to let ourselves in as if we still lived over the shop."

"Damned unreasonable, if you ask me." Beside them, Thomas looked over his shoulder from where he struggled with the key. It fell to the top step with a cold ping. "Missed again. You don't think he changed the locks, do you?"

"Highly unlikely." His lordship's patience evaporated as the young man stooped to pick up the key and failed.

"Stand up and hold this." He shoved James into his brother's arms and retrieved the key from its resting place. Seconds later, he opened the door and guided the inebriated pair to a Louis XV settle. Groping his way in the dark to a switch, he turned up the gas-lit chandelier overhead.

"Say, you can't do that!" Thomas stood up in protest and promptly collapsed back onto the settle. "The gas isn't supposed to be lit after Father goes to bed." Ignoring him, Kieran tugged vigorously at a bellpull.

"I do not care in the least what your father does or does not permit. And after tomorrow, I shall be free to tell him so myself."

"That's what you think, old boy." James gave a snort of laughter, or perhaps contempt. "Harold Quinn never gives up a groat without a fight. If you want to live off his money, you dance to his tune."

Kieran regarded the younger man coldly. "My estate brings in an adequate amount for me to live off of, thank you. I would like to remind you that your sister comes as part of a business arrangement with him."

A bleary-eyed footman arrived a few minutes later, struggling into his livery jacket. Consigning Thomas to this unfortunate individual, his lordship hoisted James to his feet and ordered the servant to lead the way to their bedrooms.

As he staggered through what appeared to be miles of hallways, he gave thanks that the Quinn brothers slept in neighboring chambers. Bundling the portly young man onto his bed, Kieran gasped for breath and regarded him with a jaundiced eye. Then, without a word, he turned on his heel and left the room.

The evening had been one long alcoholic binge for the Quinn brothers, interrupted only by a visit to Madam Sweet's brothel for what they termed "horizontal refreshments." Already disgusted with the family he was marrying into, Kieran partook sparingly of the alcoholic refreshment and bypassed the women completely. An habitué of elegant salons in London, Paris, and Rome, the tawdry entertainment provided at the Quinns' favorite house of ill-repute failed to impress him.

Not that he expected more from his fiancée's family. The stench of sweat and cheap perfume from the bordello left a sour tang in his mouth. Hopefully a drink of his future father-in-law's excellent cognac would overcome it. As he made his way toward the study, he fought back the bile that rose in his throat. His engagement had given him plenty of time to assess the family. Only the need to look after his tenants kept him from bolting this neo-Gothic monstrosity they called a house.

He had approached Harold Quinn the previous summer, when the American had rented a house for his wife and daughter in London. Not only did the man run the most successful passenger ships plying the Atlantic, he retained ownership of his grandfather's fishing fleet. Kieran had approached the magnate in hopes of interesting him in backing the fishermen sailing from the one harbor in Rossburn lands. The old man had listened to his proposal in silence, then dismissed him with a promise of an answer within a week.

Striding down the dimly lit marble stairs, Kieran

tightened his jaw at the memory. He had had no choice but to agree to Quinn's insolence. Ever since the potato blight had spread from Ireland to Scotland in his father's time, their tenants had struggled to make a living. His father had nearly beggared the family, trying to take care of their people. It had taken years for the two of them to increase income from the private demesne to the point where the lord's family could live comfortably off of it. Little extra remained to help the tenants.

Despite the social solecism of an aristocrat engaging in trade or industry, he had determined to start some venture to provide employment for his tenants. His family had held their lands since before the Normans had invaded England, and the sense of responsibility for their people ran deep in Rossburn blood.

Even so, he had refused to pay the other man's price the first time the old man informed him what it was.

"You're mad." He had regarded Quinn with revulsion. The other man's brows beetled. Evidently, the magnate did not hear many blunt assessments of his character.

"Mad or not, boy, that's the offer. You want my help, you take my daughter." Sitting back behind the large desk in the Mayfair library, he laced his hands over his stomach. "Take it or leave it. It won't be repeated, and don't think you'll get any help from any other businessman on either side of the Atlantic." The corners of his withered lips quirked. "I've put the word out that you're a bad risk."

"What?" Kieran erupted from his chair. "I made sure that proposal was more than fair to any investor. By God, you'll not call me dishonorable, sir."

"Not dishonorable, no." The American regarded his steepled fingers with half-closed eyes. "Let's just say I left out a few details when I discussed your ideas with other men in a position to help you."

"Just enough to make me sound like I don't know what I'm doing." He could not keep himself from adding quietly, "You bastard."

The other man waved the obscenity aside. "Been called worse, with more cause. The price of doing business." His pale blue eyes flicked over Kieran. "Actually, you've got a good mind for a lord." In shock, he realized the man meant what he said. "And you've a lot more gumption than most of your ilk. A man who ain't willing to get his hands dirty hardly deserves to be called one."

"How very flattering, to be sure." The young aristocrat bowed.

Quinn growled. "I'm not interested in your sarcasm. Do you want the deal or not?"

The Scot bowed again. "I shall inform you of my decision within the week, sir." With that, he took his leave, determined to find another way to help his people.

He did not find one. True to his word, Quinn had poisoned the industrial world against him. At the end of seven days, Kieran had admitted defeat and accepted the American's offer, which included the hand of Diantha Quinn in marriage.

As he passed through the golden glow of the

Sienna marble foyer, he glanced at a portrait of Mrs. Quinn, along with her mother and daughter, which hung on one wall. Typically vulgar display, he snorted to himself. Nevertheless, he paused to study it closely for the first time.

Clearly a piece of self-aggrandizement for the mistress of the house, it featured the three of them in eighteenth-century garb, as if they belonged to a long-established family. Kieran admitted that the artist had done a capital job of capturing the character of his subjects. Mrs. Quinn stood in the center, preening like a peacock as she arranged a vase of flowers. To one side, her mother sat with a piece of embroidery, looking at the viewer with a sardonically arched eyebrow. Kieran smiled in spite of his foul mood. Mrs. Helford's vinegary nature appealed to his sense of humor.

On the other side, a young Diantha handed her mother a few more blossoms, her medium brown hair arranged with a lovelock curling over one shoulder. Although she looked more attractive than in her usual garb, she had clearly not inherited her mother's beauty. He peered closer, for a moment fancying a bleak expression in the dark blue eyes.

The echo of his footsteps abruptly ceased as he stepped from parquet flooring onto the thick strip of carpet leading to Quinn's study. Had the girl proved conversable, he might have borne the situation better. Most of his married friends had barely known their fiancées before marriage either, and got on tolerably well. Their wives might demonstrate the typical foolishness of their gender, but they did at least carry on conversations of more than one sentence.

Unlike his fiancée, who invariably stared at the floor during their interviews, speaking in a quiet voice only to answer questions put to her. The image of year after dreary year in the company of such a dull creature rose before his eyes. And dear God, after tomorrow he would have to bed her if he hoped to beget an heir.

"Ugh." He shook his head. He had only agreed to marry the girl. Visiting her bed had not been in the contract he had signed. If worst came to worst, his cousin Barclay could inherit the title after he died. Or rather, Barclay's children could, since he was two years younger than his cousin and heir.

He did not consider Miss Quinn unattractive. True, she would never match her mother's remarkable looks, but her face and figure were well enough. No, it was her spiritless demeanor that repelled him. He opened the study door and stopped dead.

To his amazement, the subject of his sour thoughts appeared in front of him. In her nightgown and a hideous bright green wrapper.

"Miss Quinn!"

"Lord Rossburn!" She must have scrambled to her feet when she heard the door open, for she stood stiffly in front of an overstuffed chair. His gaze took in the lamp, the glitter of cut crystal on the small table beside her, and a heavy book of some sort lying half open at her feet.

For once, her eyes met his, wide with guilt. They glittered strangely, and he caught his breath at the realization she had been crying. Doubtless nerves, he thought to himself.

"Forgive me for interrupting, madam." He shifted uncertainly on his feet under her glare.

"Can't you wait till tomorrow to start interfering with me?" She plumped herself back into the chair, curling her legs under her. "You're not my husband yet; I shall do as I please." He noticed that she formed the words carefully, as if struggling to force them out.

Still somewhat at a loss, his lordship groped for a reply. "I had no notion of disturbing you, Miss Quinn. By all means, continue reading." He moved toward the liquor cabinet. "I only wish to drink a cognac before returning to my hotel."

"Well, that is a fortuishus—fortu—" After a few more attempts to pronounce "fortuitous," she gave up. "It's your lucky night." She held up an empty snifter under his shocked gaze. "Papa keeps his spirits locked up, but I had the same thought. I wager you don't even know where he keeps the key."

Glancing inside the open cabinet, he saw an empty space in the line of crystal decanters. Wrenching his gaze back to his fiancée, he gaped as she held up the missing container.

"I have no idea what this is, but I highly recommend it." She swirled the liquid around its interior, and giggled. "It tastes like fire going down, but do you know, I have not felt the least draft for over an hour."

Striding over, he relieved her of the decanter despite her protests. Up close, alcohol-scented breath confirmed her words. His fiancée had indeed imbibed a good portion of drink.

He examined the level of cognac remaining. "How much of this have you had?"

"I don't precisely recall." Under his incredulous eyes, she wrinkled her brow as she pondered the question. "I remember bringing the decanter over after my second glass because I kept tripping when I walked over to refill it."

"Never mind." He bit off the words before returning the decanter to its place and shutting the cabinet doors. Seeing the key in the lock, he turned it and faced her once more. From her position in the large chair, she regarded him with a puzzled expression.

"Aren't you going to have your drink?" She picked up the snifter again, peering mournfully into its empty bottom.

"You need to get back to your room at once, Miss Quinn." He ignored the mulish expression on her face. "As it is, you shall feel quite wretched tomorrow."

"Ha!" She ejaculated the syllable bitterly. "I shall feel wretched anyway." She shot him an unexpectedly shrewd glace. "So will you."

Thrown off balance for a second time, he resorted to his most formal manner. "I assure you that I shall feel nothing of the sort on such a momentous occasion."

"Stuff!" She straightened in the chair, tensing her body as if to spring. "You came in here for a drink for the same reason I did."

"And what reason is that?" Wondering if her family had forbidden her to speak for fear of exposing a shrewish nature, he braced himself in case she flew at him.

"You don't want to marry me any more than I want to marry you." She did not make a move to attack him, but her accurate assessment of his feelings startled him into taking a step back.

"Whatever gave you that idea?" Never mind that she spoke the truth; one did not betray one's emotional state in public. He paced a few steps to the dark fireplace, dropping his eyes.

"You only like pretty women. Everyone says so." The anger left her voice. "I mean, look at me."

Although not a command, he lifted his eyes and did as she said. Miss Quinn stood once again, regarding him steadily from her place in front of the chair. Even with those appalling nightclothes tied at her waist like a pudding bag, he could detect the slim curves they covered.

For the first time he found himself able to examine her face. Brown tendrils gleamed around a firm jaw where they had escaped the thick braid hanging down her back. Her mouth with its full, curved lips hinted at sensuality.

"I have mirrors, you know." Her voice broke into his thoughts. Although slightly slurred, it held nothing but a matter-of-fact acceptance of her appearance. It occurred to him that part of her reticence in their courtship might result from growing up with a beauty for a mother. Certainly they had conversed more in the last quarter of an hour than they had in the months previous.

"Oh dear." She swayed suddenly and clutched at the armchair for support. She stared at him accusingly. "The room is tipping!"

He sighed. Moving toward her, he picked up the book from the floor. It had fallen open at a page detailing the mathematical composition of a Palladian building.

"You were reading this?"

She shrugged, her face closed. "Just thumbing through it." A bitter smile twitched across her lips. "I like to look at the pictures."

He shelved it and returned to her. "Allow me to escort you." Holding out an arm, he waited for her to take it.

Instead, she put her hands behind her back and tried to step away from him. Stumbling over a leather-covered hassock, she nearly fell. His hands shot out to catch her and she grabbed them with a gasp. Holding her upright, he prayed for patience.

"Apparently I am doomed to assist inebriated members of your family to their bedrooms tonight." As she emitted an outraged shriek, he scooped her into his arms and strode out of the library.

"Put me down!" She struggled for a few minutes, then ceased. "Bother! You're making things spin again!" With a small groan, she buried her head in his shoulder as he strode toward the foyer.

"That's the cognac, not me."

"Really? Why on earth do men drink so much of it, then?" She raised her head for a moment, winced, and let it fall to his shoulder again. A silent laugh shook him. Clearly she was a stranger to spirits. Something inside him relaxed slightly and he chuckled at the absurd situation.

"At least you're easier to carry than your brother." She did not reply, merely linking her arms around his neck. To his surprise, he enjoyed the soft weight of her body. Her chest rose and fell in a deep breath and he wondered if she had fallen asleep. He cautiously set one foot on the bottom step.

He nearly lost his balance as she burrowed her face farther into his neck and inhaled again. "You smell wonderful."

"Thank you. If you don't mind, it would be most helpful if you did not move excessively while I'm going up the stairs."

"Mmmmmmmm." She sighed contentedly, and he had hopes of getting her to her chamber undiscovered. If word of this episode got into society, both their reputations would suffer. A moment later, she lifted her head slightly. Risking a quick glance at her face, he saw her staring at the carved banisters with an intent expression.

"Do you know something?" She asked the question in a ringing voice, and he hushed her.

"No, listen to me!"

"Miss Quinn, I beg you not to awaken the servants."

Obligingly, she lowered her voice. "I've always thought those carvings look like something from an overambitious wedding cake."

"An apt observation. Pray be quiet." A sheen of sweat broke out on his brow. While his fiancée weighed considerably less than her brother, he had not carried James up the staircase. His breathing became more labored as he neared the top.

"You sound like my mother. She never wants me to talk either." Kieran felt a flash of sympathy for the woman as his fiancée whispered on. "Do you know, she picked out the banisters herself? In France. And the gargoyles. Hello, boys!" She sang out the greeting and waved at the statues. In the light from the foyer below, he could have sworn the damned things smirked at him.

"They are indeed revolting, but I must ask you to remain silent." Having finally reached the top of the stairs, he set her on her feet and leaned on the nearest gargoyle, gasping for breath.

She stood staring at him, swaying slightly on her feet for several seconds. Then she slowly folded into a pile on the floor, looking up at him in confusion.

At least she remained conscious, he thought grimly. "Right, give me your hand." He took the proffered appendage and pulled her to her feet, none too gently. "'Once more unto the breach.'"

"*Henry the Fifth*, Act Three, Scene One." She nodded sagely as he hefted her into his arms once more. "Do you care for Shakespeare, your lordship?"

"He's tolerable." A low ache began to spread

across his back. "You appear to be familiar with him, however. Have you attended the play often?" He rolled his eyes at the ridiculous conversation.

She shook her head. "Oh no! Mother would never let me see one of Shakespeare's plays. They're dreadfully improper." Her voice lowered at last. "She doesn't know I read them. I stole the book from my brothers." She giggled. "That was five years ago and they still haven't noticed it's missing."

"Very clever of you, but we really must not wake up the rest of the house." He whispered in hopes of encouraging her to do the same. At the sight of the footman outside her door, he stopped short. To his alarm, the girl failed to take his subtle hint.

"See, Eoghan, I said I'd be back!" He tried unsuccessfully to hush her. "Do you know, Lord Rossburn hates the banister, too."

The servant met his eyes in horror. "Mary, God, and baby Jesus, I'll be sent back to Belfast for sure."

"Is there a discrete female you can fetch to help get Miss Quinn, er, settled in?"

"Wait here." The stripling scurried off into the shadows.

He eased her back onto her feet, this time sliding an arm around her waist before she collapsed again. He strained to listen for any sign that they had been overheard. Thankfully he heard nothing until the brush of feet on the hall carpet and a circle of candlelight heralded the return of the footman.

His relief vaporized when he recognized

Mrs. Helford. She came forward to assist her granddaughter.

"Granny!" His fiancée almost literally fell into her arms. "Lord Rossburn and I were enjoying some cognac in the library!"

The old woman pinned him with a ferocious glare. He held up both hands. "I assure you, madam, when I entered the library in search of refreshment, Miss Quinn was already there. In an advanced state of inebriation, I fear."

She scrutinized him for several seconds before addressing the girl. "Diantha Susanne, is that true?"

She giggled. "I got into Papa's best liquor, and there's nothing he can do about it." She tried to snap her fingers, then stared at her hand in bemusement when she failed. "It did taste odd at first, but I got used to it easily enough. Lovely stuff!"

"I doubt you'll think so in the morning." The dry tone of her grandmother's voice sailed over her head. Mrs. Helford sighed and addressed him.

"I suppose it's a blessing that you found her instead of my fool daughter and her husband." She muttered to herself. "What did they expect, keeping the girl locked up like one of their collections? You there!" The hovering manservant snapped to attention. "Get down to the kitchen and warm a large pot of coffee—you and nobody else. If anyone asks, you're taking it to me. Bring it here and mind no one catches you."

Nodding, the young man hurried away.

"You can safely turn Diantha over to me, young man." She spoke with the crisp air of a military officer. At the mention of her name, the girl looked up before sagging back onto her shoulder. Alarmed, Kieran reached to relieve the small woman of the burden. She waved his assistance away impatiently.

"You get yourself back to your hotel. I've a great deal of work to do if she's to show up at the church unimpaired."

He regarded the pair of them with concern. "I quite understand, madam, but will you not need help getting her into bed?"

Despite the circumstances, the old woman chuckled. "My late husband weighed nearly two hundred pounds in his prime and I certainly helped him to bed often enough. Now shoo!"

On the short walk to his hotel, Kieran shook his head in disbelief. Despite her condition, he had enjoyed his fiancée's company more in the last hour than he had in the previous six months.

More by Bestselling Author
Fern Michaels